Claire was born in Edinburgh and grew up in the small village of Mayfield in Midlothian with her parents and sister, and where she continues to stay with her two sons. She was an active member of the local primary school, high school and church fundraising committees and often helped with different projects.

She has always loved travelling, but the family holidays to visit her great aunts and uncles on the Isle of Skye were considered the best times of her life.

To my dad.

Claire Walker

The Feather

Austin Macauley Publishers™
London • Cambridge • New York • Sharjah

This is a work of fiction. Names, characters, businesses, places, events, locales, and incidents are either the products of the author's imagination or used in a fictitious manner. Any resemblance to actual persons, living or dead, or actual events is purely coincidental.

A CIP catalogue record for this title is available from the British Library.

ISBN 9781398445710 (Paperback)
ISBN 9781398445727 (ePub e-book)

www.austinmacauley.com

First Published 2022
Austin Macauley Publishers Ltd®
1 Canada Square
Canary Wharf
London
E14 5AA

I would like to thank my sons, Jordan and Lewis, and the rest of my family for their continued support. Alan and Sandra Marshall, Edgar and Sheena Peter, John and Jean Stirling, Affie and Richard Morley for their friendship, encouragement, support and prayers. Gorebridge Creative Writers, especially Jim Green, Heather Brown and Frank Taylor who always had a constructive word for my writing. My friends Sharon Corse, Trudy Stewardson and Jackie Moffat who have shared many laughs and tears and of course a few glasses of prosecco.

Thank you to all the people at Austin Macauley Publishers who have worked on bringing this book to completion.

And to all the people I met along the way and shared a story with, thank you.

Chapter One

Squashed like a sardine against the window on a cold and damp Number 3 bus to Mayfield from Edinburgh is an hour of my life I could be spending doing something important or at the very least enjoyable but, it was my little piece of space. My time to dream about all the possibilities this world has to offer. My time to be a fairy tale princess, an explorer, an accomplished artist. The possibilities were endless. There was no point in even trying to bring the car into town, especially during rush hour, and then the thought of trying to find a space to park and walking for twenty minutes through the throngs of tourists or people just trying to get to work. I was better off just getting the bus.

"Where are you off to tonight, darling?"

And then there were also reasons to take the car! Well, that was one way to bring me back down to earth. I'm not sure why I attracted all the old, drunk men, but it was a talent I had been improving on these last few years.

"Just home," I answered politely with a smile.

"You're too good-looking to be going home on your own," he said loud enough that had some looking around to see if he was right and others looking desperately out of the windows so he wouldn't pick them to talk to.

I laughed. "That's very kind, but I don't think you're seeing very clearly at the moment," I tried to joke, and it did produce a couple of chuckles from around the top deck of the bus.

"I know what an angel looks like when a see one," he continued. This time the bottle he had been drinking out of was pointed towards me to accentuate his remark before taking another swig and wiping his mouth on the sleeve of his black jacket.

I bet it wasn't just angels he had been seeing. I smiled, hoping the next stop would be his. I was on until the end of the line, so if he stayed on, there was no escaping him. I took a quick look out the window into the darkness.

We left the town, and we were heading our way into Midlothian. Small communities that had built up as Edinburgh expanded outwards into the farmland that surrounded it, but even now, the new housing estates were taking over the greenbelt and joining together communities that were losing their own identities.

The bell sounded for someone to get off, which tore me from my thoughts.

"It was a pleasure, miss," the man said, swaying and bumping off the seats as he made his way to the stair.

"Bye," I called after him.

My Granny always said it didn't cost anything to be nice to people. I watched as he stumbled his way up the road before the bus passed him, and he was just another face in the night.

I thought about him for a while. What his story might be. I was one of the lucky ones, but who knows what the future has in store for us.

I folded my arms around me as the bus emptied, and the icy cold fingers of winter crept their way in, piercing through my coat with a shudder as the only sign they were there.

As if it wasn't bad enough that I was on the bus until the very last stop, I had a bit of a walk back to my house too. The slippery pavement sparkled like a yellow brick road for me to follow, only the light from the moon illuminating the way ahead down a pathway between the houses on one side and a field on the other.

I held my breath as a man in a white suit appeared from one of the side streets. Not a John Travolta flashback, but it looked quite stylish. His hair was silver, not grey, cut short at the sides with a flop on top neatly combed back, and a pair of mirrored sunglasses, which was strange, seeing as how dark it was. He walked towards me, and I instinctively gripped the keys I was carrying a little bit tighter, scared, in case the evening took a sinister turn.

I took another quick look at him, my mouth opened slightly, and the breath I had been holding in escaped in a white mist before me into the icy air. There was something about him. I knew I was staring rather than taking a glance, but he was captivating. I dropped my eyes as he passed. What was that? I couldn't believe the feeling I had had, like my stomach had just flipped inside me.

I increased the pace, glad to see my house come into view. I breathed a sigh of relief as the key locked the front door behind me and my hand went out to feel for the light switches. I was home at last. I turned the heating up as high as it would go and kicked my shoes off before putting the kettle on.

My mind went back to the man on the bus, and I wondered who he was going home to tonight. He probably had more of a family than I had. My dad had died suddenly a few years ago, leaving me devastated, then my mum passed a few years later.

I walked into the living room and picked up the remote before deciding against another night of mind-numbing television. I made a cup of green tea before noticing the red light blinking on the answering machine. I tapped my fingers on my cup—hoping it wasn't someone trying to get me to sign up to some new crazy scam. I pressed the button, holding my breath.

"Hey, Gracie, you seemed to get all the crazies on the phone today. I hope you're okay."

Luckily, it was just Niven, which made me smile. She had been my best friend since we started working together almost ten years previously at one of the local call centres. We had been inseparable until she got married and had kids. We were still good friends, but the days of staying out all night drinking then going to work the next day had definitely come to an end. It was good, she had Darcy, and he had certainly calmed her down and in the process had calmed me down too, allowing me to spend more time painting, which I loved more than anything.

"So, what's the gossip with Amelia then? You wouldn't have thought she needed to work with those Louboutin shoes! I think she wears a different pair every day. She's completely out of place around here. Anyway, I need to go before Darce has a complete meltdown. See you tomorrow, luv ya."

I chuckled to myself. Niven was always direct to the point.

Amelia was a bit strange. She had joined the company at the end of last week with about twenty others, and she was one we had earmarked not to make it to the end of the month, let alone the obligatory twelve-week probation period.

She had been placed with me to listen in to my calls, to get trained, and since then, she had tried continually to be my friend, but there was something off about her, something that had my stomach in knots every time I was with her. Maybe she was just a bit lonely, but no one else liked her, and I seemed to get dumped with her at every break and lunch, which meant people I used to enjoy having a chat with wouldn't come near if she was there.

I switched off the lights, went upstairs and into my room to change out of my work clothes and exchange them for the usual and more comfortable shorts and T-shirt combo. I caught a side-on image in the full-length mirror I had leaning against the wall and was quite impressed I was still looking as fit as I was. I wasn't the best at keeping to regular mealtimes, and then when I did decide to cook, it was whatever was easiest to throw in a pan. It wasn't that I couldn't cook and when I had people over, I really enjoyed it, but I could never see the point when it was just me. There were also the local takeaways, which I think I was single-handedly keeping open.

I tied my shoulder-length dark brown hair into a knot at the back of my head. I liked having my hair a bit longer, but I hated it in my face when I was trying to work. When I put the light on in the bedroom turned studio, a smile spread across my lips. My little piece of heaven. Photographs and paintings adorned the walls, and benches and shelves held an array of paints and canvases for me to develop into something spectacular well, that was the idea anyway. I looked on at the easel and brushes that were lying, ready for me to paint my day away. It was my sanctuary, the one place I could be me. I sat down and began to paint. I never had any idea what I was going to paint before I picked up the brush. A thought or a feeling, a landscape picture I had taken previously while out for a drive, was usually the inspiration for my creations.

I stayed up longer than I had planned, making it into another day and another missed meal for my art, but it was worth it to sit and be completely consumed by my work. Even calling it 'work' was a stretch when it brought me this much joy.

At least it was Saturday, and I had the next two days off work to enjoy. I did need food though. As I looked through the cupboards and fridge, I tried to remember when the last time was, I placed an order to get some shopping delivered. I thought about taking the car to one of the bigger supermarkets but guaranteed I would end up with a full trolley and spending a fortune, and all I needed was something for my dinner tonight.

I walked over to the store. Through the park that had been my playground for many a lunchtime from school. Mayfield had been my home since I was born twenty-nine years ago. A lot had changed over the years, more houses, and more of our facilities being taken away or incorporated into the new high school. Our local shops overlooked for the bigger supermarkets, with better prices and out of town retail parks or online shopping was a new and easy option for this fast-paced life we were all leading. I was just as much to blame but going to the local shop where everyone knew your name and asked how you were doing because they were genuinely interested had long since gone.

I walked the aisles with my basket swinging, looking for the inspiration I needed. How could shopping for food be so mundane and time-consuming? I'm not sure how many times I walked up and down the aisles before settling on an instant meal in a pot and a sharing bag of crisps. Well, that was lunch sorted, with a takeaway for dinner, and a supermarket delivery tomorrow.

"Grace Grimes! I thought that was you. You haven't changed a bit." The man standing in front of me said cheerfully.

Well, it was always a danger going to the local shops that you would bump into someone you knew from school.

"Aaron, hi." I tried to look as happy as he did right now, but to be honest, after thirteen years away from high school, he was the last person I wanted to see, and the years had not been kind to him.

"You look great, did you get married, kids?" he asked in a way that had me wondering if the next words out of his mouth were going to be, we should get a drink sometime.

"Thanks, no, no husband or kids." Which should make you happy. I thought to myself. "You?" I asked, trying to be polite.

"Married, divorced and four kids, three boys and a girl."

"Really!" subtle as usual. I looked on at the larger-than-life man that now stood in front of me compared to the athletic kid from school, wondering how he had managed to get a woman to sleep with him on more than one occasion.

"Do you still stay here? I haven't seen you in here before?" he asked, putting his hand out to hold onto the shelf next to him. The sweat stain under his arm was the cue I needed to leave.

"Busy. Anyway, I need to get going, but it was nice seeing you again," I lied before starting to walk away.

"We should get a drink sometime," he called after me.

"Yeah, let's do that," I called without turning around and raised my hand to wave as I continued to walk away from him. Not in this lifetime or the next. Note to self, if I needed food, get it in town before coming home.

After a day of housework and a run-in with Arron, all I wanted to do was go to my studio and immerse myself in my art. I had wondered if I should try and see if anyone would like to buy some pieces, but I wasn't that confident, and I wouldn't have a clue where to start.

I sat consumed in my painting of a scene from Loch Lubnaig, Callander, and singing along to a playlist I'd made on my phone entitled work, which was belting through my Bluetooth speaker when a knock at the door, which could have woken the dead, startled me. I paused my music and ran down the stairs. I opened the door expecting police, firefighters or masked burglars, hoping not Aaron!

Chapter Two

I swung the door open to be confronted by a bottle of prosecco pushed towards me. "Hey Gracie, get the glasses." Bryce and Nic pushed past me, giving me a quick kiss on the cheek before making their way into my kitchen.
"Please, come in," I quipped.

"Oh, shut up, like you were doing anything." Laughed Nic, his leather jacket handed to me to hang up before pulling two glasses from the cupboard.

Bryce and Nic had both worked for the same company as Niven and I but had both made it out. Bryce had started working for one of the large banking firms in town, and Nic had gone back to work with his dad in his joinery company.

Nic was a lovely guy. He was tall and thin, and he always kept his light brown hair cut short and at least a days' worth of growth on his face, but it suited him perfectly. He did, on one occasion, shave it off entirely and looked about twelve. Since then, he kept it neatly trimmed. He was always there if you needed to talk, worked hard, and he could make some of the loveliest pieces I think I had ever seen out of wood. I had more than a few of his creations scattered around the house. There was never anything between us. We were and always would be good friends.

Bryce, on the other hand, had shared my bed on more than one occasion, and he was the complete opposite of Nic. He had a gym membership and spent nearly every morning there before going to work. He was still tall, but muscly and not out of proportion to his body, his dark hair was short at the back but longer on top, which meant he was always running his hands through it. We knew we weren't going to spend the rest of our lives together, but it didn't stop him from trying.

I jumped up onto the island, my usual seat when people came over for drinks. "So, what brings you two out?" I asked, wondering where I fitted in on their Saturday night drinking plans.

“Can’t we just come over for drinks without there being an ulterior motive?” asked Bryce discarding his suit jacket over one of my dining chairs. The tailored shirt underneath accentuating his well-toned body, and his tight-fitting trousers only making me stare, which I knew I shouldn’t.

“No! You forget I know you two, now spill,” I said, pointing to each of them.

“We couldn’t decide what we wanted to do,” confessed Bryce.

“And we thought Grace has a—” Nic started to say, taking over from where Bryce had left off.

“Large drinks collection?” I jumped in laughing.

“Big heart. Is what I think Nic was going to say?” Bryce said, laughing at his joke. “So what’s new with you, Miss Grimes? How’s work been without me?”

“Dull, I miss you both. There’s this new woman, Amelia, that I’m training.”

“Oh, now I’m interested,” chimed in Nic. “Please tell me she’s single and has a.”

“Big heart!” laughed Bryce.

“You’re going nowhere near,” I scolded. “She’s a bit weird, and she’s driving me nuts.”

“Okay! Steady, wouldn’t want you to tell us what you really thought,” said Nic while pouring the drinks.

“Sounds like you could do with a drink.” Bryce handed me a glass filled with prosecco. He was right. This was exactly what I was needing.

“I take it we’re phoning for a Chinese, Auld Mother Hubbard?” asked Nic while looking through my empty cupboards and fridge. “We could take a run over to the store for some cans?” he suggested.

“No! Definitely not,” I shot back.

“Don’t tell me you were banned?” joked Bryce.

“I wish. I was over earlier and bumped into a guy I used to go to school with.” I recalled screwing my face up as an involuntary shudder only added to the memory.

“Long lost love?” asked Nic.

“Not even close,” I said before taking a large drink.

“Had the years not been as kind to him as they have been to you?” asked Bryce.

“I hope I don’t look that bad. The sweat patches were enough to put anyone off, well, not anyone. Would you believe married, divorced, and has four kids!” I recalled.

"See, how does that even happen, and I'm still single?" Said Nic finishing his drink and reaching for the bottle to pour another.

"The perfect girl is out there for you," I said, smiling at him.

"I think I might have missed my chance."

"What a sorry excuse for a party!" exclaimed Bryce. He got off his seat, grabbed the bottle from Nic, and placed it on the island next to me.

"I'll put some music on." Shouted Nic as he connected his phone to the Bluetooth speaker. A classic rave tune boomed through the open plan kitchen, diner, living room.

"Nice," commented Bryce.

I drained the last of the bottle into my glass. "Could you get another from the fridge?" I asked Bryce.

"Only on one condition." He looked at me with a slight smirk crossing his lips. "What are you up to, Mr McKinley?"

He placed the bottle from the fridge on the bunker and held out his hand.

I shook my head. "I haven't had nearly enough to start dancing," I protested.

He wasn't taking no for an answer and took my hand and pulled me down from the island.

He spun me around the kitchen, and we were both laughing.

"Now, this is a party." Nic came in-between Bryce and I. "Mind if I cut in?" I put my arms around Nic's neck as we continued to dance.

"What do you two look like?" Bryce shouted over the music while opening the next bottle.

"You're just jealous," Nic shouted back.

His hand that was on my shoulder began to run down my back, and I knew he was trying his hardest to wind Bryce up.

I spun out of Nic's arms and went over to Bryce. I was having too much fun to have Bryce going in a huff.

I stood behind him and draped my arms over his shoulders. "I hope one of those is for me?"

I came round to stand beside him and took my glass from his hands.

"We need to have a big party like we used to, Grace, get, Niven, and Darcy over." Suggested Nic.

"We really should. It's been far too long," I agreed.

Bryce put his hand around my waist, but that wasn't how I wanted this night to go. I retook my seat on the island.

"Pour me one of those, and I'll get it in a minute," said Nic excusing himself.

"Alone, again," I noted.

"Keeps happening." Bryce smiled, his eyes piercing into my soul. He moved, himself in-between my legs. His fingers brushed stray pieces of hair behind my ears. "Why do you have to be so beautiful?" he asked, kissing my neck.

"Bryce. I thought we had agreed," I said, wriggling free from his advances.

He took his glass and looked outside the patio doors. "What if I've changed my mind?" he asked, turning to face me.

"We agreed one year. One year to see if we still felt the same, then we would give it a try," I reminded him.

"Do you know how hard it is to be in the same room as you and not touch you, not kiss you? Do you not feel it?" he asked desperately.

I jumped down off the island and picked up my drink. "It's only been three months." I went to walk away.

"Is it because you're waiting to see if something better comes along?" he asked directly.

"I don't want to get too serious with anyone just now, that's why I said a year, and you agreed," I said, defending myself.

"Or maybe it's because you don't want to get too serious with me?" he placed the glass on the bunker and walked past me grabbing his jacket just as Nic was coming back in-to the kitchen.

"Nic, The Hole has an eighties' night, do you fancy?" asked Bryce.

"Yeah. Grace, you coming?" Nic asked, not reading the atmosphere.

"No, I've got stuff to do. You go, and I'll hear all about it later," I said, trying to sound more positive.

"See you later. Catch." Nic kissed me on the cheek and squeezing his jacket between his hands like he wanted to say something but couldn't before joining Bryce, who had already made his escape out the door without saying anything more.

I went to close the door, but not before noticing a lorry parked in the street. I wondered if that was my new neighbour. The For Sale sign had been in the garden for months. I hadn't seen anyone coming to view it, then all of a sudden, the 'Sold' banner went up, and work vans had been appearing day and night to rip everything out and replace it. I ran up to my bedroom window to get a better view. The removal van had its crew moving boxes and furniture, but there was no sign of the people who had bought the Henderson's old place.

I sat on my bed, wondering who the new owners would be. I'm not sure if it was the encounter with Bryce or if I was just feeling a bit lonely, but the thought of a young, handsome, dark-haired single man moving in was front and centre in my thoughts. I laughed at myself. It was more than likely a family.

I was the only single person who would buy a five-bedroom house. My dad had always said buying property was a good investment. When he died, I used some of the inheritance money to buy a place that I could live in for the rest of my life or sell for a good profit and move to California, which was always one of my life-long ambitions.

I laid back on the bed. There hadn't been anyone serious in my life for a while, and I was certainly feeling my age. As long as I wasn't going to end up a lonely, old spinster, I think I'd be happy, even if it did mean spending the rest of my life with Bryce.

Chapter Three

Another week completed at work, and a weekend of painting to look forward to. If only I could catch this bus, then into my pyjamas, something to eat and cuddled up in bed with a film. I was walking about as fast as I could without running, turning, occasionally to see if the bus that was coming up the Bridges was mine. The early dark nights and rain forcing me to screw up my eyes to see the bus numbers. There was no time taken to admire the majestic sights up the Old Town and Edinburgh Castle or over to the left the imposing shadow of Arthur's Seat, a now dormant volcano in the heart of the city.

On one of my turns, I noticed the man from the other night, white suit and silver hair. Maybe he was a performer leftover from the festival. I gave him a side glance as he passed me, then continued watching that cute butt disappear in front of me.

I'm not sure what happened, but the next time I turned around, my foot slipped off the pavement. Luckily, I didn't fall on my face, even if it felt like I had. As I tried to walk, nonchalantly away, the limp that now accompanied me was slowing me down. I turned in time to see my Lothian bus whoosh past me at speed. I walked quickly, hoping to catch the now disappearing number 3 bus but to no avail.

"Not your night?" A voice came from behind me. Well, that was the understatement of the year.

I smiled. "No, not really," I said, bending over to rub my ankle.

"Looks like you could do with a trip to A&E," the male voice suggested.

I stood up, the man was looking concerned, or maybe it was impatience that he couldn't get past me. He was extremely good looking, which made me look around to see if he was speaking to someone behind me.

"It's fine," I answered, trying to move out of the way. "Here, let me help you," he offered.

He took hold of my arm and helped me into the bus shelter. I tried not to lean too heavily on him, but I was grateful for the support.

"Thank you. I should be fine now," I said, trying to give him an out.

"Yeah, I'm not so sure. I think you need to go to the hospital and get that x–rayed just to be on the safe side."

His dark blue eyes bored deep into mine like he was hypnotising me with each syllable. "It's fine, honestly. I'll put an ice pack on it when I get home," I answered, not wanting to spend a night in A&E when all I had been looking forward to all night was dinner and bed; come to think of it; if he played his cards right, it could still work. I smiled more at my thought than at him, but it seemed to have the same effect.

My boot was becoming increasingly tighter. I bent over to take the zip down, but the pain caused me to make a noise loud enough to have the man looking more than a bit anxious. He walked out into the middle of the road and hailed a taxi coming up from Princes Street. He put his arm around me and practically carried me, dumping me in the back seat.

"Edinburgh Royal Infirmary, please," he said to the driver before turning to me. He lifted my leg and foot gently across his knee and carefully took my boot off, which had me wincing in pain and grabbing hold of his arm.

"You're better getting your boot off before it swells too much, or they'll need to cut it off," he said, the unease evident in his voice.

"What my foot!" I asked, shocked.

He laughed. "No, your boot."

I did feel more than a little stupid for that comment and laughed nervously. "I'm Grace," I offered.

"Nice to meet you, Grace, Gabriel," he replied.

"Ha, like the angel." I laughed. I was definitely on a roll tonight.

"Just like the angel." He smiled.

I studied his face, the dark stubble looked like it was newly trimmed, which accented his strong, defined jawline, and his hair was short but slightly messy on top, styled that way rather than he couldn't be bothered doing it before he left. I sat there wondering how lucky I could get, then realised I was making my way to the hospital, so not that lucky! I closed my eyes, the pain beginning to make me feel a bit nauseous.

"That's us here," he said, nudging me slightly.

I opened my eyes and sat up, grabbing my bag to pay for the taxi.

"I've got it." He leaned forward and paid the driver before opening the door and helping me out.

I put my toes on the path to get my balance, but the pain shot up my leg and had me grabbing for Gabriel's arm again.

"Yeah, you're not walking." He bent over and picked me up and began to carry me to the reception desk.

There wasn't any point in arguing, and anyway, there was no way I could get there myself.

"Name?" asked the receptionist without looking up from her computer. "Grace Grimes," I answered.

"Address?"

"30 Rowan Tree Gardens, Mayfield, Dalkeith."

"Date of birth?"

I paused, wondering if Gabriel would drop me on the floor and walk away. "11-9-93." I braced for impact, but I was still in his arms.

"What's brought you here tonight?"

"I tripped off the pavement and hurt my ankle."

"If you want to take a seat and someone will call your name. Next."

Gabriel carried me over to a row of plastic seats and sat beside me, pulling my leg back over his.

"Thank you, Gabriel, but you don't need to stay. I could be here for hours yet," I offered.

Friday night in A&E was not a pleasant experience. It was always busy, and you could be waiting half the night, depending on what emergencies there was. It was more than likely from some drunken nights out.

"I'm not going to leave you now, and anyway, isn't that what neighbours do?" he asked, with a grin crossing those perfect looking kissable lips.

"I have no idea what you're talking about," I said, shaking my head and looking more than a little confused.

"I'm the person in the van that's moving into number thirty-two. It was you I saw looking out of the bedroom window the other day." He was laughing at me and for good reason.

"I thought I was trying to be very inconspicuous," I answered, moving uneasily in my seat.

"There won't be a job at MI5 waiting for you, put it that way," he joked.

"I'm sorry. It's the quietest street you moved into. Not much happens," I tried to apologise, feeling mortified that he had seen me at the window.

"You don't need to apologise. At least we can share the taxi home." He remarked.

"Well, I'm paying this time. It's the least I can do."

"Let's wait and see what the doctors have got to say first."

I sat staring at the television, trying to read the subtitles of the news that was playing without sound, anything to try and pass the time. Gabriel had gone to get himself a coffee and a tea for me as the waiting area filled with more and more people.

"It was a machine I'm afraid, all I can say is it's wet," he said, handing me the small cup.

"Thanks. It might keep me awake until my name's called," I said before taking a sip of the lukewarm drink.

"No, it's not," he said, shaking his head.

"No, it isn't," I answered back immediately laughing, knowing exactly what he was meaning.

"So, who else do you have moving into the house with you?" I asked, knowing it was absolutely none of my business.

"No one. I've just moved into the area," he answered, taking another sip of his coffee.

"Big house for one person."

"Who stays with you?" he asked.

"Touché." I smiled back at him.

"Grace Grimes." A nurse called from the side of the waiting area.

"Here," I shouted, putting my hand up like I was back in primary school. Gabriel picked me up and walked towards the nurse.

"I'll get you a chair," she said, taking one look at me.

Gabriel put me down and wheeled me into a cubicle before helping me onto the bed.

"What happened here then?" she asked. She seemed nice enough. Older so had probably heard more than her fair share of stories.

"I was walking to get my bus home, and I turned round to see if it was coming, and I slipped off the pavement," I recounted my story.

"Right, well, let's take a wee look." She smiled widely, which scrunched up her plump rosy cheeks, putting me at ease almost immediately.

I didn't take my eyes off her face, looking for any tell-tale signs that this was worse than you'll be fine, take a couple of paracetamols for the pain.

"I'm going to have to re-design your wardrobe, I'm afraid." She produced a pair of scissors from a drawer. "I hope these weren't your favourite socks and jeans?"

I looked at her, wondering why she had asked me that.

"Grace, they need to cut your sock and jeans off." Explained Gabriel.

I looked at the bulge between my sock and my skinny jeans. There was no way anything was getting past that.

"I'll step outside." Gabriel excused himself.

"The doctor will be in shortly to assess you." She smiled before opening and closing the curtain behind her.

"Hey, is it okay if I come back in, or would you rather have me wait back at the reception?" Gabriel asked, popping his head around the curtain.

"You're fine, come in." My leg was lying outside the covers, and a pillow had been placed under it to keep it stable. "I bet this isn't what you had in mind for tonight?" I tried to joke.

"No, but I don't mind. I wasn't going to be doing anything tonight anyway," he said, sitting on one of the hard plastic chairs next to the bed.

"What do you do?" I asked. Might as well get all the information I can while I've got him trapped here.

"I'm in requisitions," he replied.

Well, it explained the suit. "Sounds important." Almost immediately, I wished I hadn't asked. Now I knew he was way above my pay grade.

"It is, but my boss is exceptional." He tried to explain.

I leaned back on my pillows, the interrogation over for the time being. The rush of nausea washed over me again. I closed my eyes and tried to breathe through it.

I felt him holding my hand. "Can I get someone for you?" he asked.

I nodded my head slowly but not slowly enough as the dizziness increased.

Chapter Four

I woke to find my hospital room full of people. "You call this a party?" I tried to joke.

"There she is." Nic was first to notice and came over to the bed to hug me.

"Don't scare us like that again." Niven hugged me as the tears streamed down her shocked looking face. She stayed close as she moved her short light brown, bobbed hair behind her ears. She was lovely looking and had the most amazing blue eyes, like some Caribbean Sea which had all the males at work swooning over her and some of the females too, but she only had eyes for Darcy. They had met on one of our many drunken nights out and had been inseparable ever since.

"Who knew tripping off a pavement could cause such a reaction," I said, looking at all the worried faces.

Darcy pulled Niven away from me. "Give her some air. How are you, Gracie?" he ruffled my hair like a father would a son.

He wasn't as tall as Bryce and Nic, but he wasn't short either. He was the father to the group, always there with words of advice or encouragement. His blonde hair was swept back behind his ears and held in place with his glasses. The look of anxiety on his face meant there was certainly something to be concerned about.

"I'm fine, honestly. One night in the hospital, and you're all acting like I was at death's door," I tried to reassure them.

"You had to get surgery on your ankle. We were worried." Bryce sat on the bed and held my hand. He grasped it tightly, making it look small in his. He brushed his thumb over the back, trying to reassure me, but this didn't feel right.

"But you're fine now," Nic called over the top of him, trying to raise the tone.

I looked around the room, hoping to see Gabriel, but he wasn't there.

"Those flowers are gorgeous," I exclaimed, seeing a large bunch of white roses on the bedside table, with a card placed next to the vase.

Bryce let go of my hand and stood up with a huff. I looked to Niven for an explanation.

"They're from Gabriel. He was the one who brought you in," she said as if I wouldn't remember.

"I know who Gabriel is," I cut in.

"He's stayed with you since you came in," she said, looking at Bryce apologetically.

"He's my new neighbour," I said, trying to sit up before Niven ran at me, pushing me back down.

"We know. Don't move! You're not allowed to move."

For the first time, I looked down at my swollen leg with more colours than a rainbow and a halo with metal pins keeping my ankle straight.

"Not, a sprain then?" I laughed.

"You broke it, and then because you tried to walk on it." Nic went through all the gory details, some of which I could have done without hearing.

A nurse came into my room. "Nice to see you back with us, Miss Grimes. I want all of you out of here in the next five minutes. You can come back during visiting time," she ordered them before leaving us to say our goodbyes.

"I'll come in tomorrow. Do you want me to bring anything from the house?" asked Niven.

"Everything you would expect."

"I'll take a run over before I come in." She kissed me on the cheek and gave me another hug before standing back.

Darcy put his hands on her shoulders to reassure her. "If you need anything, just let us know."

"Thanks, Darcy."

"Are you sure we can leave you, and you're not going to get into any more trouble?" Nic joked, squeezing me tightly until I squealed.

"I promise." I laughed.

I looked over at Bryce, who was standing against the wall. There was an awkward, shuffling, and staring before Nic, Niven, and Darcy left the room.

"You better watch before Nurse Ratched comes back and finds you here," I teased.

"Why do you do that, try to make everything a joke?" he was serious now.

"There's no point having everyone crying," I tried to reassure him. "Come here." I held my hand out for him to take.

Bryce walked back over and took up his previous spot on the bed facing me and taking my hand in his.

"I'm fine, honestly."

"I don't know what I would have done if I'd have lost you." The emotion was building in his voice and his eyes had a shimmer to them.

"Hey, I'm fine." I smiled. "I'm not going anywhere."

"So, who's this Gabriel then?" he questioned.

"He's my new…"

"Neighbour. Yes, we all got that. I mean, why does he never leave your side and bring you expensive flowers?" he butted in, almost accusing.

"Bryce, I don't want to get into this right now." I let go of his hand. This was why we were never going to be together.

"What, he moves in, and you two are what? An item?" he was angry and jealous, a trait that I had had to contend with on more than one occasion.

"Is that even a phrase anymore? No, we're not an *item*. He was kind enough to help when I needed him, and the fact I passed out while he was watching me, he probably feels guilty." I looked to the door, wondering if the five minutes were up yet.

"Do you even want me to come back to visit?" he stood up and folded his arms in front of him like a petulant child.

"Of course, you can visit, but you can't be like this. We're friends, Bryce, that's all I want from you." I tried to explain for the hundredth time, still unsure whether he was going to accept it.

He pushed his hands into his jeans pockets and blew the air out from his puffed-out cheeks. "If that's what you want," he conceded grudgingly.

"It is." I smiled, hoping it would do the trick this time.

"Five minutes is up," the nurse said as she came back in. She never even looked at Bryce as she spoke. Instead, she walked straight to me. Knowing her request would be carried out. Her hair had been pulled tightly back and tied at the back of her head, which gave her a serious, no-nonsense look.

"Catch." Bryce walked out, letting the door bang behind him.

"Bit of a temper that one?" she commented and left me wondering if she had been on the wrong side of one of his outbursts. It was a different nurse to the one I had when I came in.

She looked to be in her forties, seemed nice enough, and had the mark of Bryce.

"He's harmless, he just gets worked up sometimes," I wasn't sure who I was trying to convince, but it certainly wasn't the nurse.

"That other one who comes to visit, now there's a gentleman," she commented, giving me a look of approval as she went about checking me over.

"I don't know him that well," I confessed, knowing she was talking about Gabriel.

"Then my suggestion, get to know him." She smiled. "Now rest and let that ankle heal. The doctor will be in later to take a look." She squeezed my arm and smiled, trying to reassure me which on this occasion was working.

There was nothing more boring than lying in a hospital bed with nothing to do and not being able to move. The clock I had been watching never seemed to move, and I had fallen asleep and woke three times already. All I could think of was Gabriel, and why just as I wake up, he's not here and if he had given up and decided not to come back.

The room was probably a standard design used all over the country. Not that I was that well versed, having only been in hospital to visit my parents when they were dying.

I closed my eyes again, hoping sleep would consume me for a bit longer, but the fact I had been sleeping since I arrived it was probably the last thing my body wanted. All I could picture was Gabriel lifting me in his arms and carrying me through the A&E department. If nothing else, it made me smile.

"Nice dream?"

I quickly opened my eyes. "Gabriel," I blurted out with a little too much enthusiasm.

He put his bags down next to the wall and came over to the bed. He took up the same position that Bryce had earlier, this time though there was an excitement building in my chest. I had wondered if I had made him too perfect in my thoughts, but he was just as breath-taking as I remembered.

"Hey." He almost whispered. "I brought a bag of your things; Niven was at the house and asked if I could bring it in for you."

I couldn't stop staring at those deep dark blue eyes. "Thanks. And what's in the other bag?" I asked, hoping it was a large box of chocolates.

"Monopoly."

Oh well, a girl can dream.

"What's with the face?" he asked, laughing. "I thought you'd be glad of something to do," he said, squeezing my hand playfully.

I hadn't even realised the disapproving look I had let show on my face. "Thank you for the flowers; they're gorgeous," I gushed. Way to bring it back.

"I'm glad you had something nice to wake up to," he said.

If it hadn't been for this leg, I would have pulled back the covers and dived at him, throwing my arms around his neck and kissing him with such passion that he wouldn't know what hit him. Yeah, it was the leg that was stopping me!

"I woke up to a room full," I told him.

"Were they all here? I told them just a couple at a time. I hope they didn't tire you out too much," he asked disapprovingly and sounding concerned at the same time.

"I think sleeps the last thing I need there's not much that's going to tire me out," I joked.

"We'll see about that." He got up from the bed and went over to retrieve the bag with the Monopoly in it. He put it on my trolley and then pulled out a well-wrapped golden box with a big black bow tied perfectly. "Now, you're smiling. Well, at least I know how to keep you happy," he said, handing me the gift.

I opened it, wondering what it could be, my mind racing through the different ideas. "Chocolate." I laughed.

"You don't like chocolate?"

"I love chocolate. I was hoping the Monopoly box was chocolates," I confessed.

"These aren't your run of the mill chocolates. Close your eyes and open your mouth," he said, taking one of the small round chocolates from the box.

I giggled, wondering how many times he had used that line.

"Grace." He scolded and rolled his eyes at my infantile joke.

I did what he asked me to do.

He put the whole chocolate into my mouth in one go. Not how I would usually savour chocolates, biting off small bits instead. He knew best. The runny chocolate centre mixed with the soft milk chocolate coating had my taste buds buzzing. I had to put my hand up to my mouth. I was having way too much fun over some chocolates.

I opened my eyes.

"Enjoy that?" he asked with a strange look on his face.

I think I was blushing. "Don't get out much," I joked.

"I think we'll put these over here." He put the lid back on the box and put it on the far side of the unit next to the bed.

I tried to sit up.

"Here, let me help you," he offered.

His strength was certainly an asset as he pulled me up the bed into a sitting position and made sure the pillows were perfectly placed behind me.

We set up the Game of Thrones Monopoly with a glass ring stain on the board. "Is this mine?" I asked, surprised.

"Niven said it was your favourite." He shuffled the cards and set up the pieces. "Do I even want to know about the stain?" he asked with a slight smirk on his face.

I screwed my face up. "Probably not." He didn't need to hear about one of my drinking games.

"No," he shook his head. "Which piece?"

"House Lannister."

"Why?"

"It looks like the Lion Rampant."

"A proud Scot?"

"Something like that. I never asked where you're from," I questioned. The thing was I knew absolutely nothing about him.

"I'm not really from any one place, I moved around a lot, so I don't call anywhere home." He rolled the dice starting the game.

"Have you ever been to a place that you've wanted to stay?" I asked, hoping this would be one of those places.

"There have been places that I wouldn't mind going back to, but I haven't found the perfect place yet."

"Maybe Scotland will be the perfect place," I said, hoping.

"I think that will depend."

"On."

"You ask a lot of questions," he observed.

I shrugged my shoulders. "How are you going to know anything if you don't ask?" I moved my piece landing on one of his holdings.

"Good point. That will be four silver stag tokens."

Five times around the board and he'd bought most of it with me landing in jail on nearly every turn. If this had been one of my drinking games, I think I would have passed out by now. We were having fun, and I hadn't even noticed the time until a yawn escaped.

"Right, that's enough for one day," he said, picking up all the castles and holdfasts from the board.

"Please don't go just yet?" I pleaded.

"I'll stay, but only on one condition," he offered.

"And what condition would that be?" I asked in my best seductive voice.

"You lie back down, and if you feel tired, you go to sleep,"

Well, it wasn't what I was expecting rather what I was needing. "Deal."

He packed everything away and sat on the chair next to the bed. "You look tired."

"What game are you bringing tomorrow?" I asked while trying to keep my eyes open.

"What have you got?"

"There's a key under Jeremiah in the back garden, have a look for yourself," I teased.

"Jeremiah?" he looked at me quizzically.

"You'll recognise him straight away."

"I see."

There wasn't much talk after that. I thought I heard Gabriel saying goodnight, but I was too tired to open my eyes, or reply for that matter.

Chapter Five

"Tell me everything? Did mysterious Gabriel come to visit last night?" Niven asked, coming to lie on the bed next to me.

"He did, and he brought me chocolate." I laughed.

"Oh, he's a keeper," she joked. "Where are they?" she asked, looking around.

"Gold box on the unit." I pointed.

She leaned over and picked up the box, opened it, and put one in her mouth before offering one to me. "Bloody hell." Her hand shot to her mouth. "Where did he get those?"

"I know, right!" I knew straight away the sensation she was experiencing.

"If that's the chocolates, can you imagine the sex?" she waved her hand in front of her face.

"Niv!" I said, sounding shocked.

"Like you haven't thought about it!" she exclaimed before putting another chocolate in her mouth. "You better take these away from me. Poor Darcy doesn't stand a chance." She laughed.

I put the lid on the box and gave her them to put back. Niv was always full of fun; even the way she dressed was bright and cheerful.

"Is he coming back today?" she asked.

"I told him to find Jeremiah and bring another game. Hopefully, one that doesn't have the remnants of one of our infamous drinking games plastered all over it. Thanks for that, by the way," I scolded, staring at her from the corner of my eye.

"Oh yeah, I forgot about that."

"Yeah." I giggled.

"Do you not worry about him going through your house? What if he's rummaging around in your underwear drawer?" she gasped.

"It won't take him very long, and there's nothing there that would turn Bryce on, let alone Gabriel. Anyway, he has to find the key first."

"I'll send him a clue." She smirked before turning her head away.

"And how will you send him a clue?"

"Well, someone had to keep him informed about how you were doing,"

"Niven, Marshall!"

"What? Can't a girl help out her best friend?" she asked, nudging me, giggling.

"It's like a dream come true, Niven and Grace in the same bed." Nic burst into the room in his usual over the top fashion. "Thank you, God!" He looked up to the ceiling with his hands clasped together.

"In your dreams, Nicky boy!" exclaimed Niven.

"Always Niv. Now budge that ass over and give me a piece of that action." He squeezed himself onto the bed beside me like some human sandwich.

"I think we're going to need a bigger bed," I said, putting on the voice of Brody from Jaws.

"Who's been eating chocolate? Don't get cheap on me, ladies," he asked, reaching over and fumbling his way around in between Niv and I, which had us both squealing and laughing in equal measure.

Niven reached over and dropped the box into Nic's hand.

"Wow! They are damn fine chocolates, I bet those cost." Nic turned the box in his hands, looking for a label or some other marking.

"I never thought about it," I said, wondering if I should have.

"They're handmade, not two of them are the same, and you can see the design they've put in on the top. That's to show it's from a particular chocolatier." He tried to explain.

"From one craftsman to another," I commented.

"You have to appreciate good quality. I keep telling you both that's what you get with me, quality." He dropped one of the chocolates on top of Niv and me, which made us squeal again and move a bit quicker than he had expected. Niven managed to grab hold of me, but Nic started flailing as he tried to grab hold of the bed before falling on the floor.

We were all laughing hysterically when the nurse stormed in. "What is going on in here?" she shouted. "This is a place for sick people!"

Niven and I stopped straight away, including eating our chocolate, but when Nic popped up beside the bed looking like a wee boy caught with his hand inside the biscuit tin, we couldn't contain ourselves any longer and burst out laughing again.

"I'm going to get the doctor," she spat before turning on her heels and storming out of the room.

The whole performance had us looking at each other and bursting out laughing again. "We should go before we get you into trouble," said Niven scrambling to get off the bed in a hurry.

They both hugged me before making their escape holding on to each other as they sneaked out the door like two hapless burglars. I pulled the covers over me and pretended I was sleeping. It worked when I was a child, who knows, maybe it still would.

The door swung open.

"They were just here!" the nurse tried to explain.

"But they're not here now. How about we let Miss Grimes get her rest?" the doctor reprimanded her.

"Yes, doctor."

The door closed behind them, and I was able to breathe again. I would need to watch it with that nurse. All the other ones seemed to be very nice, but I had taken an instant dislike to this one, and to top it all, she had scared away my friends, leaving me on my own again.

When Gabriel arrived, later on, he could tell almost immediately something was wrong. "You, okay?" he placed the leather bag down next to the chair that he had slung over his shoulder.

I shrugged my shoulders and continued to pick at the side of my trolley table.

He looked at me, trying to study my face. "I found Jeremiah, the Bullfrog!"

"Did Niv help you?" I asked, still concentrating on what I was doing.

"Yeah. Have I missed something? Did I do something wrong?" he asked, pushing his hands into his trouser pockets.

I stopped what I was doing and looked at him. The anger and disappointment had bubbled to the surface, and the tears began to roll down my face. "We were just having a laugh, then the nurse came in and started shouting at us, and Nic and Niven had to leave, and I've been on my own all day, and I'm so bored and…" I blurted out in one breath before I had to stop and breathe in again.

He didn't wait for an invitation. He sat on the bed in front of me, ready for me to bury my face into his chest. I sat there and cried for what seemed like way longer than the situation deserved before pulling back to grab a tissue from the unit.

"I'm sorry," I finally managed to say through the sniffs.

“I’m sorry for leaving you here on your own. It won’t be happening again,” Gabriel said, sounding angry.

“What did you bring?” I asked, looking at his bag. “Cluedo?” his voice hadn’t lost the edge to it.

“Set it up. I’ll be Miss Scarlet,” I said, trying to smile and trying to break Gabriel out of the mood I had put him in.

“Have you got any of those chocolates left?” he asked, trying to catch a glimpse of my reaction from the corner of his eye.

“I think there might be, but Niven and Nic had a couple. Nic thought they were handmade.” It was more of a question than a statement.

“They were for you to enjoy,” he said, looking straight at me.

“Sorry.”

He stopped what he was doing and looked at me dismayed. “Why are you apologising? And yes, they were handmade. I had them sent over from Belgium.”

I looked down at the trolley. “I thought you were angry. You didn’t need to go to all that trouble for me.”

“I am angry, but not with you, and who are you to tell me how I can and can’t spend my money?” he smiled. “Roll.”

I picked up the dice. “Thank you.”

“I hope you don’t mind, but Niven told me about your art studio, so I had a look. You’re very talented,” he complimented.

Trust Niven to tell him. It usually took me a while, if ever, to tell someone about my art.

It always made me feel a little self-conscious telling people. “It’s what I love most.” I stopped playing.

“Have you ever thought about putting on an exhibition?” he asked.

“I wouldn’t know where to start. I’m not sure if I even have enough good quality paintings to put on something like that.” I shrugged my shoulders.

“Maybe you need to get home and get painting again,” he suggested.

“I would love that,” I gushed, probably too emphatically.

“Now that’s the smile I was hoping to see when I first came in.”

We both jumped when the door opened unexpectedly. The doctor walked in for the second time today, but there was no way I was going to pretend I was sleeping this time. He was an older gentleman, short and stocky and he never had the nurse with him.

"Miss Grimes, how are you feeling today? I heard you weren't eating," he asked, sounding like I was in trouble again.

"I wasn't hungry," I tried to explain.

"You need to eat to keep your strength up. I can't allow you to go home if you're not eating!" he scolded.

My eyes dropped to the trolley, and I could feel the tears welling up behind my eyes.

"Could I have a word with you in private?" Gabriel stood up waiting for the doctor to lead the way.

It was funny watching how the doctor fumbled his way around some words of protest as he sorted the thick glasses on his nose before taking another look at me, then Gabriel, and decided to do as he was asked.

I don't know what was going on with my hormones. I was never usually this much of a cry baby.

Gabriel and the doctor came back in, and I sat up, wiping away the remnants of my latest breakdown.

"Well, Miss Grimes, it looks like we'll be sending you home," he said, looking to Gabriel for approval.

"Really, but what about this thing?" I asked, lifting my leg and wishing I hadn't.

"We can get you back in as an outpatient," he confirmed.

I looked at Gabriel, who had his hand up to his face like he was evaluating the situation and the doctors' performance.

"When can I go?" I asked excitedly.

"If you want to get your things together, I'll get a porter."

"No," jumped in Gabriel. "I'll carry her."

"That works," he said, nodding his head.

I tried to stifle the smile that was on my lips. I think the doctor would have done anything Gabriel told him to.

"Right, well, yes. I best be going." He sounded flustered. With one last look at Gabriel, he left the room.

"Do you always get everything you want?" I asked, surprised at what had just taken place.

"I'll tell you later," he said, looking straight at me. I could feel my cheeks flush at that comment.

He dumped my bag on the bed and helped me to sit up. "Is there anything I can help you with before I go?"

"Where are you going?" I asked, not wanting him to leave now.

"I was just going to wait outside until you changed."

"Oh, right. I don't think so." As long as Niven had packed everything I needed.

Gabriel left, and I rummaged through my bag. I managed most things on my own, but my pants and jogging bottoms were never going to fit over that contraption. I sat there, wondering what to do.

There was a knock at the door. "Is it okay for me to come back in?" Gabriel asked.

"Sure." I rolled my eyes.

"Not ready yet? I thought you would have been dying to get out that door," he commented.

I swallowed and looked down at my leg, trying to pluck up the courage to tell him what was wrong.

"I can't get my pants and trousers on," I said, embarrassed, which was never usually a problem for me.

Gabriel laughed into himself. "I'll be back in a minute." He came back in with a pair of scissors.

"Give me your pants," he asked, holding out his hand.

I handed him my shorts, and he cut up the side of them.

"What are you doing?" I asked, bewildered by what I was watching.

"Leg," he ordered, holding his hand out.

I lifted the leg that was fine, and he slipped my pants on. "Pull them up."

The look on my face must have been a picture. Gabriel turned around, and I pulled them up, holding the two ends together at my hip.

"How am I going to…?" but before I could finish, he had taken the two sides and tied them together. Ingenious really. "Cool, but I don't think that's going to work with these," I concluded, picking up my trousers.

He took the scissors and proceeded to cut the legs off, turning them into a pair of shorts. "Perfect. What did we ever do without scissors?" Gabriel laughed.

We packed up my room, and we were ready to go. "What about my flowers?"

"I'll buy you more." He picked me up.

"Wait, my card." He carried me back to the unit, and I picked up the card.

"Ready?" he asked before moving again.

I nodded my head. We got more than a couple of stares as he carried me through the hospital like Richard Gere in an Officer and a Gentleman and into the car park. I wondered what kind of car he drove and scanned the rows trying to pick his one out. His keys were already in his hands, and with one press of a button, the boot opened on a large black Lexus.

"Is that where I'm going?" I joked before he placed me in. "I was joking."

He went round to open the back door then came back to pick me up and place me in the back seat with my foot outstretched. It was far from comfortable, but due to our hastiness, it was going to have to do. I managed to get a seatbelt around me before he got in the car, and we were heading home.

"Call Niven." Gabriel spoke out loud.

"Gabriel is everything alright?" came Niven's voice through the car sound system.

"I've got Grace in the car. I'm bringing her home. Any chance you could meet us there?"

"Yeah, sure. Leaving now."

The line went dead, and I rested my head into the seat.

It was just as much of a palaver getting into the house, but at least I was in my bed, relaxed, television, bathroom, and who could forget, studio.

"I'll leave you two to it. I need to get back to get the kids tucked in for bed." Niven hugged us both before leaving us in the bedroom.

Gabriel waited until the front door had closed before he began to speak. "You're all mine now." He whispered.

"And what are you going to do with me?" I smiled back at him.

"How about we have some food first, Chinese?" he offered.

"Sounds better than that hospital food."

He went to stand up from the bed.

"Wait." I grabbed his arm to stop him from moving. "Thank you for this, for getting me home," I said, sounding serious.

"It was my pleasure," he said, leaning over me before kissing me on the forehead.

I held onto his jacket so he couldn't move too far away. We looked at each other before he moved back in. I had never been more ready in my life to kiss someone. I closed my eyes, feeling his breath on my face, waiting anxiously for that first kiss. His lips brushed over mine. I gasped as I felt him pull away. I could have stayed like that for the rest of my life, and it wouldn't be long enough.

"I should phone for food," he said, standing.

He left me lying, breathless on my bed. I had slept with men who hadn't left me feeling this good, and that was only a nearly kiss!

Chapter Six

Gabriel had set me up in my studio before leaving me alone to paint. I sat on a chair; my leg outstretched on a stool with a pillow for comfort. I sat staring at the blank canvas. There was nothing more frightening. I suppose it must be the same for a writer, an empty page just waiting to have words written to create a picture in the mind of the person who was reading. Well, it was the same for me sitting here, only I was giving the person the visual all they had to do was find the words to convey the emotions the piece of art was making them feel.

I closed my eyes and let the pictures of my life run through my mind. What makes me happy, what brings me joy? What was I feeling at this precise moment? I picked up a brush and began to paint. No artists block this time, although Gabriel block was a new feature. I couldn't stop thinking about him, which had me smiling and gasping for breath as my mind included the missing parts from that nearly kiss.

"Grace?" came a call from the front door.

"Hey," I called back as the butterflies made me giddy with excitement.

I could hear Gabriel bounding his way up the stair and into my studio. "Still sitting there?" he asked, smiling, knowing there was no way I could go anywhere on my own.

"Funny! How did your meeting go?" I asked.

"Good. This painting is amazing," he commented as he knelt beside me, his hand resting on my knee.

"I'm not sure it's a bit dark." I tilted my head slightly as if seeing it from a different perspective was going to change it any.

"What's at the man's back?" he asked.

"You, okay?" I asked, noticing a look of terror crossing his eyes.

"Yeah, fine," he said, deflecting me back onto his question.

"I'm not sure. I think the man is protecting the girl, maybe a cape, her superhero." I turned my head to look at him.

Gabriel looked at the picture a bit longer than I was expecting then turned to face me. "Maybe we should let it dry." He stood, picked me up, and carried me through to my room.

I arranged the pillows at my back while Gabriel did the same for my ankle.

"Your family must be missing you?" I asked, hoping I could find out a bit more about him.

"Yeah, and I miss them." He came to lie next to me. My heart skipped a beat having him this close.

"You?"

I shook my head. "Dad died ten years ago, mum a few after that. I have a lot of aunties, uncles, and cousins, but we only really see each other for weddings and funerals,"

"You can share my brothers." He smiled. He moved closer, his hand reaching over to move a stray piece of hair away from my face.

I looked into those deep blue eyes wanting him more than I think I've ever wanted anyone in my life.

He moved closer, and I took a deep breath wondering if this time, he would kiss me properly, although I would settle for one of his nearly kisses even if it did leave me wanting more.

He smiled as if he could understand every thought that was passing through my brain.

I closed my eyes as my heart rate began to increase. I was sure Gabriel could hear the pounding coming from my chest. He moved closer. His breath, his lips, the door!

"Grace!"

You have got to be kidding me! Niven!

"Hey, okay. Bad timing? I should…" she said pointing towards the door.

"No, it's fine. Could you sit with Grace for a bit? I need to go and collect a few things from home," he asked, jumping from the bed and making a hasty retreat, not waiting for an answer.

Niven turned to face me, and mouthed, "Did you see that?"

"I think I might have." I laughed. Always one for stating the obvious was Niv.

"Tell me everything, how was he?" she threw her coat onto the chair in the corner of the room before jumping onto the bed next to me.

I blew the air from my puffed-out cheeks. "Yeah, the chocolates weren't even close."

"Blew your mind?" she asked, teasing.

"He would have had a certain someone not interrupted," I said, staring at her.

"Sorry. Darcy always says I come with Niven timing." She closed her eyes and sighed. "What are you going to tell Bryce?"

Damn, I hadn't even considered him. "I'll think about it."

"You need to tell him it's not fair to keep him hanging on," she said, turning her head to look at me.

"I know, but how many times do you think I'll need to tell him before he gets the message?" I huffed.

"I think the fact that Gabriel will be around may be enough to convince him," she said with a 'you know I'm right' look on her face.

"Do you think he'll ever talk to me again?" I asked with a hint of sadness to my voice. As much as I didn't want to be in a relationship with him, he was still a good friend, and I would miss him. I turned my head and stared again at the ceiling.

"You'll need to give him time, Gracie."

She always called me Gracie when she was telling me something I didn't want to hear or consoling me.

"I'm missing you at work. Amelia keeps asking after you." She laughed.

"I'm sure. Who's she latched onto now?" I asked, wondering if they would keep her.

"Well, that's the funny thing, she doesn't hang around with anyone. She goes out to her car at breaks, and she goes out every lunchtime," she informed me.

"You should follow her," I suggested with a gasp.

"I could be like Poirot!" She laughed. "International detective. I could put on my best German accent."

"Was he not French?" I suggested.

"I'll IMDB it." She scrolled through her phone. "Belgian!"

"Who knew?"

"Not us," she said, laughing.

"I wonder what her story is," I asked, determined to know more.

"I'm not sure I want to know. There's something about that woman that scares me." Niven shuddered.

"I wouldn't worry about it. Just stay away," I suggested.

"Anyway, I should get going and let you get back to well whatever you two were in the middle of," she teased.

"You've probably scared him away."

"He's not going to be away for long, trust me." She picked up her coat. "Catch."

I lay there for a bit before picking up my phone and sending a text.

"Coasts clear."

"We need to get a chain," he replied.

"Kinky."

"For the door!"

"I want you."

"Patience."

"Are you busy?"

"I got caught up in a couple of things, will you be okay for at least the next hour?"

"I'm sure I could find something to do, lying in bed, on my own…"

"No!"

"Why?"

"That's my job."

"Staff reviews are due. You'll need to do better!" I smiled.

"Does the boss get an appraisal?"

"Only if it's favourable."

"Let me get on with my work, and I'll be over as soon as I can."

"Catch x."

"X."

I let the phone drop beside me and closed my eyes. Damn! I needed to pee.

I threw the covers off, sorted my pyjamas, and edged my way over to the side of the bed. I took a deep breath and stood up and promptly fell straight back down again. Breathe! I tried over, and this time managed to stand, although I felt a little queasy. I hopped over to the bathroom door and held on. Who knew going to the bathroom could be so tiring?

I made it back to bed without incident, but I wondered if I should phone the hospital and get a set of crutches. It would save waiting to get Gabriel to carry me everywhere unless that was his plan all along. To keep me trapped in my bed like the guy from Misery. I was too tired to think about it. I was glad I was back in my bed.

I was walking up the Bridges, turning my head occasionally to see if my bus was coming. "Miss." I turned around.

"Gabriel?"

"You're going to miss your bus."

I turned back as it went past, not stopping at the bus stop. "I've missed it."

"Yes, you have! You're mine now!" Amelia stood where Gabriel had been only moments before.

"Amelia?" She looked different. She was staring at me like she wanted to kill me.

"Run, Grace!" called Gabriel.

I began to back away, but I couldn't take my eyes off her. She started to walk towards me.

"Gabriel!" I called, but he was on the ground. He was different too, there was a glow surrounding him, and there was something on the pavement beside him, blood! I managed to turn and run, but her hand caught my shoulder.

"Grace!"

"No!" I screamed, my eyes darting open. Gabriel was sitting next to me with his hand on my shoulder.

"You're, okay, I'm here," he said, trying to soothe me back into this reality.

"I think I was dreaming." I tried to regulate my breathing. The fear still present with me.

I sat up and ran my hand through my hair. I went to get up.

"You think? Where are you going?" he asked, concerned.

"Bathroom."

"I'll help you." He went to pick me up.

"No! I can do it," I said, pushing him away. I hopped my way to the bathroom and ran the tap, splashing some cold water on my face. What was that? I thought to myself as I tried to slow my breathing. I dried my face on the towel placing it back on the heated rail and returned to bed. Gabriel was leaning against the wall with his arms folded in front of him.

"You, okay?" he asked.

I got back into bed and pulled the covers up leaving my damaged leg exposed. "Bad dream."

"I got that much." He had that angry tone to his voice again as if I had upset him.

"What?" I asked, knowing there had to be more. I had been around Bryce for long enough. I could tell when I managed to piss people off.

"Talk to me." His voice softened.

"Give me a minute," I closed my eyes hoping the vision of Amelia wouldn't be there or Gabriel lying in a pool of his blood.

The bell on the door went. "Tell them I'm sleeping," I called after Gabriel as he ran down the stairs to see who it was.

"Bryce," said Gabriel, and there was that edge again.

"Can I come in?" Bryce asked.

"She's sleeping." Gabriel cut him off.

"Can I see her; I won't stay long?" he pleaded.

"She needs her rest. Phone her later." Gabriel suggested.

I heard the door closing. I could tell Bryce would have just walked away.

"That was Bryce," he said, leaning against the door frame with his hands pushed into his jean's pockets.

"I heard. I'm sorry for pushing you away. I'm just used to being on my own," I tried to explain.

"You don't need to do that with me." He looked hurt.

I put my hand out to him. "Come here." It was the first time I noticed he had changed out of his suit and into a pair of jeans with a shirt.

"You changed?"

"I wanted to relax. Maybe I should go and let you get some rest," he suggested.

"I think I've had enough rest." I sat up. "Please," I asked again.

This time he walked over to me, put his knee on the bed next to me before leaning forward. Our faces were close together, our mouths slightly open, ready for what was to come. His mouth pressed against mine, and he didn't disappoint. His hand moved slowly over my body, squeezing me in all the right places. He wasn't rushing, but this felt way more intimate than anything I had experienced before. I opened a couple of buttons on his shirt and pulled it up his body while he helped remove it over his head, exposing his muscled body beneath. I gasped, as his hands continued the exploration of my body. His mouth had moved away from mine and was finding new ways to excite me.

"Is this, okay?" he breathed next to my ear?

Was he kidding? "Yes," was all I could manage to say.

I ran my hand through his hair, and I let a breath escape next to his ear. "I want you."

He moved and hit my ankle, which had me gasping and grabbing his shoulders and not for the reason either of us had expected.

"Grace, I'm sorry." He knew straight away what had happened. He jumped up and moved my leg back onto the pillow, a look of shock on his face.

I lay back with my arms over my face breathing steadily to take the pain away.

"I'm so sorry, can I get you anything?"

"It'll be okay in a minute." I hoped anyway.

He knelt next to the bed and pulled my arms away from my face. Luckily the tears were rolling into my hair from the sides of my eyes.

"I've hurt you, I'm sorry." He looked like he was in more pain than I was.

"It was as much my fault." Luckily the pain had begun to dissipate. I put my hand out and touched his face. "We just need to be more careful," I suggested.

"I think we should maybe wait until you get that thing off, at least," he said, looking at me longingly.

"I don't think we need to wait that long." I smiled.

He leaned forward and kissed me. "What am I going to do with you?"

"I could think of a few things." I let my hand run down his chest.

Chapter Seven

The hospital delivered the crutches, and I had my appointment to go back to the hospital for a check-up. I couldn't wait to get the thing off and take a proper shower without having to put my foot in a bin bag first.

Gabriel had been trying to keep me occupied with the latest Blu-ray movies and a new PlayStation. My days spent as an army operative were the only thing keeping me sane. Nic had come over, and with his skills, I nearly finished the campaign, granted it was on the lowest skill level but still. I had never seen the fascination before, but I couldn't put it down, and it was scary how quickly you got involved in the game.

Gabriel would bring food in with him when he came home from work. Our nights spent talking about nothing in particular but feeling at ease in each other's company. I was getting used to cuddling up with him at night to watch a film or to carry on one of our weird conversations. What *would* happen if you were driving down the motorway and pulled your keys out of the ignition?

I was beginning to wonder where Gabriel went all the time. There were all these secret meetings he had to get to, and he always seemed to appear just when I wanted him to. Niven said it was a coincidence, but I was having a hard time believing that. I never was one for coincidences. Maybe I was expecting too much.

If everything had been fine with my ankle, I would have had work and my painting, and we probably wouldn't have seen each other until the weekend. I knew I was just bored lying here all day with no one to talk to.

When he had left last night, I hobbled my way to the window and watched him walking next door to his own house. I wasn't sure what he was doing once he got in, but he had some mad lighting system set up where all the lights in his house would come on at the same time, but then they would go off just as quickly.

I had been keeping up with my painting too. The dark man was always saving the girl. I had no idea where I had dreamed up that concept. I know Gabriel had helped me after the accident, but this was more like the man was saving the girl's life.

"Grace!" Gabriel ran up the stairs checking all the rooms.

It did make me laugh as I spoke to myself after every door opened and closed behind him. "Cold. Warm. Warmer."

He burst through the door of my studio, the only logical place. "Boiling!" I smirked. Paintbrush in hand.

"What?" he asked, looking puzzled and out of breath.

I shook my head. "What's got you all in a spin?" I asked, pointing my paintbrush at him.

"You phoned me. You sounded like you were being attacked. That's why I'm here."

I laughed. "I think your Spidey senses are off, Gabe. I never phoned you, and I've been sitting here all day."

He stood with his hands on his hips, trying to regain his breath and his composure, but he did not look happy. "Let me see your phone."

I unplugged the phone from my earphones and handed it to him. I watched him as he played around with it before handing it back to me.

"There was no phone call."

"As I said, I haven't moved from here."

He looked at me perplexed, wondering how I had managed to phone him without actually doing so.

I put my paintbrush down, eased my leg off the stool, and hobbled over to the door where he was still standing. I grabbed a handful of his coat and pulled him down so I could kiss him. "I'm sorry you got a fright, but I'm fine. Now that you're here, maybe we could." I bit my lip and looked up at him through my eyelashes. It was my best seductive move, and one I hoped was going to work.

He smiled. "I suppose I could stay for a little while." He wrapped his arms around my waist and leaned in for a kiss, which I was more than obliging.

"How about we get you out of these work clothes?" I teased, pulling his tie off and draping it around my neck.

"It looks better on you anyway." He picked me up and carried me through to the bedroom.

He placed me down gently, and I moved his coat off his shoulders, letting it drop to the floor. He didn't seem that concerned, and I continued to undress him. Opening each button and kissing the exposed skin beneath. I stared into his eyes while I removed the belt from his trousers and slowly pulled the zip down. I let one hand discover him while the other reached up to the back of his head, pulling it down. I bit at his bottom lip which seemed to produce the desired effect.

"You'll need to lie on the bed. I can't kneel," I spoke next to his ear.

He kicked his trousers off before picking me up and placing me on the bed. He moved me back, lying on top of me, still kissing me. This time his kiss was more forceful, his hand finding its way under my top. He pulled it up and over my head. He moved me slightly to the side to unhook my bra, which seemed to fall off without any effort. Our lips skimmed each other's, and I could taste his sweet, warm breath. His hand went to the side of my neck, clearing the way for his moist lips while slowly kissing where his fingers had been only moments before. The stubble from his face scratching me in the tiny movements of his mouth opening and closing as he moved over my skin.

"Where are you going?" I asked as he got up and stood at the side of the bed.

He smirked. "I think it's going to take a little more effort to get your shorts off." I lifted my hips off the bed as he knelt beside me, exposing me to him for the first time. I tried to keep my eyes locked on his, but he was looking elsewhere. It did make me feel like a nervous teenager again, and I was sure I was blushing. I dumped my shorts unceremoniously on top of the pile next to the bed. He removed his shorts, and I was the one looking down his body.

The sparse amount of hair over his chest, the little molehills of muscle on his abdomen, and the darker, thicker, snail trail, taking me on a journey; I would never want to return from. The smile, my unexpected gasp made, across his lips only made me desire him more. He knelt in-between my legs, and I was ready, anticipating what was about to happen, but also a little nervous at the same time. He moved on top, his body pressing against me, his mouth and tongue mixing with mine. My fingers ran down the length of his spine, and I felt him shudder.

He let a breath escape on my neck. "I want you," I whispered.

He kissed me again.

His phone rang, and he looked up.

"Leave it!" I demanded.

"It might be important."

"This is important!" I shouted back.

"Two minutes." He reached onto the unit for his phone, forgetting about my ankle, and kicked it off the bed.

"Argh! Gabriel!" he rolled onto his side to look at his phone, and I sat up on the side of the bed. This wasn't happening!

"Check your phone. It's Niven. She's been trying to get you."

I rolled my eyes at the ceiling. "My phone's fine." I reached over to check it while Gabriel forced his phone into my hand.

"Niv, this better be good." I chuckled.

"I got a text from you saying you needed a lift."

"I don't know what's wrong with it. Gabriel got a strange phone call from me too. It must be a crossed line or something." I wasn't even sure if that happened with mobiles, but it was the only explanation I had, and I had a naked man lying next to me that needed my attention.

"Okay, I'll let you go. I hope I wasn't interrupting anything?" Niv laughed. I hung up the phone and sighed.

"Everything okay?" Gabriel asked.

"I need a new phone." I turned to hand him back his phone. I leant over and rubbed my leg, the pain still not dissipating.

He got off the bed and knelt on the floor in front of me. "I'm sorry I banged your ankle again." His fingers ran up and down my leg.

I rested my hand on his shoulder. I screwed up my face and reached for my top from the pile on the floor. "Do you get the feeling someone's trying to tell us something?"

Gabriel stopped me from putting my top on. "You're not going to let a small interruption halt proceedings, are you?" he asked, smiling at me.

Anybody else, and I think I would have just put my top on and got cuddled into bed, but this was Gabriel. The more times we keep putting it off, and we might never get the chance again.

"I'm not sure what if the ceiling falls down?" I answered sarcastically.

"If it does, I'll be on top to protect you."

"Well, when you put it like that." I kissed him, and he stood up, moving me back onto the bed but forgetting to lift my ankle first as he managed to get a direct hit on it again! "Bloody hell Gabriel!" This time I stood up, went to my chest of drawers, and took out a pair of pyjamas before locking myself in the bathroom.

I sat on the toilet as I got dressed. It wasn't Gabriel's fault, but it was so frustrating having this big bloody contraption attached to me. I sighed and opened the door. Gabriel was getting dressed.

I leaned against the door frame. “I’m sorry, Gabriel. It’s not you that I’m angry with.”

He stood up, tucking his shirt into his trousers and fastening them. He stood in front of me and put his arms around me. “I know.”

“Please don’t go,” I asked, hoping I hadn’t pushed him away.

He looked into my eyes. “I should be getting back and let you get some rest.” He kissed the top of my head and left.

I hobbled over to the window and watched him walk away. The bright light illuminated every window in his house when he entered, and I put it to mind that I would need to ask him about that. “Night Gabriel,”

Chapter Eight

I had decided to make a nice dinner for Gabriel as a thank you for taking care of me these last few weeks. I had music streaming through my phone and into the speaker. I was happy.

The doorbell interrupted my rendition of some eighties' classic, but I was at the door in a flash, a new skill I had acquired with the help of my crutches.

"Amelia?" I sounded as surprised as I was to see her standing there as if she had just walked off some catwalk.

"Oh, you poor thing," she said as she barged past me and into my house.

I stood thinking about what had just happened. I closed the door and followed her into the kitchen.

"What can I do for you?" I asked, hoping it was something quick.

"Why Grace, I've missed you terribly." She wiped a non-existent tear away from her eye. "When are you coming back to work?"

"I'm not sure. I need to wait and see how I get on at the hospital." I turned the gas down on my pots as Amelia seemed to be casing my home. She was flitting from one thing to another, like a butterfly in a greenhouse.

"In that case, maybe we could have a girl's night in?" she produced a bottle from her bag.

"I'm not meant to be drinking with the tablets I'm on." I tried to let her down gently.

"I noticed you had a new neighbour."

I wasn't even sure how she knew that considering the sign had been taken down from Gabriel's garden. Had she been here before? This whole thing was making me feel uneasy.

"I'm sorry to rush you, Amelia, but I have a friend coming for dinner," I tried to explain, hoping she would get the hint and leave.

"Of course. Well, it was lovely to see you. I'll leave this with you, for when you can enjoy it fully." She placed the bottle on the bunker and made her way back through leaving the front door open as she walked to her car.

I closed and locked the door. Grateful that she had left, but I felt uneasy. I had the feeling that if she came back again, I wouldn't be so lucky a second time.

I finished making the dinner, unable even to lift the bottle she had brought and move it to the fridge. It sat on the bunker like some sort of recording device. If it had eyes, it would have been like one of those paintings where they follow you around the room.

I plated up, checking the time for when Gabriel would be back. He was always on time, and I hoped tonight wouldn't be any different.

I had been sitting at the table playing with the food on my plate for the last hour. Playing on my phone, checking for any messages, but nothing. I picked at the food, but it wasn't as good as it could have been when it was hot.

I looked at the bottle of wine that Amelia had left. "Stuff it!" I got a glass from the cupboard and poured some of the sparkling white. I took a quick sniff, not that I had any idea what I should be looking for, but it smelled amazing. I took a sip, and the bubbles exploded over my tongue. I giggled to myself and put my hand up to my mouth. What was it just now with chocolate and now wine? In a little while, there would be no need for Gabriel to be here at all! Maybe he shouldn't be here if he couldn't even message me to tell me he was going to be late.

I turned the sound up on my speaker, finished the wine in my glass, and poured another. I was doing my best to dance on one foot while holding onto the island. The bottle was like the magic porridge pot, never-ending. Maybe Amelia wasn't so bad, after all. She could bring me wine like this anytime she wanted.

It didn't take long for the effects of the wine to take hold, and instead of dancing, I was stumbling my way around the kitchen. It had gotten dark, and the little glow from the fairy lights was blending together. The thought that I should probably stop went through my head, but this was as much fun as I had had in a long time. I finished the glass and another when the door opened, which made me jump, which in turn made me laugh.

Gabriel came through to the kitchen. "What's going on here?"

"I'm having a party for one." I giggled raising a finger at him.

"Really?" he walked over to the island and picked up the bottle. "How much have you had?"

"That's the funny thing. It doesn't run out! It was the gift that keeps on giving!" I slurred.

"I think the party's over." He switched the music off.

"Spoilsport." I threw my arms around his neck. "Take me to bed, Mr," I burst out laughing. "I don't know your surname."

I wasn't sure what happened next, but I was upside down. "Are you carrying me?" I asked, not believing what he was doing.

"If you're going to act like a child, I'm going to treat you like one!"

"Oh, Gabriel's angry!" I looked down the flight of stairs. "Quickly put me down. I think I'm going to be sick,"

For the first time, he did what I asked him. He held me up against the wall in the hall and looked at me.

"I missed you," I slurred as I tried to focus on his face.

"So, you thought a bottle of wine was going to take my place?" he looked at me incredulously.

"It was."

"But not now."

I shook my head carefully. "Where were you? I tried to message," I asked, wondering why he was so late back.

"I'll explain tomorrow when you've sobered up a bit."

I leaned in and kissed him. I didn't want to wait any longer.

"Grace," he said, trying to stop me, but I was a woman on a mission, and I leaned back in. He relaxed into me and began to kiss along my neck, shoulder. His mouth came up and joined with mine. I slipped my tongue into his mouth, and he pushed me back onto the wall.

"What have you taken?" he shouted at me.

"You're hurting me!" I tried to wriggle from the grip he had on my arms.

"What did you take, Grace?" he shouted again. I tried to focus on what he was saying. "Grace!" he let me go and ran down the stair.

I heard a glass smash and wondered what was going on. "Gabe?"

He appeared at the bottom of the stair with the magic bottle. "Where did you get this?"

"Amelia brought it over," I confided like a guilty teenager. "I think I'm going to be sick."

Gabriel sprinted up the stairs two at a time, grabbed me, and ran me into the bathroom. It was not pretty. I hated being sick at the best of times, but I couldn't stand properly, and my body was aching.

"I'm sorry," I said, trying to grab for some toilet paper to wipe my nose and face.

"It's okay, it wasn't your fault," he said, kissing the back of my head.

He picked me up and carried me in his arms this time through to my room. He stood me in my bathroom, switched the shower on, and took my clothes off. He held me with one hand as he began removing his shirt, trousers, and shoes while walking me into the shower. He stood behind me, holding me as the water ran over us. His arm steadied me around my waist. I put my hands forward onto the wall in front of me.

"I'm sorry." I felt so stupid.

He placed his hand next to mine on the wall and kissed my shoulder. "I'm sorry for shouting."

I ran my fingers along his muscled arm. I turned around and kissed him, holding onto him. He pulled my hair back from my shoulders, kissing me, feeling me. I put my hand inside his shorts.

"Don't," he whispered and brought my hand up to his mouth and kissed my wrist.

"Don't you want to?" I asked, looking at him.

His eyes were closed, his head hung forward.

I put my hands on his face. "Gabriel, this wasn't your fault."

"I think it might have been," he confessed. He switched the shower off and grabbed a couple of towels from the rail.

He carried me through to the room and picked out a clean pair of shorts and a T-shirt pyjama combo.

I dressed and put the towel around my head. I thought that after being sick and having a shower, I should be feeling better, but the pain in my head and the nausea weren't going anywhere soon. I turned to see where Gabriel was. He was standing, his arms folded in front of him, staring out of the window, the towel wrapped around his waist. I hobbled over to him and kissed his back.

"Talk to me," I asked.

He turned around and held me tightly against his body. "There are things about me you don't know, and I can't tell you. It's for your own safety."

"Hitman?" I joked.

“This is serious, Grace.” He went to move away, but I squeezed him tighter.

“I don’t want you to leave.”

“It might be for the best. I think someone got close to you that shouldn’t have.” He admitted letting his hands fall onto my shoulders.

“Then we need to be more careful,” I offered.

“I can’t be with you twenty-four hours a day. I can’t give you the protection you need.” He insisted.

“I have money. I have a house in the highlands we could go to?” I begged.

“I’m falling in love with you, and I don’t want to hurt you.” He declared.

“Then don’t. We can make this work, but you have to be honest with me,” I pleaded.

He kissed my forehead, and I closed my eyes, which had me hobbling quickly to the bathroom to be sick again. I should have remembered I’m always sick twice.

He waited until I had cleaned up then pulled me closer and kissed me. He lifted me, and I crossed my leg around his waist. He walked me over to the bed and kissed me as he removed my clothes again. I just hoped there would be no more interruptions. He arranged the pillows higher up for my leg to rest.

“Better?”

I nodded, and he removed the towel from around his waist, exposing him again and making me gasp again without realising I was doing it. The little smile crossed his lips, which was a nice touch, but I did need to get myself under control. His hand went down to position himself while moving inside me. The deep intake of breath and my head pressing back into the pillow had a concerned look appear on his face.

“Are you okay?”

“Yes, you?” I asked in bursts, staring up into his eyes, not wanting to move too soon.

He didn’t answer. A quick nod of the head was all that he afforded me before his head was next to mine. My fingers feeling through his dark soft hair as each long movement of his body built up the euphoria inside me. He kissed me, pressing his mouth hard onto mine, and taking my hand, and holding it on the pillow beside us. He was moving quicker, and I wasn’t sure how long either of us would be able to last. My legs squeezed against his hoping this feeling I was experiencing rushing through my body would last forever. His head sunk into my shoulder; his breathing laboured. I wrapped my arms around his body, holding him tightly as the last moments of our lovemaking left his body. I had wanted him since the first moment we had met, and I was never going to let him go, no matter who was after him.

Chapter Nine

My eyes flickered open. Was Gabe still here, or had he crept out in the night. Not that I could blame him. I had been sick even more during the night, which was enough to put anyone off. I moved my foot back, not wanting to turn around, but just a gentle nudge would tell me if I was still sharing a bed.

Nothing! I know I was a bit out of practice, but I didn't think it was that bad. I closed my eyes as my mind flashed through a montage of hot and steamy flashbacks. I let out a sigh as my cheeks burned at the thought and wishing he had waited for me to wake up before he left, and maybe it wouldn't have just been a memory.

I turned over as the sheet lay crumpled where his body had been next to me only hours before. My hand went out to the pillow, the indentation where his head had rested. I ran my fingers gently over the white cotton. It was then that my finger touched something that had no place being there. I sat up quickly, the sheet falling off my naked body, as I picked up the foreign object and twirled it around my fingers, wondering how a feather had appeared in my bed.

It wasn't a goose or duck feather. It was large enough that would have made writing with it look ridiculous, I ran it along the back of my hand, but the trail of blood it left was more indicative of a razor blade, but how could that be? I recoiled at the pain that was now coursing through my hand. I jumped out of bed and hobbled into the bathroom.

The red droplets were splashing off the white porcelain sink faster than I could grab a towel. It was looking like I had just committed some atrocious acts rather than swiping a feather across it.

I sat with my hand raised and a towel wrapped around it to try and stop the bleeding.

Where had the feather come from in the first place? It wasn't like we were doing some S&M stuff, and with what just happened to my hand, I was glad about that! I laughed to myself and brought my hand down to take a look at the damage. Well, at least the bleeding had stopped, but I now had a lovely straight red line across the back of my hand and no reasonable explanation to go with it.

I bandaged it up anyway and followed the blood trail back to my bed. I sat down and carefully picked up the feather. It was as white as snow, apart from my blood down one edge. The calamus was as strong and as heavy as iron as I twirled it around my fingers. I held it up to the light. It was almost translucent had it not been for the spectrum of coloured light that now danced across my bedroom wall.

I sighed and took it through to my studio and clamped it to my easel. I gathered my brushes and paint and prepared myself for an afternoon of painting something other than my heroic mystery man.

I sat back after hours of painting. The woman in the painting was lying on the ground.

Her throat slit, and the feather, with the same blood splatter as mine, lay beside her. The streetlights shone down on her like the stage lights on a west end production. Who would ever suspect a feather as a murder weapon? As long as they didn't pick it up, it would remain with the rest of the rubbish on the street. The perfect crime! I sat looking at it, imagining all the different scenarios of how the woman met her untimely death and who the murderer was.

There was a point where I imagined Gabriel coming up behind the woman to help her as she stumbled. The feather slicing across her neck in a swift, unnoticed action. He laid her gently down on the pavement, dropping the feather in the gutter before shouting for people to come and help. The police would be none the wiser, as there would be no murder weapon, and who would suspect a Good Samaritan coming to the aid of a beautiful young woman?

Gabriel. I picked up my phone, three twenty. I wondered where he was, as he was never usually this late. Anyway, I had a crime scene of my own to clear up in the bedroom. My hand was nipping, and I was feeling tired after changing all the sheets and putting another washing on. Luckily, I hadn't been sick. Whatever had happened last night, the effects had finally worn off.

I couldn't stop going over it. Did Amelia put something in my drink? Was that what Gabriel had tasted? But why? Was she the one who was after Gabriel? My head was swirling with all the questions. Where was he?

I sent him a text. "Gabriel, are you okay?"

I threw my phone down on the bed. Niven! I stretched back over to retrieve it.

"Hey, have you spoken to Gabriel?"

"Yes, did he tell you what happened?"

It sounded like we were having two different conversations. "No, tell me what?"

"Somebody stole my bag at work, then sent Gabriel a text saying I had been in a car crash, and could he come and pick me up."

"How did you find out?"

"Gabriel came to the house to see if Darcy had come to get me. How weird is that?"

"Yeah, weird."

"Are you okay? Were you looking for Gabriel?"

"Yeah, it's fine, probably still at work,"

"Well, if you need me, just shout."

I tapped the phone off my chin. What was going on? I tried calling Gabriel's phone. Answer machine.

"Gabriel, hi it's, Grace. Could you message me, so I know you're, okay?" It didn't take long for my phone to beep with a text message.

"Grace, I'm fine. We'll talk when I get home."

Well, at least I knew he was still coming back, and nothing had happened to him. I put a film on and got into bed, anything to take my mind off what had happened.

The film finished and the next. I got out of bed and went to see if any of the lights were on next door, but it was in complete darkness. Why was Gabriel taking so long? I checked my phone, nothing. I was getting scared, especially after what Niven had told me. Amelia!

What if Amelia had stolen Niven's bag to get Gabriel away from me. Was she trying to get at Gabriel through me?

Maybe the idea of heading north was a good one after all. At least we would be safe there, no one knew about the house. I don't know why I had never mentioned it, but it was my place of refuge, my sanctuary. We could go after I had been to the hospital and hopefully get this damn bear trap off!

I went into my cupboard and pulled out a bag and began to pack some clothes and other things I would need and just in case I put my driving licence and passport in too. I went to my chest of drawers and pulled out the bottom drawer, put my hand inside, and found the key to the house taped on the underside of the next drawer up.

I spun it over in my fingers a few times, wondering if I was going to be opening a Pandora's Box by going back. I hadn't been there for such a long time that it might not be liveable. I used to love being there, but I was older, and all the memories that I had were just that, memories. It was just a house. There was no warmth, no aunties, and uncles to keep me entertained, and my dad wouldn't be there to tell me about what it used to be like when he visited as a child.

I used to love hearing how his mum would put him on a steam train in Edinburgh on his own at five or six, and he would travel over to Glasgow and on to the West Highland line heading for Mallaig. He would see the Bonnie Prince Charlie monument and Glenfinnan Viaduct, but it was when he saw the white sands of Morar that's when he knew his train journey was nearly over. Then he would have to get the ferry over to Portree, where his auntie would be waiting for him with a lift up in the post van.

Changed days. I can remember being picked up from school on a Friday and driving up.

There weren't the new motorways and stretches of dual carriageways where you could overtake. The tapes of John Denver, Neil Diamond, and Simon and Garfunkel were the soundtrack to my childhood as I looked out of the window at the passing scenery.

I wiped at a tear that was slowly running down my cheek. There were times when I thought about my dad that my heart felt like it was ripping in two. I wasn't sure what happened, everything would be fine, and then either a song or a phrase that my dad would use or sometimes it was nothing at all and a wave that some Hawaiian surfer would be proud of would come crashing in and hit me full force in the chest.

I sat on the floor of my room and just cried.

"Grace!" called Gabriel, closing the door behind him.

"Up here." I wiped at my face hoping that Gabriel wouldn't notice.

"Hey. Have you been crying?"

Well, that worked!

"Just memories." I tried to smile through the pain that was still welling up inside.

Gabriel came and sat down on the floor next to me, he put his arm over my shoulder, and I cuddled into his chest.

"I'm sorry if you were worried," he said, stroking my hair.

"It wasn't that. I mean, yes, I was worried about you, but this, this was reminiscing."

"Do you want to talk about it?" he asked.

"No. It was silly. Anyway, where were you?" I held onto his shirt, hoping he wasn't going to move.

"Were you going somewhere?" he asked, looking around at all the bags and drawers lying around slightly perplexed.

"We need to talk." I stood up and sat on the bed.

"Sounds serious," he said, taking his jacket and shoes off before getting himself comfy beside me, pulling one of the pillows up at his back.

"You never told me about Niven having her bag stolen," I began.

"You weren't really in the best state of mind to go into detail." He tried to explain.

"I know, but you were away before I woke up, and we didn't have a chance to talk about last night," I pointed out.

"Sorry. I had to be somewhere. There wasn't any time." He wasn't looking at me when he spoke, and it made me wonder if he was trying to hide something.

"You said last night that you thought someone might be trying to get to you. I think it might be Amelia."

Gabriel sat up and turned to face me. "Has she been back today?" he asked.

I shook my head. "No. She would have been working yesterday, and she knows Niven and I are best friends. Then if she knew about us, she could have used Niven's phone to message you, knowing the coast would have been clear to come to the house. She left the bottle for a reason. You knew right away that there was something in the wine. Maybe she was trying to get at you through me."

Gabriel studied my face for a while before speaking. "Maybe that job at MI5 isn't an absurd idea after all. I think she's been playing you for a while now," he suggested.

"How did she know?" I turned to look at him.

Chapter Ten

"Know what?" he asked, studying my face.

"She began working with me at least a week or two before we met, so how did she know that we were going to know each other?" I was trying to figure it all out while Gabriel sat there quietly. "Gabriel?" I looked at him intently.

"She couldn't have known." Gabriel tried to reassure me as he ran his hand over my back.

"Were you following me?" I asked incredulously, pulling away from him.

"What? No!"

"It wasn't a coincidence that my new neighbour was just happening to be walking up the Bridges at the same time as I trip off the pavement." I couldn't believe what I was saying, but he wasn't exactly trying to refute the accusation. "I'm going to go away for a few days after I've been to the hospital," I informed him.

"I'm not sure if I can leave just now."

"I wasn't asking you to come. I need some time on my own." I had no idea what was going on, but I also knew I wanted no part of this.

"Grace, please. Don't leave me. I'll tell you what you want to know." He pleaded.

"Were you following me?" I asked him.

"Grace, anything but that."

I scoffed. "I think you should leave."

"No. I can't tell you that, but yes Amelia has been trying to get close to you so she can hurt me." He blurted out.

"And why does she want to hurt you?"

He scrunched his face up. "I can't tell you that either."

"It seems to me you can't tell me very much." I shook my head in disgust. "What's the point?"

"Don't say that!" he stood up and walked over to the window. He ran his hands through his hair, desperately looking around for anything that could help him get away from this line of questioning.

"I'm not from around here!" he exclaimed.

For the first time tonight, I believed what he was saying.

"Where are you from?" I asked, wondering if an answer was going to be forthcoming considering the way he was reacting.

"I'm not of this world."

I sat staring at how intense he was looking, then burst out laughing.

"Grace, I'm trying to be serious here." He folded his arms in front of him.

I put my hands out in front of me. "Okay, okay. I'm sorry, right, I'm ready," I took a breath to try and stop myself from laughing.

"If you're not going to take this seriously."

"Are you an alien?" I gasped. "Is that why your house lights up at night?" I asked, surprised.

"What? Did you see that? No! I'm not an alien."

"So, you're not a little green man, then?" I smirked.

"Is this you being serious?" he was getting exasperated, and I think I had wound him up enough for one night.

"Stand up." He ordered while closing the blinds and switching the lights off. I did what he asked.

He began to unbutton his shirt. "Gabriel, I don't think this is the time."

He removed his shirt. "Don't be scared. Promise me."

"I promise," I answered nervously. "Wait, you don't have a big head with dripping wet fangs or anything? Please tell me you don't walk up walls because that would freak me out. That's one of my pet hates, that and someone lying under the bed!"

He gave me a strange look. "Nice to know, and no, no fangs."

I took a step back.

"Can I show you now?"

"Wait."

"Grace!"

"Are you hideous? Is that why you're so good looking in a human body?"

He shook his head, laughing. "Right, that's enough."

I took a deep breath and watched him, half ready to run to the bathroom and lock the door.

He closed his eyes as a light began to emanate from his body before he changed. "What the hell are those?" I screamed, seeing two perfect wings appear behind him. In the same instance, they disappeared, and he ran for the door.

"No way, you're not going anywhere!" I'm not sure how I managed it, but I hit the door about the same time as he got to it.

"Let me go," he asked. His breathing was fast, and he couldn't look at me.

"No. What was that?" I asked again.

He rested his head on the door. "I'm sorry, I didn't want you to find out like this."

"Find out what? Who are you?" I asked, resting my hand on his shoulder. I wasn't angry anymore. I just needed to know who or what he was. "Are you a bird?"

"No!"

"But the wings?"

"What did you say to me when I first told you, my name?" he lifted his head from the door and looked at me.

"I can't remember," I answered honestly.

"I said I'm Gabriel, and you said."

"Just like the angel," I responded, all emotion gone from my voice.

"Grace. Say something." His hand ran down my arm, but my mind couldn't comprehend what he had just told me.

I sat back on the bed. "You're an angel?" I repeated.

"I'm an angel,"

"You said you were in requisitions?"

"I am, of souls."

"Mine?"

"Everyone. I'm here to help."

I looked up at him, bewildered. "Really?"

"I'm sorry, I couldn't tell you." He sat next to me.

"What about now? Are you in trouble for telling me?"

"Probably. I couldn't lose you like that."

"What happens now?" I didn't want to hear the answer.

"That's up to you. I can ask my brother to come and help protect you here, or you can go away while I try to sort this out, then I can come and get you when it's all over. If you want someone to go with you, I can arrange that too," he offered.

"Can I see them again?"

"Grace, I'm not sure."

"Please." I put my hand on his arm. He had done what I asked and told me the truth.

Now it was my turn to be there for him.

Gabriel stood up, he closed his eyes, and the same light protruded from him before his wings appeared behind him.

"They're beautiful," I commented. I stood up. "Can I touch the feathers?"

"You can, just be careful." He warned.

I giggled and held my hand up. "Been there."

He took hold of my hand. "What happened?"

"There was a feather on my pillow, and I picked it up to inspect it and cut myself," I said, rolling my eyes.

"I'm sorry I should have been more careful," he offered.

I reached out, and he moved one of the wings closer to me. I ran my hand down the feathers like you would petting a dog or cat. They may have looked like ordinary feathers, but there the similarities ended. They were like an old-fashioned chain mail nothing was going to get through.

"They're strong, powerful," I said, tracing the outline with my fingertips.

"They need to be. I have to be able to protect myself as well as humans." He was trying his best to explain, but every time he answered one question, I had another twenty just waiting in line.

"Can you fly?" I asked, smiling.

"Yes." He smirked back. "Let me hold you."

I nodded. "Where can I put my hands?"

He took them and placed them around his neck. "I've never done this with a human before." His wings came round, encircling us in a cocoon of feathers.

"Have you ever made love to another human?"

"No, you were the first." He whispered into my ear. He began to kiss my neck.

"Make love to me."

"Grace, I don't think we, I should. Not when you might be in danger." His hand ran up and down my back.

"Please."

"Are you *sure* you want me to?" he asked.

"Sure, sure!" I giggled. It was something my dad used to say.

"Well, when you ask like that, how could I refuse?"

"You don't!" I smiled.

He picked me up and placed me onto the bed, removed the rest of his clothes and found his way in between my legs. He kissed down my body while his hands pulled my top up and over my head. His mouth continuing to explore every inch of me as his wings, holding the weight of his body, freed his hands to move and caress my body.

"You're a quick learner." I inhaled as he found every part, I wanted him to. I scrunched my fingers into his hair while he spent some valuable time between my legs.

He moved back up to kiss me, his tongue finding mine as his hands cupped my face. "I'm never going to let you go," he said, easing his way inside me, staring into my eyes. "I love you," I blurted out, wanting him to know how I felt about him.

"I love you," he said in a breath. He pulled my leg up the side of his body as his movements intensified.

I grabbed at his back as tiny sounds of pleasure escaped my body, which only encouraged him more in his endeavours.

"Never leave me, Grace." He blurted out, holding me tightly.

We were both being very loud, and I didn't care if the whole street heard us. I never wanted this night to end.

Chapter Eleven

I couldn't help but stare. I woke early from a relaxed sleep, all the thoughts from last night still running through my head. I mean, going out with an angel was a first for me. I sat up in bed with a cup of tea. Gabriel was still sleeping next to me; his wings hadn't retracted and covered the side of his body that was exposed. He had his own insulation blanket. I was like a curious child and couldn't help myself, but I just wondered how warm it was. There was no need for a sheet by the looks of things as his powerful looking legs peeked out from under the feather blanket.

I moved my hand under his wing to touch his shoulder. I was right; it was warm. Well, if we ever got caught in a snowstorm, we'd be fine.

"Good morning, Miss Grimes." He mumbled without opening his eyes.

Busted! "Good morning. Do you have a surname?" I asked quizzically.

"No, it's just Gabriel." He smiled.

I put my cup down on the bedside unit, and leaned forward and kissed him, which he reciprocated.

"Open your eyes," I ordered playfully.

"No," he teased.

"Why?" I kissed him again.

"I'm not ready to start a new day."

"But think of what this new day could bring?" I ran my finger down the side of his face and along his lips.

He grabbed my hand and pulled me into his chest, covering us with his wing.

"You're not going anywhere." He opened his eyes as his hand touched my back like he was looking for his car keys.

I laughed. "Lost something?"

He closed his eyes and sighed. "You got dressed." He huffed.

"Take them off then," I answered him teasingly.

He laughed and opened his eyes. "What am I going to do with you?"

"Anything you like."

He laughed and kissed me, probably hoping I would give up. "You've closed your eyes again!" I joked.

"I'm exhausted!" he said, grinning like the cat that got the cream.

"Do angels even get tired?" I asked, not believing they did.

"It's different on earth."

"In what way?"

"We don't have sex crazed women for a start," he joked as the side of his wing moved gently down my arm.

I giggled. "You can't tickle me with your wings; that is not allowed!" I scolded.

"I can't?" he scrunched his face up. "Really?" before I knew what was happening, his wing had flicked my arm away and was squeezing into my side, which had me squealing.

"Okay, okay!" I conceded.

This time his wing moved my body closer to his. It was funny how he could move them as he was still in the same position as before.

"How do you do that? With your wings, I mean?" I was curious.

"It's just like having arms and legs. You can move them all independently of one another. Wings are the same." He explained.

"Cool. Is it sore when they go out and in?"

He opened his eye and smirked.

"You know what I mean," I sighed, letting my hand fall onto his elbow.

He laughed. "It doesn't hurt, but I feel more myself and relaxed when I can lie like this or walk around with them out."

"Are there others like you on earth?" I wondered.

"Not exactly like me," this time he opened his eyes and sat up on his elbows. "The earth has lots of angels, but you can't see them. There would even be angels in your room."

I instinctively looked around. "Why?"

"They can be here for protection, prayer, praise and worship, love, anything." He smiled as he was talking.

He was talking about angels the same way I would talk about my painting.

"Are you the only angel in human form on earth at the moment?" I asked.

"So many questions. I'm the only angel on earth, at the moment that can walk around in human form." He was choosing his words carefully.

"How? Are you a special angel?" I teased.

He wasn't laughing this time.

"You are a special angel! Is that why you're here?" I asked, shocked at the realisation.

He sighed and retracted his wings. "History lesson over for today." He got out of bed and began to get dressed.

I sat up. "Gabriel, I'm sorry if I ask the wrong questions. I was genuinely interested. I don't know that much about you," I tried to explain.

He sat on the bed next to me, put his hand up to my face, and kissed me.

"I need to be careful with what I tell you. I've never done this before, and I don't want to do or say anything that could harm you or me or anyone else for that matter," said Gabe, trying to clarify the situation.

I smiled, leaning my forehead against his. "I trust you," I said before kissing him tenderly.

"That means a lot. I love you, Miss Grimes."

"I love you too, Gabe. Now, are you going to get those trousers off and get back into this bed?" I smirked, pointing at him.

"Same goes." He smirked back.

It didn't take long before we were both lying next to each other.

"You're going to go down in history as the first human to kill an angel." He managed to say as he was totally out of breath.

"And a special angel at that!" my breathing just as laboured.

"I'm an archangel."

"That good, is it?"

"I'm the boss."

"Is it allowed to be caught sleeping with the boss?" I giggled.

"I better be the last boss you think about sleeping with!" he reprimanded.

He took me back in his arms, kissing me again.

"So do you know, God?" I asked with all seriousness. It wasn't something that I had ever considered, I remember someone saying once that you should never discuss politics or religion; I've stuck to that.

"You can't ask me anything about that," he answered back.

"But there must be heaven because you're an angel."

"Archangel," he corrected.

"Archangel. Heaven?"

"There's the Heavenly Kingdom."

"Wow!" I said in disbelief. "Can you go back and forward when you want?"

"Yes."

"Can I go with you?"

"No." His eyes dropped.

"What about when I die."

"Grace don't." His eyes began to sparkle with the tears that were filling them.

"But I have you here. I have you now!" I smirked before kissing him again.

He pulled my body next to his. "Is this too weird for you?"

"No. So are you the top boss or just a supervisor boss?" I teased.

He chuckled to himself. "I am one of the chief messengers. I'm higher than the angels." He explained.

"Only one of?" I goaded him.

"I have brothers."

"How many?"

"Three."

"Why are you here then and not one of them? Could they not be trusted?"

"I wanted to come."

"You offered to come here? Are you crazy?"

"I have you, so no, not crazy."

"Have you been back to heaven since we met?"

"I have."

"Did you tell them about us?"

"We talked about it." He began to look uneasy again.

"They didn't approve," I sighed.

"Hey, they don't know you like I do. And it's not you per se, but the fact that I'm with a human." He sat up, holding my hand, kissing it.

"You're breaking the rules." I looked up at him.

"Way more than you could ever imagine."

"I like that." I smirked.

"Do you now?" he moved back between my legs as he began to kiss me.

"You won't be sent back?" I grabbed his arm, the shock that I might lose him hitting me.

"Boss!" he laughed, kissing down my neck.

"Are there girl angels?" I asked, wondering.

He stopped kissing me. "Are you asking me that?" he pushed himself up, so he was right over the top of me, waiting for the next question.

"I was only wondering if."

"If I had been with half of the girl angels in heaven?" he tilted his head slightly, and a smirk crossed his lips so quickly I think I would have missed it.

"Have you?" I chuckled.

He shook his head, kissed me on the forehead, and rolled onto his back.

I lay there knowing I had gone too far, but it was also a question he wasn't going to answer. I turned away from him, pulling the sheet under my arm.

"Grace. Turn round," he asked.

I don't know why it was bothering me this much I had been with other men before Gabriel, so why wasn't it okay for him to be with other women? It was because I wasn't part of *his* world. I was a human, and I had no idea about his past.

He moved, so he was pressed into my back, his knuckles running up and down my arm. "Talk to me."

I wiped at the tears that were flowing down my face. "I don't know anything about heaven. I don't know how things work." I closed my eyes.

He kissed the side of my head. "I'm sorry, Grace. I never meant to hurt you." He kissed my shoulder. "Turn round so I can hold you," he asked, the pain evident in his voice.

"Give me a minute." I touched his hand.

He moved away from me, and I felt my heart ripping in two. He had done what I asked, and it was killing me. He wasn't going to fight for us, for me.

I wiped my face and turned around.

He was sitting with his arms wrapped around his knees. His wings were out, and they were wrapped around his shoulders, slumping forward just like the rest of him.

"Gabriel," I spoke as my voice caught.

He turned to face me; his face wet with tears.

"Hey." I jumped up, kneeling next to him, cradling his head against my body. "Please don't cry."

"I've never done this before, and I've made a mess of everything." He sobbed. I moved to sit on top of him, wrapping my arms around his neck. "I love you."

He put his hands on my hips and rested his forehead on my shoulder. "You turned away from me."

"I'm scared that I'm going to lose you. I don't know anything about your world, and I feel like you're trying to keep me away from who you are." I cupped his face in my hands, tilting it up so I could look into his eyes.

"What can I do?" he asked.

"Talk to me. Help me to understand," I tried to explain.

His mouth found mine as his arms wrapped around my body, squeezing me against him. "I haven't slept with any angels. It's not what we do."

"But you can?"

"No," he shook his head. "We don't have the same desires or impulses that you have here."

"But you do. Is it because you're an archangel?" I let my finger run over his bottom lip.

"Partly, and I'm on earth. I'm in human form, which means I have all the feelings of an ordinary man, all the desires and emotions." He bit my chin playfully; his hand went up into my hair and pulled tilting my head back so he could kiss down my throat.

"I'm sorry for turning away from you; I shouldn't have done that," I said as he continued to kiss me and touch me.

"Make love to me," he whispered as he gripped my shoulder.

He was ready for me to slide on top of him. I dropped my hand down between my legs, guiding him inside of me. He breathed next to my ear as my hips undulated over him.

"I love you, Grace" He leaned back on his wings, pulling my hips into him.

"Gabriel." I grabbed his shoulders, my nails pushing into his skin.

"I want to feel you come." His mouth was open, trying to suck in as much air as his lungs would allow.

For once in my life, I wasn't going to say no, but then before I knew what was happening, he flipped me onto my back, his wing catching my ankle. He never missed a beat, as each movement, each thrust inside me had me grabbing hold of him. He pulled my leg further up his body.

"Grace."

"Come inside me!" I couldn't believe he was making me come again. "Gabe!" The two of us looked at each other, sweating, and completely out of breath.

"Grace, you *are* going to kill me!" The two of us laughed as he kissed my forehead and rolled onto his back.

I let my arm fall over onto his chest. “You’re one to talk. Bloody hell Gabriel what was that?”

He kissed my hand and turned his head to look at me. “Makeup sex.” He smiled.

“I’ll need to argue with you more often.”

“Please don’t. I don’t know if I’ve got the stamina to keep up with you.”

Chapter Twelve

Gabriel drove into the hospital car park, and I shuddered uncontrollably. The large white imposing building of the Edinburgh Royal Infirmary was never a place I wanted to end up in, but it was a far cry from the old Victorian infirmary in the centre of town. I've always hated hospitals at the best of times, but this was the hospital where I had lost my dad, and it was the hospital I had to come back to get this bear trap off my leg.

"You alright back there?" asked Gabriel looking in the rear-view mirror with his sexy, sultry eyes.

I blew the air out my cheeks. How did I get so lucky to have that, I thought? "Fine."

Gabriel helped me out of the car and gave me my crutches. We made our way to OPD6 and waited with all the other patients for the nurse to call our names.

"Grace Grimes?" Gabriel and I stood up.

"We need to get an x-ray first. You won't be able to go I'm afraid," she explained, looking at Gabriel.

"That's fine; I'll wait for her."

"Okay, if you're happy with that, Miss Grimes?" she asked, staring into my eyes.

"Yes, that's fine." She ushered us through to another waiting room.

"I don't think she likes me," he observed.

"She was making sure it wasn't you that broke my ankle," I remarked.

"You're kidding?" he looked shocked.

"They don't know you, and they're on the lookout for people being abused or trafficked," I informed him.

He sat, staring at the wall.

"Gabriel, stop worrying; they do it with everyone that comes in," I reassured him.

I held his hand, wondering who was here for who.

After my x-ray, we went back to the first waiting room again and sat for an eternity watching the faces of people coming and going. It was a while before it was my turn and ushered into an examination room.

"Hi Grace, my name is Dr Corse, and I'll be helping you today." He looked to be in his fifties with an athletic frame, which was confirmed by the bike helmet hung on the back of his door and sports bag under his desk. "I've been looking at your x-ray," he said, pointing to the computer screen where my ankle with all the pins holding it together was on full display. "And I think we can take this off now and get you doing some physiotherapy and home exercise to strengthen your ankle and get you walking properly again. It looks good, no infection, which is a great sign, and there's new bone starting to grow around the fracture points."

"That's a relief. So, when can I get rid of the bear trap," I asked expectantly.

He laughed. "I've heard them called a lot of things. How about Thursday? I can schedule you in?"

I could feel my shoulders slump. I thought it was just a couple of screws to take out, but it looked way more of a Meccano set experiment. "Thursday is fine." I tried to smile.

"Great. We'll see you then."

I hobbled my way back to the car, not even waiting on Gabriel paying for the parking ticket. The tears were streaming down my face, and I just wanted to get away from this place.

Gabriel beeped the doors, and I got in the front for a change. It was boring, lying around all the time.

"It's only another couple of days." He put his hand to the back of my head. I looked out of the window.

When we got home, I dumped my coat on the floor and went up to my room and slammed the door. I slumped onto my bed and buried my face in my pillows and cried and cried and cried.

"Right you up!" Niven pulled at my arm.

"What is it? What time is it?" I must have cried myself to sleep.

"It's party time, now get up, everyone is downstairs waiting on you." She tried to coax me.

"I don't feel like it."

She was having none of it. "I don't care what you feel like. Now get your backside out of that bed, or I'll get Bryce to move it for you!"

With the look on her face, I knew she wasn't joking. I sat up, and she handed me a towel before switching on the shower.

I stood under the water, and she was right; this did feel better. The only thing that could top it off would be for Gabriel to join me, but maybe not if there were people in.

I got dressed and went downstairs, where the party sounded like it had started without me. The music was on, and the chatter and laughter emanating from the kitchen made me smile.

"Call this a party?" I said, walking in to find my open plan kitchen full of my friends.

"Looking good, hun!" Nic came over and gave me a big squeeze of a hug that had me squealing loudly and everyone else laughing.

"Hey, Gracie Baby." Bryce came over and kissed me on the cheek. Gracie Baby was his pet name seeing how I was the youngest out of us all. He hadn't used it in a while, and it was nice to see him again.

"Hey, Bryce." I put my hand up to his face kissing him back.

"We brought presents." Exclaimed Niven excitedly.

I smiled and went over to the table where Niven brought out pictures drawn by her children. Along with a couple of bottles of prosecco.

"Awe, they're so cute. I can see where they get their artistic talent," I joked. Niven's stick people were infamous amongst the group.

"We can't all be amazing artists like you," she rebuked me.

"They need lessons from Auntie Grace." Darcy kissed my cheek.

"And who's looking after my two precious babies so you two can come out on a school night?" I asked, looking between them.

"My mum offered." Darcy shrugged his shoulders.

"You know you're not getting them back for at least a week." I laughed.

"It's a sacrifice we're prepared to make." Darcy kissed Niven, and with her blushing, I knew just what they would be doing while they had the house to themselves.

I looked over at the other side of the kitchen where Gabriel was standing, with his legs crossed against the bunker. He had settled for a more casual look for the evening with a tight-fitting T-shirt and jeans.

"Can I have one of those?" I asked, looking at the glass he had in his hand. He needed to stop looking at me like that when we had company!

He poured a glass and brought it over for me.

"Toast. To Gracie Baby! Woo!" everyone raised their glasses and joined in with Niv.

Gabriel's hand moved down my back. "I hope you don't mind." He whispered into my ear.

"I love you." I smiled back at him.

"Where's the Twister?" shouted Nic above the music.

"Are you kidding? How am I supposed to do that?" I asked, horrified at the suggestion.

"Gabriel can help you," Niven answered with a smirk.

Bryce had already hit the games cupboard and pulled the mat out.

"We don't have any jelly shots!"

"There's a bottle of tequila in the cabinet, and you know there's a stack of plastic shot cups."

Gabriel looked at me, confused.

"Yeah, you're going to get drunk." I rolled my eyes at him.

Bryce and Niven filled the shot cups and placed them on the coloured circles, ready for the game to begin.

"Who goes first?" asked Gabriel.

"Gracie Baby. It goes youngest to oldest; what age are you?" questioned Niven.

"Oh, he's way too old. He can go last, so he knows what to do," I interrupted.

"Red, right, foot." I bent down, picked up the tequila shot, and downed it before putting my right foot on the red circle.

Nic was next, followed by Darcy, Bryce, and Niven. "Gabriel's turn." Squealed Niven clasping her hands together.

I hadn't seen anyone look as uncomfortable as Gabriel did right now, which made me chuckle slightly at his predicament. The look he gave me back, I knew I was going to pay for it later.

"Red right hand." He walked over, bent down and picked up the shot, and drank it. He never took his eyes off me before bending back down and placing his hand on the mat.

It was my turn next. "Blue left hand." It was a simple move, blue being the next row of colours on the mat, but Niv's left foot was already occupying the circle next to me. I did my shot and moved my hand to beside Gabriel.

"HOT!" exclaimed Niven waving her hand in front of her face.

Gabriel and I gave each other a knowing look before the next round began, and it was back to his turn.

"Green right foot." Everyone began to laugh because it was the opposite side of the mat. "Nic, pass me the shot."

Nic obliged, and Gabriel drank the shot, pushed my head down so he wouldn't kick me in the face, and flipped his legs over, his right foot landing perfectly on the circle on the other side of the mat. A side plank with arm fully extended and me crouching in the space under his arm.

"That's not fair. I don't want to play anymore." Huffed Nic. Which had the rest of us laughing. "Oh, come on, he's not even tensing,"

"Gracie Baby, you've got this. Show what our side can do." Darcy encouraged. I spun the counter and laughed, closing my eyes.

"What is it?" asked Niven enthusiastically. "Red right hand,"

"How the hell is she going to do that?" asked Bryce.

Gabriel lent forward and got my drink. "Go for it; I've got you."

I finished my drink and reached out to the top of the matt. Gabriel put his arm around my stomach, holding me for support.

"Go, Gracie Baby." Called Nic.

The board was filling up fast, and I wasn't sure how many more moves we were going to get, but I hoped at least another time of Gabriel moving.

It was back to his turn as all our arms and legs were getting a bit shaky, the drink proving an obvious hindrance.

"Yellow left foot."

Gabriel was now over the top of me, holding me up from the floor. He kissed me, and I could have crumbled right there.

"Right enough of that, you two, you're putting me to shame as it is." Called over Darcy.

"Can someone spin for me?" I shouted over the music.

"Green, left, foot." Called out Bryce.

"No way is she going to be able to do that," said Nic.

"Well, I'm not betting against her." Joined in Darcy.

Niven handed me the drink.

"I've got you. Move your leg under me. Slowly," Gabriel whispered in my ear.

"Nobody move! I'm going to get my phone and get a picture of this because no one would believe me," Niven said.

We saw the flashes going off as she took the pictures; what we hadn't realised was everyone else had got off the game and were standing watching. They continued to play along, stamping their foot on the mat for effect, but no one was playing except Gabriel and me.

"Your turn Gabriel. Red left hand." Niven called out giggling, as she handed Gabriel his drink.

He moved his hand from around my waist and down my leg. He continued kissing the back of my thigh before making his move. There were still flashes going off, and I was glad I was going to get to replay this.

"Game over," laughed Bryce.

"How can you two turn a kid's game into that? We're buying one for the house," said Niven slapping Darcy.

We stood up while everyone clapped.

"Who wants a proper drink?" asked Gabriel, heading for the fridge.

"Oh, yes, please," called Niven. Gabriel turned around and smiled.

"I'll have a beer," I said, raising my hand.

"So, where do you work out?" Bryce began to talk to Gabriel, and Darcy went over to join them.

I was glad they were all getting along together, especially Bryce and Gabriel. I joined Nic and Niven on the couch.

"He is so good for you." Beamed Niven.

"Yeah, I have to admit I wasn't sure, to begin with, but he's been there for you." Nic complemented.

I looked over at Gabriel, smiling and chatting away. "Yeah, he's perfect."

"I wouldn't go that far." Nic butted in.

"Okay, so he's not as perfect as you, but who is?" I teased.

"If only you meant it, Gracie," he said, kissing the side of my head.

The party had gone into the early hours and left a few of us more than a little worse for wear.

"Right, I'm calling it." Bryce stood up and held his hand out for Gabriel to shake, which he did. "Thanks for a great night, mate,"

Everyone reciprocated the sentiment with hugs and coats adorned, as a taxi arrived to take them all home. We waved goodbye and closed the door. I was more than a little drunk, but nothing like the other night.

As soon as the door closed, I turned to Gabriel. “Thank you. That was just what I needed.” I pushed him up against the wall and began to kiss him. “How about we take this upstairs?”

Gabriel picked me up and carried me to my bedroom. It was the most tired I had seen him all night, and he didn’t even seem that drunk.

“You can’t get drunk, can you?” the realisation hitting me.

He dumped me onto the bed. “No. You, on the other hand,” he said, pulling my shorts off.

I smirked. “It was your idea to have a party.”

“Yes, it was. Tequila shots and Twister never entered my mind,” he said, shaking his head.

“I don’t know what they’re teaching you archangels these days!” I teased.

He laughed. “Turn over, Gracie Baby.” He whispered. “Maybe I could teach you a thing or two,” he said, unbuttoning his jeans.

I took up the same position I had while we were playing Twister. His hand felt up the back of my thigh, finishing on my hip, where he held me tightly. His other hand placing himself before each thrust of his hips, had me gripping the sheets in front of me as the euphoria coursed through my body.

Chapter Thirteen

There was nothing I enjoyed more than waking up in Gabriel's strong arms. I tried to carefully prize them from around me so I could go to the bathroom, but every time I moved one arm, the other grabbed tighter. After five minutes of this, I realised he was awake!

"Gabriel!" I said, pushing his shoulder.

When I came back from the bathroom, he wrapped his arms around me as his mouth found mine.

"You brushed your teeth," he noted.

"I didn't want to kiss you with stale drink, morning breath."

"Thank you."

"Don't know how you taste so sweet all the time?" I commented.

"Archangel!"

"Really?" I asked, believing him.

"No, I was up earlier."

"You're a nightmare!" I laughed.

"What do you want to do today?" he asked.

"Don't you have work to go to?"

"Not today. Today I'm staying home with you," he said, squeezing me just a little tighter.

"I've got you all to myself?" I kissed him. "What will we do all day?" I sighed before laughing.

"Not all day." He tickled me, which had me squealing and trying to get away from him, a pointless exercise in hindsight.

It felt nice to be in his arms.

"What are you thinking?" he asked, kissing my forehead.

"How much I'm enjoying you taking the day off." I smiled.

"The other night had me thinking. You said you don't know that much about me or where I'm from, so if you want, I'll try to answer some of your questions.

There might be things that I can't tell you, but that's not because I don't want to. okay?" he said, looking serious.

"Really?" I asked, wondering what my questions would be.

"Really. However, I want something in return." He smirked.

I smiled. "What did you have in mind?"

"Not that!" he said, placing his forehead against mine. "I want to know more about you. What your life is like."

"I think I can manage that. How many questions do I get?"

He laughed. "I'm going to regret this. You can have as many as you like."

I sat up on an elbow. "Do you have a house?"

"Not like this."

"Why?"

"There's no need."

"Where do you eat and sleep?"

"We don't sleep, and we eat together. Heavenly food doesn't require cookers or fridges. We have provisions for everything we need."

I turned onto my back, this was going to take a while, and I wanted to be comfortable.

"You, okay? I haven't put you off already?" he asked.

I turned my head to look at him. "No, it's just something I've never thought about before."

"That's why I said, you can ask me anything. I want you to be a part of my life, whatever that looks like."

I reached out and touched his face.

He moved his head to kiss my palm. "Can I ask you something?"

"Eek! Depends." I was never very good at talking about myself.

"Why aren't you married?"

I blew the air from my puffed-out cheeks. "Starting with the easy questions first? I don't know. I just never felt that spark with anyone."

"You've been out with other men?"

"Yes."

"Bryce?"

"Yes."

"I'm surprised there wasn't a spark there; you seem to get on well," he said, no longer looking at me.

"It's complicated. We're better as friends."

"Have you made love to him?"

"We've spent some nights together."

"What about the other men you've been out with; did you make love to them?" his eyes remained closed.

"I've had sex. I don't think I've made love to anyone apart from you."

He sat up beside me. "Is there a difference? And why would you have sex with someone if you didn't love them?" he asked, looking perplexed.

"Things are different on earth," I said, using one of his lines hoping he would drop it.

"You're not getting off that easily."

"To fill a need. To be close to someone if only for one night. To feel loved." I played with a loose thread on the cover.

"Is that the same for most people on earth?"

"Probably. I don't know."

"Why didn't you wait until you found someone you loved before having sex?"

"If I did that, I might never have had sex." I laughed, looking up at him. "Anyway, tell me about your job, what is it you do?"

"I'm a messenger, so I tell people about things that are going to happen either in their lives or in the world so they can prepare, or so they understand what's going to happen. Have you read the Bible?"

"No. We did the main stories in school, but it's not something I got into," I tried to explain. Which was a bit weird considering I had an angel in bed beside me?

"Do you know the story about Mary, the angel telling her she was going to have a baby?"

"Yeah, I know that story," I said, rolling my eyes. Every school pupil in Britain for the last however many years had had the pleasure of the annual Christmas Nativity play.

"Well, I was the angel sent to give her the message."

"Wait, so you're Gabriel, the angel, from the Bible?" I sat up.

"One in the same," he said, laughing. "Who did you think I was?"

"I take it there's not more than one Gabriel?"

"No, we all have individual names. I'm *the* Gabriel, the archangel."

"Damn! I am sleeping with the boss!" I said, shocked.

Gabriel started laughing. "Come here." He pulled me into his body.

"Are you sure this is allowed? Am I meant to bow to you or something?" I pushed myself away from him, panicking that I had done something wrong.

"I'm not here like that. I'm in human form." He tried to calm me down.

"If you weren't here in human form, would that be different?"

"Completely. I would be bigger, stronger and my voice would make you quiver,"

I don't know why that made me giggle; whether I was nervous or the thought of quivering under him, he had made me feel things that I hadn't felt before, but quivering wasn't one of them.

"Do you have special powers?" I gasped.

"If I was here as an angel."

"Really, like what?"

"I can compel you to do things, I can…"

"Wait, wait. You can compel me to do things?" I said, looking at him incredulously.

He laughed. "I haven't." He put his hands up in front of him. "Remember, human form."

"And if you weren't in human form, what would you compel me to do?" I smirked.

"Considering what we've been doing, I wouldn't need to compel you to do very much!" he joked.

I took a sharp intake of breath. "You're going to pay for that!"

"I was joking." He was laughing as he tried to get me to cuddle into him.

"You might need to *compel* me if you think I'm going to have sex with you now!" I teased.

"I don't think I will."

"Oh, really!"

In a move quicker than a blink of my eye, he grabbed my waist, pulling me next to him, and after a flash of light, his wings appeared; we rose until my back was touching the ceiling, his body pressed against mine.

I squealed. "Gabriel! Don't let go!"

"I've got you. Close your eyes and relax."

I closed my eyes, but my white knuckles were an indication that I was anything but relaxed.

"Make love to me," he whispered into my ear.

"Are you kidding?" my eyes darted open.

"First time for everything." He squeezed my thigh as he moved it along his body. "I never thought you'd be scared to try something new." He teased while kissing down the side of my neck.

"Please be careful." I shook my head. "I can't believe I'm doing this."

"You'll need to help me out here."

I took a breath before letting go of his shoulder and guiding him inside me. He took my hand and held it against the ceiling as he began to move.

"Gabriel!" I never wanted him to stop.

He slowly brought us back down, turning so he placed me perfectly on the bed. "How was that?" he asked.

"Yeah, definitely a first." I put my hand up to my mouth. "Can I still ask you questions?"

"Depends."

"On?"

"Ask."

"I asked if you could fly, and you said yes. Can you take me flying?"

"You want to fly?"

I shrugged my shoulders. Now I had the chance; I wasn't so sure. I was bad enough on the ceiling!

"How about I take you out tonight," he offered.

"Do you teach angels how to fly?" I asked.

"That's not part of my job description."

"Do you have baby angels in heaven?"

"We have new angel beings that are created but not how you create." He kissed my shoulder. "Do you want babies?"

I thought about his question for a moment longer than I probably should.

"I take it that's a, yes?"

"It's not something I've desperately wanted, but I love when Niv and Darcy's children, Violet and Charlie, are over, and I suppose I have wondered what it would be like." I smiled at him.

"I always wondered too what it would be like to be a father like you have on earth, to create a living being."

"Is that something you're able to do while you're on earth? I mean, you say you're in human form, so does that mean you have all human traits?" I sat up holding the sheet against my naked body.

Gabriel sat up on his elbow. "Now, that is complicated. Angels aren't supposed to have sex with humans because the life created is evil and causes a lot of problems. The fact that I'm not here as an angel changes things slightly, but I still need to be careful. Archangels have a slightly higher power, so I'm not sure exactly what would happen in that situation."

"So, if we continued this relationship, we shouldn't have children?" I asked, already knowing the answer.

"I'm sorry." He looked just as disappointed as I felt.

"I suppose it's better to know. Where are you going to take me flying?" I asked, not wanting to think about children anymore.

Chapter Fourteen

It was a cloudy night, which Gabriel said was good because we wouldn't be spotted by people on the ground as easily. That and the fact he had told me to wear dark clothes we should be fine.

"Are you ready?" he asked, leaning against the doorframe to the kitchen.

"I'm a bit nervous. How good a pilot are you?" I asked, playing with my hands anxiously.

"Well, I haven't crashed yet." He smirked.

I shook my head at him. "Not funny!"

"It was a little bit," he continued to laugh at me as I walked past him.

He beeped the car doors, and I got into the passenger seat and turned the heating up as soon as Gabriel started the car.

"Are you sure you're ready for this?" he asked, keeping his eyes focused on the road in front of us.

"As ready as I'll ever be." I laughed nervously.

"I can't wait to share this with you." He reached over, squeezing my hand in his.

"Just don't drop me. One broken ankle is enough."

"I won't drop you," he said, taking a quick look over.

He stopped the car in amongst the trees on a forestry road. You couldn't see the main road from where we were; come to think of it, you couldn't see anything once the headlights were off.

"How are we going to see where we're going?" I asked, worrying about tripping over something and hurting my ankle.

"I can see." He clicked his seatbelt and began to take his jacket and T-shirt off. "Will you not be cold?"

"No, I'll have you to keep me warm." He smiled over at me. "Time to go."

We got out of the car, and he stood behind me. He held my arms while he kissed my neck then wrapped his arms around me. "Hold on to my arms." He whispered into my ear.

The light flashed, and he brought his wings around us before opening fully behind him. "Are they bigger tonight?" I asked, surprised.

"They need to be to carry you." He laughed and kissed the side of my head.

I felt my feet lift off the ground, and he wrapped his legs around me, snug against his body.

"Is this, okay?"

I nodded my head. I didn't mind flying in an aeroplane, but the take-off and landing were always the parts I found scariest and had me grabbing hold of the armrests, this time; I was grabbing hold of the arms of my pilot.

"Have you got your eyes shut?" he tried to move to see.

"Squeezed shut!" I exclaimed. The air was blowing over me and the constant rhythm of the beat of Gabriel's wings was giving me something, other than being hundreds of feet up in the air, to think about.

"Relax, I've got this. Open your eyes."

I held on tighter as if that was going to make any difference, took a deep breath, and one at a time, I opened my eyes.

"Wow!" I couldn't believe how beautiful it was from up here. The street lights marking a trail through the earth like the constellations above us.

"Impressed?"

"How could I not be?" For someone afraid of heights, this was incredible. I felt completely safe in Gabriel's arms.

"Do you trust me?" he asked.

"I don't like the sound of this." I held his arms a bit tighter.

He turned us on to his back, then after a while of just soaring, he turned and swooped down over the coast and across the sea.

"Let go."

"Are you crazy? Don't let me go," I said, panicking.

"I'm not going to drop you. Allow your arms to dangle. I promise you'll enjoy it."

I could hear the teasing smirk in his voice and not wanting to be made a fool of, I dangled my arms as the salty water from the sea sprayed through them.

"Is there anything you'd like to see while we're here?"

"The Forth Bridges." I loved when you flew back into Edinburgh Airport; the flight plan would swoop out over the Forth and pass over the bridges on its descent.

We flew over the rusty painted colour of the rail bridge, under the road bridge, and over the new Queensferry Crossing with its large white cables. He twirled us around while we flew back under the rail bridge so I could see every part of the engineering spectacle.

We landed on the Isle of May, off the Fife coast. It felt a bit funny having my feet on land again and a bit dizzy.

"You okay there?" Gabriel asked.

"Just getting my legs used to being on land again."

He held me as he sat down and placed me on his knee, his wings wrapped around us to keep the wind off.

"This was where my maternal grandparents met. My granddad came from England and was part of the forestry service. He was working here, and my granny was living in Fife. She took a boat trip for a day out, and that's when they met."

"And now we're here." Gabriel said, kissing me.

"I couldn't think of a nicer way to spend the evening." I cupped his chin in my hand and kissed him back. "Can we fly home over Edinburgh?" I asked excitedly.

"I'm not sure that would be a good idea. There are too many lights, and the airspace is monitored closely over large cities." He squeezed me playfully. "How about a different castle?" he looked at me with a wide grin.

"What do you have in mind?"

He never replied before we were airborne again and flying north. I recognised some of the landscapes and scenery from Clunie Dam, the Cairngorms, and Loch Lochy, where I would stop for a break when I was driving to Skye. Our country was beautiful and seeing it like this only added to my appreciation of my birthplace.

"This is the way I drive when I'm going to Skye," I informed him enthusiastically.

"I brought you to the right place then." He nuzzled against my neck as we continued to fly.

When I saw Eilean Donan Castle, I was elated. “I love this. Thank you,” I gushed. I always looked out for it when I was going on family holidays. A landmark that meant we were close to our destination.

We flew over and around the castle before landing on one of the mountains of Glen Shiel.

“Is this, okay?” he asked. We were sitting on the side of the mountain like an eagle watching its prey.

“This is better than okay. I can’t believe you brought me here,” I said, throwing my arms around his neck. I couldn’t take it all in my eyes were darting from the castle to the mountains to the loch, trying to save every minute to memory. The sky was clear, the light from the moon reflecting off the still water of the loch; it was a night I never wanted to forget.

“I hope you don’t mind, but I was looking through one of your photo albums, and I saw a few pictures of you here in your younger days, then the large painting in the spare room and the black and white pictures you have in the lounge. You’re not exactly subtle!” He laughed as he held me tighter.

“I love it here and having you with me just makes it feel even more special.”

He relaxed his grip and moved me around. “I love seeing you this happy.” He ran his thumb over my bottom lip before replacing it with his mouth.

My tongue moved into his mouth as my fingers explored his body.

His hands lifted my top over my head and removed my bra. I shuddered as the cold hit my naked body sending a wave of goosebumps over my skin. His wings opened to shield us from the wind that was blowing along the top of the mountain. He pulled at my leggings, and I lifted myself so he could pull them off. I undid the buttons on his jeans, and he helped me move them down his legs while I positioned myself on top of him.

“I’ve never made love on top of a mountain before.” I smiled.

“We better make it memorable then,” he said, pulling my hips into him hard.

I gasped. He was more forceful than usual, and I was reciprocating with my movements. I dug my nails into his skin and bit down on his shoulder. He wasn’t gentle as his hands were groping every part of me. He grabbed my hair, pulling my head back so he could bite down my throat. The pain overtook only by the euphoria coursing through our bodies.

We held each other tightly, breathing hard but unable to move.

"I love you, Grace Grimes. If I could, this is exactly where I would ask you to marry me." He gazed longingly into my eyes, but there was a flash of sorrow there too.

I ran my fingers down the sides of his face. "We'll make this work."

He strained up to catch my mouth with his.

We stayed there, lying, cuddled together wrapped in his insulated wings, only moving to make love over and over again.

"You need to see this," he said, nudging me to sit up.

I turned to see the first ray of light pierce through the dark.

"That is so beautiful." I turned to look back into Gabriel's eyes. "I love you."

"I love you too, Grace. We should get going before it gets too light," he said, the disappointment evident in his voice.

This time there was no gentle gliding through the air, we needed to get back to the car, and it felt like we were as close to breaking the sound barrier without actually doing so. I closed my eyes, trying to ease the dizziness I was feeling at seeing everything pass before my eyes so quickly.

When we arrived back at the car, I was feeling a bit queasy, and I slumped against Gabriel.

"I've got you." He carried me to the car, which was a relief.

He opened the door, but before I got in, I held on to his shoulders and kissed him. "Thank you."

I pulled the seatbelt around me, cuddled into the seat, and closed my eyes. "Too fast for you?"

I nodded my head.

"It takes a bit of getting used to."

"Maybe the next time, we can take our time." I smiled as I opened an eye, taking a glance at him.

"I'm glad to hear you would consider a next time." I felt his hand brush over my face. "Sleep, I'll wake you when we get back."

Chapter Fifteen

I woke in my bed and wrapped in my sheet. I turned to see if Gabriel was there, but I already knew he wasn't. I was getting used to the small noises of his breathing when he was sleeping.

My mind drifted back to our adventure as the feelings came in waves over me. How could anything ever be as incredible as last night?

I went for a shower and had something to eat before taking up my usual position in my studio. My easel still had the picture of the murder scene emblazoned across it. I moved it over to the side before picking up a new canvas. The feather clipped to the easel made me smile as I began to paint. Halfway through my painting, I remembered the one from the other day with the man and woman. I changed them over, and this time I knew what was coming out of his back to protect her.

"Thought I might find you in here." Gabriel poked his head around the door.

"You're back." I smiled. "What time is it?"

"I love how you can get caught up in your painting that much that you lose track of time. Anyway, close your eyes."

I looked at him as my shoulders slumped slightly, but with the look he gave back, I knew better than to argue with him.

"Open them." He was standing holding a large bunch of flowers, like the ones I had in the hospital. "I remembered I had promised to buy you more, and I completely forgot."

"They're beautiful." I stood up.

"Just like you."

I kissed him passionately.

"Grace, I need to put these down." He tried to speak while trying to escape me. "Do I need to get my wings onto you?"

"I don't want to let you go."

"I'm just going to the bedroom to get changed."

"Take me with you."

"You're insatiable." He placed the flowers on the floor before picking me up and carrying me through to the bedroom.

He placed me on the bed before taking his jacket off and throwing it over the chair in the corner.

"So, what do you want to do now you've got me here?" he asked standing with his arms folded across his chest.

"I was thinking; I could make you forget everything you've had to do today," I teased, standing in front of him.

"And how are you going to do that?" he sighed.

I began to take his tie off and unbutton his shirt. "How was work today?" I pushed him back onto the bed, and using my tongue, began to lick and kiss down his body.

"Worst day ever!" he grabbed hold of my arm, pulling me on top of his body.

"Gabriel! I'm supposed to be doing this for you," I complained.

He put his hands behind his head. "Knock yourself out."

"I intend to!" I smirked before continuing where I left off.

I unzipped his trousers and pulled them down his legs, or at least I was trying to, but he wasn't helping me in the slightest, which had me laughing.

"Gabriel." I put my hand up to my mouth as I continued to laugh. "You could at least help me."

"No. You said you wanted to do it all by yourself." He mimicked my voice, which made me sound more like a seven-year-old!

I put my hand inside his shorts. "I'm sorry, please could you help me?" I looked at him seductively.

He kicked his trousers and shorts down his legs and onto the floor. "See what can happen when you ask nicely?"

"Thank you." I smiled at him.

I kissed around his stomach then followed the snail trail of hair like a map to the treasure at the end.

"Grace." His hand was on the back of my head as I moved my mouth over him until he came.

I lay on the pillow next to him.

"Where the hell did you learn to do that?" he asked.

I shrugged my shoulders. "Practice."

"Grace! That's not what I want to hear."

I laughed. "You asked."

He grabbed my wrists and pinned them to the bed above my head as his body pressed against mine. "Promise me you won't do that to anyone else."

"Well, not while we're together anyway." I smirked at him.

"You're not going to be with anyone apart from me ever again." He insisted.

The joking and playfulness left me. "Don't make promises you might not be able to keep." I moved my body, and he let me go.

I went to the bathroom, wondering when that sense of him leaving started. I switched the shower on and stepped in. I closed my eyes as the water fell through my hair and down my body.

I jumped as Gabriel pressed against me, his arms wrapping around me. I turned in his arms and leant my face against his chest.

"I'm sorry, I didn't mean to upset you. I hate the idea of you being with anyone else." He kissed the top of my head.

I kissed his chest. "I'm sorry too. That wasn't fair."

"How about we go back to bed?" he suggested.

"Grace." I could feel Gabriel stroking my arm to wake me up. "What time is it?"

"I need to get some work done today, but I didn't want to leave without speaking to you first."

I rubbed at my eyes as I tried to open them.

"Don't wake up. You get your rest, and I'll see you later." He kissed me a couple of times, but on the third kiss, I held him there.

"Don't leave just yet, just another five minutes." I cuddled into his chest.

"Five minutes, then I must go."

"What's more important than me?"

"My boss!"

I giggled into his chest. "Yeah, you're not going to get away with pulling a sickie. Will you be back later?"

"Of course." He began to kiss me again.

The continuous bang at the door made us both jump. We looked at each other, "Bryce?" Gabriel jumped up and ran for the door.

"Good morning, sir, I'm looking for Grace Grimes,"

"She's upstairs; is everything okay?" he asked.

I sat up and started getting dressed, wondering what bad thing had happened now.

"Could you get her for me, sir?"

Gabriel came into the room as I was heading out. "It's the police."

We went down the stair.

"Hi, I'm Grace Grimes," I said, the wave of panic making me feel nauseous.

"Sorry to bother you, there's no need to worry. We were just wondering if you had seen your neighbour, a Gabriel Lanje."

"It's Lange." Gabriel came up behind me. "I'm Gabriel. What seems to be the problem?"

"Do you live at number 32?"

"I do."

"And do you drive a Lexus hybrid rx450?"

"Yes, could you please tell me what this is about?" I could feel him tense beside me, and I put my hand on his arm.

"I'm sorry, we had a report this morning of a break-in at your property. Your car is a write off too. Would you be able to come over and help us identify if anything is missing?" the police officer asked.

"I'll be over in five minutes. I need to grab my things." Gabriel stormed past me.

"We'll probably need to get a statement from you to Miss, if that's okay, just for our records."

"Yes, of course."

Gabriel came back down the stair. "Lock the doors and call Bryce, I don't think he was going into work today, and I don't want you on your own." He kissed me and followed the police officer over to his house.

I went up the stairs and called Bryce. I looked out the window and watched Gabriel talk to the police officer. His car looked like it had gone through one of those crusher things or had been in a terrible accident. I couldn't see it getting repaired, the insurers would write it off, and he'd need to get a new one.

It wasn't long before Bryce was over, parking his car in the driveway.

We sat in the kitchen, waiting for news. "This was not how I planned today going."

"Why did Gabriel ask for me to sit with you and not Nic? I thought I would have been the last person he would want to be left alone with you," he asked.

"He knew you would be able to fight for me if it was needed," I explained.

"Is there something going on that I should know about?"

"Mind when Niven had her bag stolen at work?"

"Yes."

"Well, Gabriel got a text from Niven's phone saying she had been in an accident and would he mind picking her up. When Gabriel got to where she had told him to meet her, there was no one there. He went to her house to see if she was okay, thinking Darcy had picked her up instead. That's when he found out that someone had stolen her bag. In the meantime, Amelia from our work came over here and left me a bottle of wine, but she spiked it. Gabriel just got home in time. I was so sick."

"So, you think this Amelia is doing all this crazy shit?" he was getting angry. It was a look I had seen on Bryce's face a hundred times before.

"I'm not sure, but I wouldn't put it past her." I sat back in my chair. "I had thought about going away for a few days up North, now with this happening; I think it might be a good idea," I confided in him.

"Will Gabriel go with you?" he asked.

"I don't think so. I think Gabe will have enough to deal with." I could hear myself saying the words but going away was the last thing I wanted to do. I knew it was selfish for me to stay, and I would just be getting in the way if Gabriel needed to stop Amelia. I mean, what was I going to do with my dodgy ankle?

"If you want, I can take some time off and come with you. Someone would need to drive anyway," he offered.

"Thanks, Bryce. Do me a favour, and don't say anything to Gabriel until I've had a chance to talk to him."

"Sure." He held my hand and smiled.

There was one thing about Bryce in all our fights and disagreements; he never once took his frustrations out on me. He would do anything to protect me, and that was what I needed right now.

We were in the lounge watching a film when Gabriel eventually came back. "Hey. I'm going to grab a coffee; can I get you both something?"

"Here, let me make it. You sit and tell Gracie what's happening." Bryce got up, leaving us alone.

"Thanks, Bryce," Gabriel said as he came to sit next to me on the couch. He swung my legs over the top of his and let his head fall back.

"How bad is it?" I asked, fearing the worst.

"Everything has been smashed up. There was a goat head nailed to the wall in the kitchen, its blood spread through every room. My car is a write-off. I phoned some people who are going to come and clean the house and take the car away. I'm not concerned with things. I know they're not important." He didn't sound angry like Bryce had, but more disappointed like he was letting people down, letting me down.

Bryce came back through with the coffee.

"Are you not having one?" I asked, noticing there were only two cups.

"No, I'm going to get going. Give you two some space. Call me if you need me."

"Thanks, Bryce, I appreciate that." Gabriel raised his hand to thank him before he left. I rested my head on the back of the couch and closed my eyes.

"Grace, there's something we need to discuss," Gabriel said, running his fingers up and down my arm.

I turned my head and opened my eyes.

"You asked about heaven, but you never mentioned hell. Other forces at work on earth would like nothing better than to disrupt everything we have together."

"What? Like devil worshippers?" I asked, smiling slightly, not believing what he was saying.

"It's not a joke, Grace!" he said as he sat forward, resting his arms on his knees.

I put my hand on his back. "I'm sorry."

He turned to face me. "With angels there are,"

"Demons," I jumped in, understanding what he was saying.

He nodded his head. "I don't think everything that's happened has been a coincidence. Your phone, the crazy messages from you and Niven, the house getting vandalised, I think Amelia has a connection to all of this too."

"But you're an archangel, aren't you able to just banish them?" I asked, having no clue if that was even a thing.

"It's not that easy. I hate how the demons are getting so close and not just to me but to you too, and they're getting away with it; this should not be happening." He stood up and crossed his arms in front of his chest as he continued to pace the floor. "I think it would be best if you went away. I don't want you getting caught up in all of this, and I need to get it sorted out," he said without turning to look at me.

I hadn't seen him this disappointed since his wings first appeared.

"My bags arc still packed. I'll leave early Friday morning. I've asked Bryce to come with me. He can drive me up." I went to stand next to him.

“I hate that it’s not me going with you or that you can’t stay here.” He put his hand up to my face.

“Are you getting your brothers to come and help you?” I asked, concerned for his safety.

He rested his head on mine. “Don’t you worry about me. Also, I don’t want you telling anyone apart from Niven and Nic where you’re going. Just say you’re going away for a bit.”

“I’ll miss you.”

“You’re not away yet.” He kissed my forehead.

“Can we go to bed? It’s been a long day, and all I want to do is cuddle into you.” He took my hand, leading me upstairs.

Chapter Sixteen

We lay in bed together, holding each other. There were no words, an occasional kiss or touch. We just wanted to be there for one another. We weren't sure how long I was going to have to be away, so we agreed to spend as much time as possible together before I needed to leave.

The melancholy in the house was tangible. We slept, we showered, we ate, but we still weren't talking, well apart from an occasional word or two. We didn't want to leave the house until we had to, and that time hadn't arrived yet.

I had called Nic and Niven and made arrangements with Bryce to pick me up. My bags were packed, and I had packed a couple of boxes with cleaning products and the other with bedding. No one had been in the house for years, so I was expecting some Miss Havisham, looking cobwebs and stale food. There was one thing I wasn't looking forward to, and that was saying goodbye to Gabriel. I watched him as he slept and held him tight when he was awake. I had never been one to pray, but on this occasion, it warranted something.

When Gabriel fell asleep, I sneaked out of the bedroom and sat in my studio. It had always been my place of refuge, and this was no different. I had my earphones in playing through a playlist I used for when I was working and sat there waiting. I wanted there to be a burst of inspiration, even if it was the dark murderer or the winged saviour, but the longer I sat in front of the blank canvas, I realised that wasn't going to be the case.

"Artist's block?" Gabriel bent over behind me, taking an earbud out.

I sighed. "I thought it might take my mind off everything."

"Not working?"

I shook my head.

He kissed the back of my neck. "Come back to bed."

"I don't think I could sleep," I huffed.

"Who said anything about sleeping?"

A smile crossed my lips of its own volition.

"Why Gabriel, whatever could you mean?" I teased.

He picked me up off the stool and carried me through to the bedroom and dropped me on the bed like a bag of coal, making sure to keep hold of the leg with the bear trap attached before placing it gently on a pillow.

"I can't wait until that thing is gone!" he took a deep intake of breath.

"Me too," I sat up on my elbows, watching him.

He walked to the bottom of the bed. "What are you doing?" I laughed.

"Shh." A smile spread across his lips mischievously. "My turn!"

He bent over my leg and starting at my toes, beginning to place tiny kisses along the top of my foot, my ankle.

It made me giggle as his beard scratched against my skin, and I went to pull away from him, but he held it tightly. There was no way I was going to be able to stop him, so I continued to watch, hoping it wouldn't be too long before he made his way further up my body. He kissed as far up my leg as he could before my shorts were stopping him from going any further.

"I think we can get rid of these." He grabbed both sides of my shorts and pulled.

He hadn't been looking for a response, which was just as well because I could hardly stop myself from grabbing hold of him. Instead, I grasped the sheets as I laid back, allowing Gabriel to pleasure me like he hadn't before.

His name escaped as he brought me to the height of passion.

Without waiting, he moved up the bed, sliding inside me; it was him I held onto now. Each movement of his body felt euphoric. Feeling him like this, the weight of him on my body, his breath falling on to my neck. He pulled my leg further up the side of his body and held it there as the feelings of the final thrusts were shared between us.

"Maybe It's you that's been practising," I said, running my hand through his hair.

"You're the only person I want to be practising with."

"What's going to happen to us?" I asked, staring into his eyes.

His mouth opened, and he tried to speak, but no words were forthcoming.

"Gabriel?" I sat up, a sense of dread coursing through my veins.

He sat up beside me, sorting the pillows at his back. "Grace, I think I might have to return home for a while."

"Will you be allowed to come back?" I asked, feeling the emotion catching in my throat.

He shrugged his shoulders. “I’m not sure what’s going to happen. My main priority is to make sure you’re safe; that’s all that matters to me right now.”

“You’re making it sound like you’re breaking up with me.” I couldn’t believe what I was saying.

Gabriel took my hand in his and kissed the back of it. “I will do everything I can so that doesn’t happen, but I need to be honest with you too.” The hurt in his eyes only mirroring my own emotions.

I cuddled into his chest as his strong protective arms held me tightly, neither of us wanting to be anywhere else and at the same time a knowing in both our hearts that this could be the end for us being together.

My day for the hospital had finally arrived. We had been looking forward to this day for weeks now, but with everything that was happening, I could have seen it far enough. Gabriel hadn’t received his new car yet, so he was going to drive mine. We were up hours before we needed to leave. I sat on the island with my feet dangling as my foot bounced off the cupboard door underneath.

“Grace.” Shouted Gabriel. I turned to look at him.

“You’re banging your feet.”

“Sorry, I was thinking.”

He came around and stood in-between my legs. “I love you. Everything is going to be fine today, and today is all I’m concerned with.” He wiped the hair back off my face and kissed me. He stood back and smiled for the first time since all this stuff with Amelia had started.

“I like seeing you smile.” I ran my finger over his lips.

He held them there and kissed them. “I want to enjoy what time we have. I love you, Gracie Baby!” he laughed.

“Just you wait until this comes off; I’m going to wrap my legs around you so tight.”

“I hope that’s a promise.”

“I can’t think of anything else I’d rather do.” I looked at the clock. “Anyway, we need to get going.”

I could tell something was wrong as soon as we went outside. My tyres were slashed, and someone had smeared blood over my garage door.

I took my phone out and called the police, then Nic.

“You go. I’ll speak to the police.” Suggested Gabriel.

Nic arrived within ten minutes to take me to my appointment. "What's going on, Grace? Are you sure you're safe with Gabriel?" he asked the question that had been playing at the back of mind for a while now.

"I'm not sure." Just saying the words out loud made everything seem real. Had I been trying to hide it all away? The fact that he was an angel and demons were trying to attack us, attack me? At least I was going away. It might give us time to think about what we wanted and if we would ever work out.

I was taken through to a surgical room while Nic sat in the waiting room. I hated being in hospitals, and I hated it even more when I was the patient.

When it was over, one of the porters wheeled me back through the corridor to the waiting room. I still had crutches and a bandage to cover the holes the screws had made, but that was all.

I was lost in my thoughts when I saw a familiar face weaving in and out of the other patients and visitors. The man with the white suit! I did have to wonder if he ever took it off, but if that was his look, then who was I to judge. Anyway, it was some look, and he held my eye for probably way longer than he should have.

There was something strange about him but also incredibly appealing. Was this another one of those coincidences that he was turning up everywhere I was? I chuckled to myself; maybe he was thinking the same thing? Apart from the first time I saw him walking towards me, I suspected he hadn't even noticed me.

"There she is," Nic said, standing as I was taken back into the waiting room. "Ready to go?"

"Absolutely!" I sighed, glad at last to finally be leaving this place behind.

It was after five when we got back home. My car was sitting with four new tyres, and the garage door was clean.

"If you hadn't seen it this morning, you wouldn't believe anything had happened," Nic commented as we pulled up outside my house.

"It's okay." I put a hand on his arm and smiled, trying to reassure him everything was fine when it couldn't be further from the truth.

Gabriel opened the door and came out. "Hey. How did it go?" he asked, helping me out of the car.

"Bye Nic, thanks again," I said before leaving the car.

"Yes, thanks for taking her," Gabriel said, poking his head around the door before closing it.

Nic just lifted his hand and turned the car before driving away. I knew he was upset with Gabriel, and I didn't want that.

I went into the house and began to lift a few things from the fridge for dinner. Gabriel stood at the island. "Talk to me?"

I looked at him, but I couldn't find the words. Part of me wanted to scream and shout and blame him for everything that was happening. The other part of me couldn't open my mouth in case I started crying. I knew we were going to have to have the conversation, and I also knew I would put it off for as long as I could.

"I'm going to make a quiche salad for dinner, is that okay?" I asked, turning on the oven.

"Fine."

"What did the police say?"

"They need you to call them, and someone will come over to take a statement. The number is on the unit."

I continued to cut up the salad and get the table set.

Gabriel bent over the island, clasping his hands out in front of him. "I know you're scared, and I'm sorry about your car. I never meant for any of this to happen."

"I don't care about the damn car!"

I moved back against the bunker, crossing my arms across my chest, protecting myself for what was to come next.

Chapter Seventeen

"I think it's time to face up to the fact that we're not going to be able to be together." I couldn't believe I managed to say it without bursting into tears. Not that they would have done any good; now was a time for us to talk and hopefully be able to remain friends, although I wasn't sure how that was going to work either.

Gabriel hung his head, going over what I had just said. He pushed himself up from the island and took one of the bar stools to sit on.

"I never meant for any of this to happen. I thought I was here protecting you, but all I seem to be doing is making things worse."

"What's happening with Amelia? Did you give her name to the police?" I asked.

"No. I'll deal with her."

I rolled my eyes. "Why does it feel like you're protecting her?"

"Believe me; I'm not protecting her. I will kill her as soon as I find her. This stuff is amateur at best and probably one of her sycophants trying to upset our lives."

"It's working." I poured some water into a jug for the table.

"What can I do, Grace?"

"I don't think you can do anything. Maybe we were a bit naïve in thinking we could make this work." I took the quiche out of the oven, and we sat down to eat.

"You seem angry," he said, taking a drink of water.

"I am angry. I hate how we can't be together. I don't know; maybe I was fooling myself, thinking I could fall in love with an angel, and everything would be a big fairy tale ending."

"That's my fault. I got carried away, hoping for the same thing."

"It would've been fine if it wasn't for Amelia!" I dropped my fork onto the plate and sat back in my chair.

"If it hadn't been Amelia, it would have been someone else. It's too great a prize to hurt an archangel. I didn't think they would come after you." He let his arm fall across the table with his hand held out, ready for me.

I reached out my hand, interlocking our fingers together. "Will you need to go back?"

"Not right away, and I do need to kill Amelia first!"

"What about once this is all over? I suppose what I'm asking is if I'll ever see you again?" I could feel the tears welling up now.

He sighed. "I think it would be best for me to go away and not come back, it wouldn't be fair on you to stay, and all this could happen again."

I felt the tears running down my cheek, and I tried to wipe them away quickly.

Gabriel was up out of his seat. "Come here." He pulled me to my feet, putting his arms around me, and just holding me there, swaying me slightly, kissing the top of my head. "I will always love you, Grace."

He held me like that for a long time, neither of us wanting to be the first to let go. "I love you too." We pulled back and looked at each other.

Gabriel ran his hand down the side of my face, my neck. His mouth pressed against mine, and as much as I wanted to push him away, I couldn't.

"Make love to me,"

He picked me up, and I crossed my ankles behind his back.

"You did say you were going to do that once you got the bear trap off." His mouth opened wider, his tongue touching mine.

"I did, didn't I?"

"You need to stop, so I can see where I'm going." He smiled.

I wrapped my arms around his neck, my head resting on his shoulder as he carried me up to my room.

I unwrapped my legs, standing in front of him. Our hands were removing clothes as we continued to kiss each other. I sighed as his mouth kissed slowly up my neck. He unhooked my bra, sliding it off my shoulders and discarding it with the rest of the clothes on my bedroom floor. I kissed down his stomach, my mouth meeting my hands at his belt. I took it off before taking the button out and pulling the zip down. I pulled his jeans and shorts down his leg, kissing him, touching him. His hand was at the back of my head.

"Grace. Come here."

I stood back up, and he kissed me, his tongue pushing into my mouth, while his hands held my head. He moved me on to the bed, I opened my legs, and he forced himself inside. He wasn't taking his time, and I was glad, each thrust made in anger and disappointment that we would never be able to be like this again. I crossed my legs over his back, wanting him to go deeper inside me. His fingers interlocked through mine, pushing them into the bed. I couldn't hold on any longer, my legs squeezing around him, wanting to keep the feeling there for as long as possible, but he was moving too quickly and too hard. It was his turn to feel the euphoria I had experienced only moments before.

He kissed me before moving onto his back. He pulled me over to cuddle into his chest.

Neither of us could speak or wanted to. We both knew the significance of what had just happened. I closed my eyes, his fingers tracing a line along my arm.

We lay on our sides, looking at each other a kiss, or a touch breaking us away slowly, piece by piece.

"I wish you didn't need to go away tomorrow," Gabriel said, moving my hair away from my face.

"It's probably for the best. We could lie here for a week, and the outcome would still be the same. There would still come a day where it would be over."

"At least I would have had a week or more like this to remember you by."

I sat beside him, holding the sheet around me. I looked down at him and played with his hair, trying to remember every single part of him. "I will miss you. I'm not saying this to be mean. I think I'm just trying to prepare myself for tomorrow."

He took my hand and kissed it. "I know."

"You will wait until I get back before you leave for good? Don't kill Amelia, and then go."

"I won't. Lie back down."

"Promise me."

"I promise, Grace, I won't leave until you come safely back home, and I have you cuddled back into me. That, okay?" he asked while running his fingers down my arm.

"It'll do."

He pulled at the sheet until it dropped at my waist. "Gabe," I said, looking at him sternly.

"You can't complain to me about gravity." He smirked. "Lie down."

I cuddled back into him, and for probably the last time, his wings came out, covering us.

"I'm going to miss this." I carefully ran a finger down the inside of his wing, and it shuddered slightly. I looked at him, surprised.

"What? They're just as sensitive as the rest of me," he said, looking embarrassed. "I'm going to miss being this open with you."

"When you go back, will you know what I'm doing?" I asked.

"No, I think I'll be assigned far away."

"What if you go away and one of those demons tries to get me? Who's going to protect me? Do I get another angel?"

"You will get another angel regardless if there are demons or not. Honestly, I don't know what's going to happen. I mean, yes, you'll have an angel like everyone else to protect you, and if there's an attack, another archangel will take over your care, I don't think I'll get the job."

"Do you think you would ever come back to have a look? Like if you were curious to see what my life turned out like," I asked.

"No. Once I leave, I won't be coming back. It would be too hard for me to see you and to stay away from you."

"You could just wave across a crowded place, so I know you were still with me."

"Grace, you would hate that as much as I would." He kissed my cheek.

"What about when I'm dying, and there's no one in my room; would you come to me and hold my hand?"

"Grace, stop with all the questions."

I could feel the tears rolling down my cheeks. I pushed my forehead into Gabriel's chest so he couldn't see, that was until my body gave the game away, and I was shaking in his grasp.

"Grace, I'm sorry. I didn't mean to shout." He kissed the top of my head and held me a little tighter. "I don't want to think about you dying. When I leave, I want to remember you like this. Naked and pressed against me." He squeezed me as he kissed into my neck.

"If something did happen and I needed to get in touch with you, how would I do that?"

"Argh! Grace. How many questions can you ask?" he fell on to his back.

I turned onto my back and stared at the ceiling. I had always been the same. When I was a kid, I would ask and ask questions, to the point my dad would make something up, which of course, I believed.

"I can't think there would be any reason you would need to get in touch with me."

"But if there was a reason, just say I crashed my car or something, how would I get in touch?"

"Don't say that, Grace." His wings retracted, and he pushed himself away from me, sitting on the edge of the bed.

I sat up, touched, and kissed his back where his wings had been only moments before.

"If you need me, and I mean only in an emergency, you can pray. Ask God if I can come to you. He'll decide, so I'm not making any promises. But if He thinks I need to come back, I will. I promise, if something that bad happens that you need me here, I'll come straight away."

"I just can't get my head around not being able to see you again."

He turned around, holding me. "Promise you won't do anything to harm yourself, so I'll come back." The tears were on his face now.

"I promise. Gabriel, I would never do anything to hurt you like that." I sat on top of him, our arms holding tightly.

"Grace, promise me when I go away, you'll find someone else, even if it is Bryce, and be happy," he asked, kissing the top of my shoulder.

I pulled back. "I promise." I cupped his face in my hands and gently touched his lips with mine.

"I love you, Grace."

Chapter Eighteen

The alarm woke us from our sleep fuelled dreams; this was the day we hoped would never come, and we stayed up way later than we should have done to try and make our time together last longer. But there was no more putting it off. We said our goodbyes as we lay in each other's arms before sleep consumed us both.

I moved to get up.

"Just one minute more." Gabriel pulled me on top of him, holding me tight and his wings surrounding us.

"I need to go. Bryce will be here soon." I put my hand to his face and kissed him. His wings dropped to the side, and his arms slid off me, giving me up to the daytime.

He sat up in bed, watching me get ready and pack the last odds and ends, toothbrush, and hairbrush. The hands on the clock were moving in double time, bringing us closer to the moment when I would drive away, leaving him here without me.

When the doorbell rang its death knoll, we stopped and looked at each other. Were we doing the right thing? Only time would tell, and for now, it was running out fast.

"I'll get it." Gabriel pulled his jeans on and went to open the door for Bryce.

I finished moving my bags out into the hall for Gabriel to pack into the car. I stood looking around the room for anything I may have forgotten. I slipped my hand into my top drawer and pulled out a letter for Gabriel. One I had written while he was sleeping. One he could read and remember how much I love him. I placed it on the pillow and walked out of the room, closing the door behind me.

"Is this everything?" he asked.

I nodded my head, scared that the moment I opened my mouth, I would change my mind and beg to stay.

"Morning, Gracie." Bryce hugged and kissed the side of my head. He was subdued, knowing how much this was hurting me.

Gabriel came back in from outside. "That's the car packed. I've put the food in the back."

"I'll wait in the car." Bryce went to leave before Gabriel grabbed his arm. "Take care of her." Gabriel pleaded.

Bryce gave a nod of his head and left us to our final goodbye.

Gabriel uncrossed my arms from in front of me and placed them around his neck, then held me, pulling me close to his body. "I love you, Grace." The emotion in his voice was plain to hear.

I couldn't hold back the tears any longer. "I love you. Stay safe," I blurted out in-between cries.

He pulled back, cupping my face in his hands, kissing me. "You should go." He let his hands fall to his sides.

I held him, kissed him, and walked away. There was nothing else to say.

I got in the car and watched him standing at the door. I put my hand up to the window as Bryce manoeuvred the car, and we were driving down the street. The view of Gabriel standing watching me leave became smaller and smaller until we turned the corner at the bottom of the road, and he was gone. I closed my eyes, trying to picture him from last night. That smile, the way he would hold me, kiss me, make love to me, but that was all just a memory now.

Bryce reached over and squeezed my hand.

We were making good time. The traffic on the motorway up to Perth was light, and the next part to Dalwhinnie seemed to fly by. It was as if Gabriel had sent his angels before us to make sure the roads were clear of any obstacles.

We stopped briefly at Dalwhinnie to get something to eat and take a break. It didn't seem to matter what time of year you came; there always seemed to be snow on the mountains.

This part of the journey was always my favourite. Away from the motorways and on twisty turn roads that were a dream to drive. The only problem was I wasn't the one driving, but at least it gave me a chance to look at the scenery. I had forgotten how beautiful it was. The last time I was here, I was flying through the air with Gabriel. Everything looked different today. Bryce had never been on this road before, so there were plenty of chances to stop and rest while he took some pictures.

"I can't believe you haven't been here in years. I don't think I would ever be away from the place." Bryce commented, looking out over the mountains and lochs.

"Too many memories," I offered.

"Maybe it's time to make some new ones," he said, trying to make conversation.

I hadn't been the best travelling companion, but he didn't seem to mind, and he was enjoying the roads as much as I used to.

"Thank you for this," I said, looking at him.

"You don't need to thank me. You know I would do anything for you." He rested his head back and looked at me, smiling.

"We should be up before it gets dark, at least," I tried to change the subject, which I think he realised. He started the car, and we were off again.

He wanted to stop at Eilean Donan Castle, but I made an excuse and promised we could visit on the way home. It was too soon to see the place again. The mountains that overlooked it, our mountain where we made love, wrapped in his arms and his wings. I wiped the tears from my face. It all seemed like a distant memory now. It was never going to happen again. We were over, and it was tearing me apart.

Bryce wouldn't take no for an answer about stopping at Kyle of Lochalsh for another couple of pictures. Then it was over the bridge and the sea to Skye. He never stopped again until we arrived at the old croft house.

I jumped out to open the gate while he drove down to the house. I walked down the hill feeling like a child again, half expecting my aunts and uncles to come out to meet us. And then there was my dad. He had brought me here since I was a baby, family holidays that I would do anything to have again.

Bryce was out of the car and standing, waiting for me to open the door. It was all on the one level, kitchen, living room, two bedrooms, and a bathroom. I stood in the porch, opened the door and walked in. Everything looked the same as it had the last time I saw it. There was a lot of dust, and it needed airing out but nothing like the cobweb strewn property I was imagining.

I began opening windows, and I turned the heating on, hoping there was enough oil left in the tank for the time we were going to be here. If not, I would need to take a trip over to the peat bog and borrow some for our stay. I would go and see Mr Cameron and let him know I was here. He still used the croft for his sheep, an arrangement he and my dad had come to years previous.

"You can have this room," I told Bryce.

There was a large double bed and a wardrobe. I took the larger room only because it had a fireplace, which I used to love going to sleep watching.

I tied my hair up and went into the cupboard to get the hoover. I cleaned Bryce's room first, the bathroom, living room, and then I began in the kitchen. By that time, the heating had kicked in, and there was plenty of hot water to wash everything down. Bryce had started bringing his things in after he had gone for a walk around to explore his new surroundings.

"Are you sure you don't want a hand; I'm not completely useless, you know?" he offered, leaning against the doorframe.

"You could hoover my room and the bed; I've opened the windows," I smiled.

"Gotcha." He went through, and I could hear him busily working away.

I was glad he let me get on with tidying up. It didn't take long, and we had all our things moved in. There was enough food in the car to do us for dinner tonight, and we could do a run to the supermarket tomorrow for everything else we would need.

I made a lasagne the night before, which I heated in the oven, and I made a salad to go with it, which was in another plastic tub. There was also a bottle of wine to top it all off.

"Bryce. That's dinner," I called out to him. He had gone back outside until dinner was ready. There wasn't going to be much room left on his phone with the number of pictures he was taking.

He walked in and hung his jacket on the back of one of the dining chairs. "Wow, this looks amazing," he said while going into one of the cupboards.

I couldn't think what he was looking for; everything was on the table. When he came through, he sat down with a glass filled with small wildflowers, which he put in front of me.

"These are for you." I looked at them and smiled.

"Thank you." It was something I used to do all the time when I was a child. I used to spend hours walking around the croft. "Do you want some wine?"

"You know you don't need to ask me twice. It looks and smells fab as usual." He poured the wine and put some salad onto his plate.

"There's plenty, so tuck in," I said while filling my plate.

When we finished, Bryce cleared the plates away and washed them while I boxed up what was left. It would do Bryce a snack later.

We sat in the living room. There was no television to worry about; it was one of the things I enjoyed most about coming here, the fact it was completely different from our home.

"So, what do you think of it?" I asked.

"It's an amazing place. I can't believe you spent all your holidays here. I bet you can't wait to bring your kids here."

"I hadn't thought about it. I wasn't sure if I was ever going to come back," I explained.

"Why? You never told me what happened."

"There are too many memories. Everywhere I look, I can see my dad, aunts and uncles, family meals. We used to all sit in here in front of the fire, the adults would talk, and I would sit on the floor with my ten pence mixture and a colouring book." I smiled at the memory.

"That doesn't sound too bad." He looked at me with a puzzled look on his face.

"I never said they were bad memories. All my memories from here are wonderful; that's why it hurts so much to be here because I know how much I miss it." I wiped a stray tear away from my eye.

"Grace. Why have you never told me about any of this?" he asked.

I shrugged my shoulders. "It was too painful. Out of sight, out of mind." That was how the old saying goes, and I had done a pretty good job of both.

"How long has it been since you were last here?"

"About ten years. It was hard losing all my aunts, and uncles but when I lost my dad too, I couldn't stand the thought of coming here." I pulled my knees under my chin and wrapped my arms around my legs.

"I wish you would have let me in. maybe I could have helped in some way." He smiled over at me, and for the first time, in a long time, I realised why Bryce and I would always end up together at the end of a night out.

"Thanks, Bryce." I smiled back. "I hope you don't mind, but it's been a long day, and I would like to get to bed." I stood up.

"I think I'll sit up a bit longer."

I smiled at him; glad he was here. "Night."

I sat on the bed and looked at a picture of Gabriel and me on my phone. I wasn't allowed to call; that was one of the rules. No one could know where we were. I got changed and into bed. As usual, the Highland air had me wiped out, and I fell asleep almost immediately.

Chapter Nineteen

I woke up expecting to be first up, but I could smell bacon on the grill, and there was nothing that could get me out of bed quicker. I went through to the kitchen where Bryce had set the table with an array of bacon, eggs, sausages, black pudding, tattie scones, mushrooms, tomatoes. He had the speaker on and was singing along as he danced his way around the kitchen. He poured us both a glass of fresh orange before noticing me standing at the door.

"You've got to love a bit of seventies' music!" he said, looking embarrassed.

I laughed. "I'm beginning to see a whole other side to you, Mr McKinley," I sat at the table, and he turned the music down. "I never usually have breakfast," I confessed.

"The most important meal of the day or so we're led to believe. I thought you might like a cooked breakfast for your first morning here," he said, looking at the table.

"It looks delicious. I'm starving." I began to fill my plate.

"Is there anything you would like to do today? The weather looks okay," he said, looking out the window.

"Don't be fooled that can change in an instant." I laughed. "It would be nice to get out. I could take you down to the old schoolhouse. There isn't much left of it now, but it's a nice walk."

"Will you be able to manage?" he asked, looking concerned.

"We can take it slowly; there's no-where to be and I think we're going to need a walk after eating all of this.

I was glad to have the bear trap off my ankle, and I was able to put trainers and jeans back on. I still couldn't put my foot down completely, so I still had my crutches, but even having the weight removed was a bonus.

We walked along the single-track road, and I pointed out the different houses of the people who used to stay there when I was a kid.

"This is spectacular; it's like something from Hollywood! Imagine waking up to a view of the Cuillin Mountains like that." He was almost skipping down the road; he was so excited.

He was enjoying this way more than I ever expected he would. Maybe I should have brought him here sooner after all. Once all this stuff with Amelia, was over I should invite everyone up. It had been mine for so long, and I was desperately clinging on to an image of the past, but maybe the time was right to start making new memories.

"What are you smiling at?" asked Bryce bumping my arm beside me.

"I was enjoying being back. I was enjoying seeing how much fun you were having. You were reminding me of when I was little." I bumped him back.

"We never went anywhere during the school holidays. Dad was always working, and mum couldn't get out of bed. I just used to play with my toys in the garden. Sometimes Mrs Collins from next door would hand me over a jam sandwich or give me money to get a sweetie from the shop." He pushed his hands into his jeans pockets as he explained.

I stopped walking. "Bryce, I'm so sorry. I think we've both been a bit caught up in our own lives to share how we were feeling."

"It's not that bad. At least we've got each other." He put his arm around my shoulder as we began to walk again.

We stood looking at the small waterfall of the burn that ran past the schoolhouse. "Was that where they used to keep their animals?" he asked.

"No, that's the fank. It's where the crofters would take their sheep to get sheared, dipped, or dosed. We walked over and stood looking in. It has different pens to hold the sheep. They would shear the sheep, and as they moved through, someone else would be standing with a bucket, and something to put a paint mark on so the crofters could tell whose sheep belonged to whom. So, for instance, a red mark on the bum or a blue mark on the shoulder. Then other times, you needed to dip them so the sheep would be moved one at a time to the bath, the bit with the water, and you would have someone there with a stick to push the sheep under, then when they come out, they'd go into another holding pen then they'd be let out and herded back to the crofts. Same sort of scenario with the dosing," I explained.

"What's dosing?"

"It's like their injections, but you have to give it to them orally."

"My kind of sheep!"

A look was all that comment needed. "This is the schoolhouse my aunts and uncles went to; one of my aunties was one of the last kids to go to the school." We climbed over the fence, and I let Bryce explore. The ground was a bit uneven, and there were a lot of the roof slates lying around. I didn't want to hurt my foot again, or what would be just my luck the other one!

"Were you able to go in when you were a kid?" he asked, still looking in the windows. "Yeah, and up the stair. All the tables were still there, books."

"Really? I wonder why no one took them for a museum or something." He pondered.

"Nobody thought about all that at the time. It was just junk. The schoolteacher had a separate croft somewhere else, so when they left, the school was shut, and the kids had to walk to Portree,"

"So, the schoolteacher used to stay here?"

"Yeah, with her family." I was getting sore, just standing. "Take your time, and I'll start making my way back." I managed to get back onto the road, which was a lot easier with the crutches.

I walked back towards the house stopping now and then to admire the view of the valley with the river snaking its way along the bottom. My mind couldn't help but wander to Gabriel and what he was doing. I didn't think I was going to miss him as much as I was, but I knew this was for the best. When I got to the gate, I stopped and rested my head on my arms.

I used to love it when my dad stopped the car, and I would get out, take the wire off the gate and stand on the bottom rung as it swung open, being careful at the other side as it bumped against the opposite post. Then closing it so as not to let any of the sheep in or out, then I would run down ready for a bowl of my auntie's homemade soup.

When did life get so complicated? Even with Gabriel, as much as I loved him, we never spoke about what our future was going to be. He probably knew there wasn't a future for us however desperately he wanted one.

"Hey, what's up?" Bryce asked, standing beside me.

"I think I've made a big mistake." I turned around and buried my head into his chest.

"Hey, things aren't that bad." He tried to comfort me, but I couldn't control the sobs that convulsed through my chest.

He picked me up and carried me down to the house. "When did you get so strong?"

"I nearly dropped you the last time I tried this, and there was no way I was going to do that again. So, I've been in training ever since." He smiled down at me.

"I've left my crutches at the gate."

"I'll go and get them. I need to close it anyway."

I cuddled up on one of the couches and pulled a throw over the top of me. I never heard Bryce coming back in.

When I came too, Bryce was away, and the car was gone. I couldn't move, or I should say I didn't want to move. Why did Amelia want to hurt me? I know it was all to do with Gabriel, but she was trying to be my friend way before Gabriel turned up. Did she know he was coming to me? What did he know about me? Was I always going to be under attack?

There was a knock at the door. Maybe one of the neighbours checking to see who was squatting in the house.

"Hi, sorry to interrupt. I'm the new minister for the area, and I just wanted to introduce myself," he said, holding out his hand.

I had always been scared when the minister came to the house to visit my aunts and uncles. The black suits and hats were probably a contributing factor and the way they would stare as if they knew something that you didn't. It could have also been the number of horror movies my dad used to let me watch.

Anyway, this man didn't look scary in the slightest. He was wearing jeans and a shirt for one thing and no scary hat! He was incredibly good looking.

"Please come in. I'm Grace," I introduced myself shaking his hand.

"Daniel Nicolson," he said, reciprocating the handshake.

I never thought I would be so captivated so quickly by another man. What was the saying about busses? Wait all day for one and two turn up at once. "Can I get you a tea, coffee?" I asked, going over to fill the kettle up.

"A coffee would be great. Thank you."

"Cool, take a seat." I filled the kettle and darted about the kitchen, getting cups, coffee, sugar, and milk. "I'm sorry we don't have any biscuits, we just came up yesterday, and we haven't been to the shops yet," I tried desperately to explain.

"Don't worry, I'm trying to watch my figure," he said, patting his flat stomach laughing. Are you sure I can't help you? You seem to be at a slight disadvantage," he said, looking at my crutches.

"No, it's fine. I slipped off a kerb back home and broke my ankle. It's just taking it's time to heal, I'm afraid." I brought the kettle over and made the coffee. "Help yourself to milk and sugar."

"Would you like me to pray for healing?" he offered.

I looked at him like he had just asked me if I wanted to fly to the moon.

"I'm not sure, what do I have to do?" I asked, hoping I hadn't made him feel uncomfortable.

"Well, that's the beauty of prayer; you don't need to do anything. I'll ask Jesus to heal you, and we'll wait and see if you feel any improvement." He smiled.

He had a faint scar along his jaw, but I tried not to stare, well at his jaw anyway. "I suppose it couldn't hurt." I was willing to try anything.

"May I touch your ankle?" he asked.

I nodded my head as the power of speech had seemed to have left me in that instant.

He bent over and gently picked up my leg and put it on his knee. He put his hands on it and began to pray.

"Can I ask you to try and move it back and forward?"

I did what he asked me to do, and there was no stiffness there. "I wasn't able to do that before," I said excitedly.

"Good, now try and turn it in circles."

"No, it's a bit sore to do that."

"Let me pray again." Which he did. "Try it now."

I carefully began to turn my foot in circles. I looked at Daniel. "That is amazing. Look at that!" I exclaimed excitedly.

"Do you want to try and walk on it?" he asked, smiling at me.

"Yes, will you help me?" I asked.

"Of course." He put my foot back on the floor and stood up, holding his hands out for me to take.

I held his hands, took a deep breath, and stood up. I was keeping most of the weight on my opposite foot, but I was able to stand on it. I tried putting my weight between the two, and there was no pain.

I laughed. "I'm standing. Help me walk." He stood at the side of me, holding my arm while his other hand went around my waist. "It's all tingly, but there's no pain whatsoever! That is incredible. Thank you so much," I gushed.

Daniel let me go, and I walked back and forth from the bunker to the table. "Don't thank me; I only prayed it was Jesus who healed you."

"Well, thank you, Jesus. I'm sorry I never had those biscuits now," I joked.

"I'm just happy you're not in any more pain." He smiled.

"Would you like to stay for dinner? I'm not sure what there is, but I'm sure I could find something," I offered.

"Thank you, that's very kind, but I've got a few more house calls to make. Maybe some other time?" he asked. Well, at least it wasn't a no.

"Yes, here I'll give you my mobile number. Just give me a call when you're free. We would love to have you over." I smiled as I handed him a piece of paper with my number on it.

He held it up. "Thank you for this; I'll be in touch. I hope you enjoy your new-found freedom." He left, closing the door behind him.

I ran over to the sink and watched as he walked back up the hill to the gate. What had happened to ministers these days that they were looking that good? I tidied up the dishes and kept checking the window to see if Bryce was coming. I couldn't wait to show him my miracle.

Chapter Twenty

I was in the bedroom when I heard the car outside. I grabbed my crutches and ran through to the kitchen. I stood at the back window and took a couple of deep breaths to stop myself from laughing.

"Hey. I hope you didn't mind me going to the shops by myself?" He asked as he brought the shopping in from the car.

"No, it's fine. I take it you found everything okay?" I asked.

"Yeah." He threw his coat on a chair. "What about you, what have you been up to?" he was starting to unpack the shopping.

"Step away from the shopping," I said in my best American cop accent.

"What? Grace, come on, let me get the shopping put away." He huffed.

"Brycie boy, please step away from the shopping, "I asked nicely this time in my little girl voice and using his nickname.

He laughed. "Okay, Gracie Baby. What is it?" he said, smiling. His hands were on his hips, waiting for what I had to show him.

I dropped my crutches and pretended to hobble towards him. "Grace, stop, you're going to hurt,"

I didn't let him finish. I ran over and jumped on to him, throwing my arms and legs around him.

Luckily for me, he had been working out. He caught me and spun me around.

"What's this? I mean, how?" he asked. He put me on the bunker but didn't move away, and I didn't let him go.

"This minister came to the house, he's new, and he was introducing himself to the people who stay in this area or something. Then he said about my leg, and I told him about my accident, and he said, 'can I pray for you?' and I said 'yes,' and look, I can walk and there's no pain. Isn't that amazing?" I gushed at him.

He was laughing at me. "That is amazing. I like it when you get excited." His hand moved up my back.

I looked into his eyes, and for some reason, in that instant, all I wanted was him. He leaned in, and I kissed him. The alarm bells were sounding, but I wanted to feel him like this again.

"Gracie, I can't." He breathed next to my ear.

We sat holding each other. "I'm sorry." I pushed his shoulder back and got down off the bunker.

"Grace, we've only been here a day and a half. I don't think you've forgotten about Gabriel that quickly." For once, he was the one with a clear head.

I tried to smile, and I knew he was right; it just didn't feel like it at that moment.

"I got you something?" he smiled. He went over to the bags of shopping and pulled out a box of chocolates and a colouring book and pencils.

"Thank you, Bryce, that is lovely." I smiled.

"It's a grown-up ten pence mixture," he said.

"Did you get anything?"

"I did. I got a Sudoku. Now we both have something to do at night to keep us busy,"

We were in the middle of preparing diner when the door went. We looked at one another, and I shrugged my shoulders.

Bryce went to open it.

"Hi, I'm Daniel. I was here earlier, and your wife said I should come for diner. I hope that's still okay?" he asked.

I skipped beside Bryce.

"Hi, Daniel. Yes, of course, come in. We're not married," I informed him. He had changed from earlier, but still casual and still incredibly handsome.

"Oh right." He sounded shocked.

"No, we're not married, and we're not together. Grace and I are just friends." Bryce explained.

"Ah, I see. You never know these days," he said. "I brought some wine I didn't know what you drank, so I got one of each," he said, holding up the bottles.

"Anyone bringing wine is more than welcome. Can I take your jacket?" offered Bryce.

"Thanks." Daniel handed it to him. "Is there anything I can do to help?"

"You can open the wine," I said, pulling a bottle opener from the drawer.

"How do you like your steak, Daniel?" asked Bryce.

"Rare, please," he answered while opening the bottle of red and pouring three glasses.

We finished cooking and joined Daniel at the table.

"To Daniel. Thank you for your healing powers and the wine and thank you to Grace for letting me share her childhood." Bryce toasted before taking a drink.

Daniel and I followed.

"Shall I say, grace?" asked Daniel.

I looked at Bryce with my eyes wide. I had been away too long. It was always customary to say grace, and if you were ever in any doubt, you would wait until the person you were visiting with began to pray or picked up their knife and fork.

We sat with our heads bowed as Daniel prayed, then reached for the food the minute he finished.

"How do you two know each other?" asked Daniel.

"We used to work together, and we became friends." Bryce recounted.

"And you're both not married to other people either?" he observed.

"No, we can't find anyone who measures up," I said, squishing my face up at Bryce.

"Someone has to keep her out of trouble," Bryce interjected. "What about you? Married, kids?"

"No, none of the above, I'm afraid."

"Are you allowed to?" asked Bryce.

I giggled. "He isn't a priest Bryce,"

"Like, I'm meant to know." He shot back.

"I'm like you both, just haven't found anyone who measures up," he said before taking another drink of his wine.

I looked at him and wondered why? He was good looking and intelligent, both good qualities.

"Where were you before? You said you were new here," I asked, curious about his story.

"I was in Dalkeith for a couple of years in Midlothian, but I needed a change of scenery, and you can't get a better change of scenery than here." He smiled, looking between Bryce and me.

"Do you want to tell him?" asked Bryce.

"I stay in Mayfield, and Bryce stays in Newtongrange. We've been within fifteen minutes of each other, but we had to drive to the North of Scotland before we meet!"

"No-way! That's incredible." Daniel said, sitting back running his hands through his light brown hair. "I can't even think that I've seen you around."

"It's a big place." Offered Bryce.

"I think I would have remembered seeing Grace," he said, looking at me.

I could feel my cheeks burn at the compliment and the slight tap from Bryce's foot under the table.

"You might know Niven and."

"Darcy?" he interrupted. "I christened their son, Charlie, isn't it?"

"Yes." I sat forward, surprised. "Well, you obviously can't remember me because we're the Godparents." I laughed.

"Busted!" he said, laughing. "How are they?"

"They are great, and Charlie and Violet are just so incredibly cute," I gushed, reaching for my phone and swiping through the pictures on my phone for him to see.

"Charlie and Violet. Were they not named after film stars or something?" he asked, trying to remember.

I began to laugh. "Niven got her name after David Niven, the actor. Darcy got his name after his mum was watching Pride and Prejudice, and they decided to carry on the tradition. So, they named them after the kids from Charlie and the Chocolate Factory," I said, unable to contain my laughter any longer.

Bryce joined in.

"That's not the worst I've heard; believe me. I often wonder if parents think about their kids going to school with those names and try and find a job. It's crazy." He laughed along with us.

"How long are you going to be here for?" I asked.

"As long as God wants me here. I hate staying in one place for too long. It keeps things fresh, moving around." He smiled. "Anyway, who's for more wine?" he took the bottle from the table and began to fill up the glasses. "What about yourselves?"

"I'm not sure we're here till the end of the week, at least," I said.

"Well, in that case, you'll have to allow me to return the favour and make dinner for you both," he offered.

"We'll bring the wine," said Bryce.

"Great, I've got Grace's number, so I'll give you a call to arrange. Have you got any plans for while you're here?"

"Now my ankles better; I was thinking about taking Bryce to the Coral Beach. I used to love going there as a kid and maybe over to Staffin and the Quiraing."

"I hope you're not scared of heights," he said, chuckling at Bryce, who gave me a worried look.

"Don't worry; I'll take care of you," I said, clasping his hand in mine."

It was Daniel coughing that had me sitting back in my seat and letting go of Bryce's hand.

"I should think about making a move. It's been a pleasure. Thank you for a lovely meal and the lovely company," he said as he stood from the table.

"I'll phone a taxi," I said, picking up my phone. "The guy said twenty minutes I'll walk you up to the gate," I offered. "Bryce can do the dishes." I laughed.

We put our coats on and made our way up the road. I used the torch on my phone, so we could see where we were going; there were no streetlights here. It was a clear night, and the stars and moon were keeping the darkness away from completely consuming us, so when we reached the gate, I turned it off.

"I don't think I've ever seen stars like it in Dalkeith," commented Daniel.

"I know. I always loved it. I used to have to hold onto my dad when I was little because it made me feel like I was going to fall off the edge of the world," I confided.

"And what about now?" he asked. "It still makes me feel a little dizzy."

"Take my hand," he offered, reaching out. I put my hand in his.

"I won't let you fall," he said, turning to face me.

"Thank you." I wasn't giggling now. His intense gaze had me forgetting everything. He moved closer, and my breath caught. His hand went up to my face.

"Is this, okay?" he asked.

"Yes."

Even though I knew he was about to kiss me, I still felt shocked when he did it. I had to hold on, but it wasn't the stars that were making me feel dizzy this time. He was different from Gabriel, not in a bad way, and whatever he was doing had the butterflies dancing around my body with a flutter.

He pulled back. "I want to see you again."

"You have my number."

He looked past me. "I think that's for me," he said, looking at the set of headlights moving through the darkness.

He kissed me again before the car was too close.

"Text me when you get home, so I know you made it back safely."

I walked back down to the house smiling; but also wondering what had just happened.

"Did he get away, okay?" asked Bryce.

"Yeah." I picked up a dishtowel and started drying the dishes Bryce had just washed.

"What do you think of him?" he asked.

"I quite like him. What about you?" I was interested in what his opinion would be.

"He seems nice enough."

Well, that was probably as good as it gets with Bryce.

"I was about to go to bed if that's okay with you? I was thinking about getting up early and going for a run in the morning."

"Yeah, that's no problem; I was thinking the same thing, just not the running bit. I was hoping to get some painting done." I shrugged.

"Night then." He kissed the top of my head before leaving me standing in the kitchen.

I was in bed when my phone pinged a message.

"Hey, you."

"Hey. Get home safely?"

"Just getting ready for bed."

"I'm already in mine."

"Lucky you. I wish I could have stayed longer things were starting to get interesting."

"I know what you mean. Call in when you come to pick your car up tomorrow."

"I'll do that."

"Goodnight, Grace, sweet dreams x,"

"Night, Daniel."

The x had been deleted and re-applied a few times before I settled on no x! Well, for the time being anyway.

Chapter Twenty-One

Bryce had already left by the time I got up. I sat in the kitchen looking out the window, thinking how many times I had sat in this same position over the years. I finished my glass of orange juice and picked up my easel and paints that I had assembled before breakfast and went outside.

The light was beautiful, and the Cuillin Mountains were looking spectacular as usual. I couldn't wait to get started, so I put my earphones in and turned the music up. I loved this. There was no sitting wondering what to paint when I had a view like this to admire.

I could feel myself getting consumed in my work that was until a shadow fell across my page. I turned around sharply.

"Daniel!" I exclaimed.

"Sorry," he said, laughing with his hands up in front of him. "I called to you, but you didn't hear me," he tried to explain.

I tried to breathe easily again. "That's okay. I was a bit lost in my work." I switched the music off. "Did you see Bryce?"

"Yeah, he was over at the peats. I asked if he wanted a lift back, but he seemed to be enjoying his run. This is incredible, by the way. You're very talented," he said, looking at my painting.

"Thank you. It keeps me out of trouble." I smiled up at him.

"Why do I not believe that?" he asked, chuckling.

"Because you'd probably be right." I sighed. "What are you doing today?" I asked.

"I've got a couple of meetings, and I need to find some inspiration for the sermon on Sunday."

"I don't think you'll have any trouble finding inspiration here," I offered.

"You'd be surprised." He moved his feet uneasily.

I stood up. "Can I get you a coffee or a juice or something?" I offered as I made my way to the kitchen.

He held my arm. “Don’t go. I was thinking about last night.”

I was standing in front of him, trying to take in every part of his face and storing it in my memory.

“It’s okay, you don’t need to,” I said, trying to avoid an awkward conversation as he tried to explain his way out of it.

“No, that’s not what I meant. I wouldn’t have kissed you if I hadn’t wanted to.” His hand moved to my face.

“And what about now?” I asked, hoping he was still interested.

“Now, I don’t want to leave you again.” He leaned in, his lips joining with mine. I took a breath while he repositioned himself.

“Do you want to go inside?” I asked, wanting this to continue.

“I can’t just now,” he continued to kiss me before pulling back. “I should go.”

“Maybe once you’ve finished your meetings, we could meet up or something?” I asked.

“I would like that.” He smiled. “I should…” he let go of his hold on me.

“Yes. I folded my arms around my waist while I watched him walk away then walk back to me, kissing me again before eventually walking away.

I blew the air out from my cheeks. That man was making me feel things I wasn’t sure I was ever going to feel again. I sat back down and picked up my paintbrush as my mind wandered to Gabriel and how this whole thing was getting more than a little complicated. I let out a sigh.

I was packing up when Bryce came walking down the road. “Hey,” I called over to him.

I picked up my things and met him at the house.

“Here, let me take that,” he said, taking the easel off me.

“I can’t believe you have the energy to do anything after that run!” I observed.

“You would think,” he joked, grabbing me around the waist, which had me squealing and laughing in equal measure.

He poured himself a glass of water. “Let me see?”

I turned the painting round.

“That’s amazing. Hold it there,” Bryce said before taking a couple of pictures of it.

“Thanks, Bryce.”

"If you managed to do a painting every day we're here, you would have enough to hold an exhibition," he complimented.

"I'm not so sure about that, but painting every day, now that's something I could get used to," I pondered.

"Well, do it then. Anyway, I'm away for a shower. Catch you in a bit."

"Bryce, could you send me a copy of the picture you took?" I asked.

"Sure."

I placed the painting on top of the sideboard in the living room and sat looking at it.

There was something different about this painting, something that I wasn't able to draw from when I was at home.

I cuddled up on the couch.

I was down the croft when I heard Gabriel shouting. I turned my head to see him standing there waving.

"Gabriel?" why was he here?

Amelia walked down the road, and the fear gripped at my heart.

"Gabriel! Watch out," I tried to warm him.

He waved back, and I tried to run to get to him before Amelia did, but I wasn't moving fast enough.

"Gabriel! Please!" I screamed at him.

Amelia went to stand next to him, and I stopped running. I was watching as Amelia draped her arm over Gabriel's shoulder, and he turned round to kiss her.

"What? No! Gabriel, please!" I cried.

Gabriel and Amelia turned around to face me. Amelia took a feather from one of Gabriel's wings and ran it along his neck. The blood gushed from the wound as Amelia threw her head back, laughing. I was running again.

"Gabriel, hold on. Don't leave me!"

"Grace, be careful," he said before slumping against me.

I sat up with a gasp, my hands covering my tear strewn face.

"Grace, did you bring a charger for your toothbrush?" Bryce asked, walking into the living room. "Grace! What's happened?" he ran over to me, holding me.

"It was just a dream, but it was so real," I tried to tell him in between sobs.

"Grace, you're fine. I've got you." His reassuring words and the occasional kiss to the top of my head to soothe me.

"You need to phone Gabriel and check he's okay," I demanded.

"He told us not to phone," he tried to remind me as if I didn't know.

"Phone him! I don't care what he told us to do. And anyway, it was me he told, not you," I said, reasoning with him.

"Well you can deal with him."

"Fine!"

"Gabriel, hi, it's Bryce. I know, I know, but you know what Grace is like when she gets an idea in her head. She wanted me to check on you. She was a bit upset earlier." He turned his back, whispering so I couldn't hear, supposedly.

"Yes, she's here." He turned round to face me. "He wants to talk to you," he said, handing me the phone.

He left me to speak to Gabriel on my own. "Hey."

"Hey, Grace. Miss me?" it was good to hear his voice again.

"Always. Have you had any luck getting all this sorted?" I asked him.

"Not yet, I'm afraid. Things have gone a bit quiet down here. What about you? Are you enjoying being away from me?"

"I'm enjoying being here. I had forgotten how much I loved it. I wish you were here to enjoy it with me,"

"You never know, I might just do that, but not until I'm convinced everything is going to be okay first."

"However long that might be," I said.

"If things don't go the way we'd hoped I was thinking, I might go home. That way, you can come back and get on with your life. If I'm not here, the demons will have nothing to come after you for."

"No! No, you can't do that," I pleaded. "We can work something out. Please don't do that until we have a chance to talk face to face." I could feel the panic building in my chest.

"I won't go without seeing you first. Tell me what you've been up to?"

"We went for a walk, and I've been doing some painting, and the local minister came to introduce himself, and he prayed for my ankle, and it's completely healed. I don't need to use my crutches or anything," I gushed.

"That's wonderful news. Some of these old ministers are good at offering prayer."

"He's not that old, and he used to be the minister in Dalkeith. Would you believe he christened Niven's son, Charlie?"

"Sounds like you had a chance to sit and talk with him for a while?"

"He came over for dinner."

"Grace, I need to go. It was great to hear your voice again."

"Really? Just another five minutes?" I pleaded.

"I can't, sorry. How about I give you a call at the weekend?"

"Okay. I miss you."

"I love you, Grace."

"I love you too." I sat there holding the phone. What was I doing? All I had wanted was to be with Gabriel. But with everything that had happened, I don't know. Maybe it was Daniel that had me this confused.

I was making lunch when Bryce finally came back through.

"I thought it was women who were the ones to spend half the day getting ready?" I joked.

"It takes time to look this good." He laughed. He sat at the table and helped himself to the quiche and salad I'd prepared.

"How was Gabriel?" he asked cautiously.

I sighed. "Gabriel's fine."

"And what's with the sigh?" he asked.

Was this the best person to be discussing this with?

"Come on. You can tell me anything. Is it about Daniel?" he asked, moving his food around the plate with his fork.

I watched him for a moment before taking a bite of lunch.

"Grace, it's fine. I've seen how you were with Gabriel. Did I wish it was me? Of course, but sometimes things aren't meant to be." He sat forward, waiting to hear what I had to say.

"He thinks I could be in danger if I get too close, so he's thinking of moving away. I thought I loved him, I mean, I do love him, but if there isn't going to be a future, then what's the point of continuing with the relationship?" I was asking for an easy way out that I already knew wasn't going to be forthcoming.

"If he's not thinking of staying around, then maybe it is time to move on."

"Do you think it's a bit quick to be moving on to someone else?"

"Grace, it was a bit quick how fast you fell in love with Gabriel, but we all thought he was going to be there for you. We all thought we were going to be helping you plan a wedding before the year was out," he joked. "You need to do what feels right for you."

"When did you get so grown up?"

"I think being here has changed me."

"Once you've finished eating, I'm going to take you for a tour of the island." I smiled.

Chapter Twenty-Two

"Hey, you. That's me finished for today if you want to do something?" The message on my phone read.

We were heading back to the house when the message came through.

"Who's that?" asked Bryce.

"Daniel. He was asking if I wanted to do something," I answered.

"And do you want to do something?"

"Yeah, I think I would." I looked at Bryce for approval.

"Message him back then. I can drop you off and pick you up later, or maybe he could give you a lift home. I have some things to do for work anyway," he suggested.

"Are you sure?"

"Of course. Message Daniel!" he ordered.

"Hi, I'm in the car with Bryce. He said he could drop me off if that's okay?"

"Perfect. It's the Old Manse on the corner of town."

"Be there in around fifteen minutes."

"See you then x,"

"Well? What did he say?" asked Bryce.

"He said to drop me at the Old Manse. I'll show you where." I smiled. I stood at the door, took a deep breath, and knocked.

"Hey, you. Come in." Daniel smiled.

"I'm sorry I don't have any wine," I joked. "Who needs wine when I've got you?"

I don't know why a line like that would have the effect it did, but I giggled like a teenager on her first date.

He ushered me through to the kitchen. It looked like it had been refurbished, with its modern appliances and lovely patio doors leading out onto the garden and a view of the harbour.

"Can I get you something to drink?" he asked, switching on the kettle. "Just a glass of water, please."

"Coming right up." I watched him take a glass from the cupboard. "Ice?"

"Please." He placed the glass at the front of the fridge door for the ice and water to be discharged.

"Amazing inventions we have now," he said, handing me the glass.

"Not like when we were children making our ice in trays," I remembered.

"Or putting juice in cups and freezing it," he said, reminiscing.

"Kids don't know what they're missing these days."

I watched him make a cup of coffee while I sipped my water.

"Did you get some painting done?" he asked.

"I did." I smiled, reaching for my phone. I found the picture Bryce had taken and held it out for Daniel to see.

"Wow! I am impressed. Why aren't you exhibiting these paintings? I take it this isn't the only painting you've done?"

I squirmed uneasily in my chair. "I'm not very good at having people looking at my work."

"That's a distinct lack of confidence, not talent!" he scowled at me.

I watched a drip of condensate water roll down the outside of my glass.

"I can tell there's a story there somewhere?" he said, looking down to catch my gaze.

I looked up into his dark eyes, wondering why I was even here, let alone about to bare my soul to someone I'd only known for a few days.

"It's too long and complicated a story to be bothering with." I sat up, took a deep breath, and smiled. "You have an amazing view here." I stood and walked to the patio doors. The view across the harbour, with the mountains in the background, made me sigh, wishing I had one like this from my patio doors. I could sit here for hours just watching.

"Grace, if you need someone to talk to, it's my job to be a good listener."

"There isn't enough time in the world to go into everything in my life."

"What age are you?"

"Twenty-nine."

"Hardly your twilight years. I think you underestimate yourself."

"Could we go for a walk?"

"Do you want to go down to the beach?"

"Sure."

"Are you alright? You look a bit pale," he asked, sounding concerned. He put his hand on my arm as if he was worried I was going to fall over.

"I'm fine. I think I need some fresh air. I've been stuck in the car with Bryce for the last few hours, so it would be nice to get my legs moving.

We walked along the shoreline as the waves crashed against the rocks. It was my kind of beach. I never understood how people could lie on a beach all day sunbathing when there was so much more to do and explore. As a child, my dad would take me to play crazy golf in Croatia or walk along the shore of Miami Beach as the fish swam around our feet, anything to give my mum the peace and quiet she craved.

I looked out at the sea, the white horses dancing on the waves. "You look much better," Daniel said, coming to stand next to me.

"I feel it. Don't you love this?" I said, looking at him with the biggest smile on my face.

"I do. I have to admit the view and the relaxed atmosphere here were contributing factors to me applying for this job," Daniel explained.

"I can understand why."

"But you'll know what I mean having a house here."

"My family have been living here for generations."

"So, you didn't buy it?"

I shook my head. "No, I've been coming here since I was a baby. It was my playground growing up."

"You must hate having to leave?" he picked up a stone and skimmed it across the waves.

"I'm impressed," I said, bending over to get my stone. I couldn't resist trying to beat Daniel's four. "Eight!" I exclaimed, raising my hands in the air in celebration. He laughed along, but I could tell he was waiting for a response to his question. "I haven't been here in a while. After my dad died, there were too many memories, so I stopped coming,"

"Why didn't you sell it?"

"Same reason, how could I give up on a place that brought me so much love and joy and then there was the history connected to it, all the generations of my family who had struggled to work and make a living for their families so I could be here today." I shrugged my shoulders.

"Do you think now that you've made the step to come back, it will become a regular trip?"

"I'm not sure." A shudder ran down my back, and I instinctively hugged my arms around my body to keep warm.

He moved close to me, rubbing his hands up and down my arms. "I think it's time I should be getting you back before you freeze to death."

I looked into his dark eyes, wondering what secrets he had locked away inside them.

"Grace," he said my name in a whisper as his mouth pressed against mine.

I felt consumed in him. He had a way of making me lose all sense of the world around me. It was him and me, and I didn't want anything else.

"I would want you to come back."

He took my hand, and we walked back the way we had come, arriving at the house.

Would you like to come in for something to eat?" he asked.

"I think I should be getting back. Bryce will be wondering where I am." I wasn't sure what he expected of me, and it was too soon to find out.

"Maybe another time?" he asked, looking longingly at me.

"Of course." I smiled.

The car was twisting and turning along the single-track road. There hadn't been much conversation, and it felt like I had done my usual and managed to piss him off when it was the furthest thing from my mind.

"Pull in at the next passing place," I asked.

"Are you okay? Do you feel sick?" he asked, beginning to panic. He parked and turned to face me.

I chuckled. "I'm fine." I put my hand up to his face, and I could feel him relax into a sigh. "You were just a bit quiet."

He clicked our seatbelts, his hand holding the side of my face before he was kissing me again. There was more passion this time. No one around to see us. My head fell back as he kissed down my neck, his hands caressing me, pulling me closer. My fingers were running through his hair, holding him or moving him where I needed to feel his mouth on me.

"Grace. Why didn't you want to come back to mine?" he asked.

"There was only so far I wanted this to go, and I thought being here, I could control what was happening, and I wasn't sure what you wanted."

"And now?"

I kept my gaze on him as I slowly dropped my hand, feeling his aroused state. "I think I missed an opportunity." I smirked.

He took my hand in his and kissed the back of it. "I'm sure there will be other opportunities." He sat back, resting his head on the seat, his eyes closed.

"I think I'll need to hold you to that."

He turned his head and opened his eyes. "I'm counting on it." He smiled, starting the car and putting his seatbelt on.

I clicked my belt back in, and after another look exchanged, we were back on the road. I rested my hand on Daniel's thigh, which made him smile, and I was enjoying the closeness.

He turned the car at the gate, ready to drive away when I got out. I leaned and kissed him goodbye. He pulled me back a couple of times before he was willing to let me go.

I felt like a kid again as I walked down to the house. The excitement began to build in my body and bubble up to the surface.

"Hey, that's me back," I called out into the darkness of the living room. I checked the bedrooms, but Bryce wasn't home. It was when I came back into the kitchen that I saw the note on the table.

Hey Grace, been invited out. Don't wait up. B x

Great! And here I was rushing back so he wouldn't be on his own.

I poured myself a drink and sat at the kitchen table. I couldn't help but replay our moment in the car. It was so easy to get lost in him; nothing else mattered when I was with him, but how could I go there when I had just left Gabriel?

I jumped at my phone, signalling a message. I thought it might have been Bryce, but it was Daniel.

"Hey, you. Made it home x."

Chapter Twenty-Three

"Hi, glad to hear it. Bryce is away out."

"So, you rushed back for nothing?"

"Not for nothing."

"Ouch!"

"I enjoyed our time together."

"Me too x,"

The smile on my face was an indication of how he was making me feel.

"When do I get to kiss you again?"

It was so easy to get caught up in what was happening, but I couldn't help but wonder what Gabriel was doing right now.

"I'm guessing you're having second thoughts?"

His reply came as I continued to stare at my phone.

"It's not that. I meant what I said. I did enjoy being with you today."

"But?"

"I'm not very good at this."

"You don't have to be. Talk to me."

"I find it hard opening up?"

I put the phone down and buried my head into my arms on the table. When did this get so hard? It was like being back at school. I was too old for this! There was no reply.

I went to the freezer. Always a worthy place to end up if I'd made a mess of something. I pulled out a tub of ice-cream and a teaspoon. It didn't matter how bad the problem seemed to be, ice-cream was always better with a teaspoon, and it lasted longer.

My phone rang, and my heart sank. "Hi."

"Hey, you. I was about to send you about four different messages, but none of them felt right, so I decided to phone."

"It's okay. Maybe it's not the best thing to put in a text."

"You were trying to be honest. It's hard for me too. I think that's why I never stay in a place too long, and I don't want to get too involved."

"And now?"

"This feels different somehow. I want to get to know you better."

The smile had come back to my face. "I want that too."

A chuckle came through the phone. "I wish we had talked about this earlier, then maybe I could have still been with you."

"I would have liked that."

"What are you going to do now?"

"Ice-cream."

"Oh, nice. Flavour?"

"This is a strawberry."

"A classic. Make?"

"Lucas. Bryce insisted we bring some up."

"From Musselburgh?"

"It is indeed."

"If you weren't so far away, I would be over there in a shot."

"It is pretty good."

"I remember. I know what I'd like to do with it too!" I blushed and coughed at the same time. "Steady!" He laughed. "Maybe you could leave me some?"

"Oh, I'm not sure about that."

"Grace."

"It'll cost you."

"Whatever it takes."

I laughed again. "I'm going now before it melts."

"Grace."

"Bye." I hung up the phone laughing. A text came through.

"I can't believe you hung up on me!"

"Believe it. You should never come between a woman and her ice-cream!"

"You're mad."

"In a nice way, though."

"Definitely. See you tomorrow x,"

"Night x."

I put the phone down on the table and dived back into the ice-cream. I shivered at the thought of what Daniel could do with it. I sat smiling way longer than I should have after that conversation.

I jumped as Bryce came into the kitchen.

"And what time do you call this?" I asked in my best parent voice.

His cheeks flushed slightly, which he realised because he was now standing with his back to me at the sink.

"I met someone earlier, and she invited me out."

"Does this someone have a name?" I smiled to myself.

"Kate."

I laughed openly this time. "Bryce has a girlfriend," I teased.

He turned around. "Grow up!" he did try to walk past me and escape, but that was never going to be a possibility.

"Sit and spill," I ordered him.

"Grace," he pleaded.

"No, no, no. Nice try, now sit!" Bryce obliged if not grudgingly. I did hand him my spoon as a consolation.

"I was out for my run earlier, and she was collecting some peat, and we got talking, and she asked me over. I thought that you were away out, so I might as well take the young lady up on her offer," he explained.

"Which croft?"

"I think it's the third one over with the red roof."

"I know which one you mean. So does Kate stay with family, or is she on her own?"

"She's renting it for a year while she's studying the island or the waters surrounding it anyway. She's a marine biologist."

"You're smiling. I'm glad you found someone who makes you happy." I tapped him gently on the shoulder.

"She does. It's just a bit of a trek between here and home."

"It's not that far, and we could share a car journey now and again."

"We'll see. Now I'm going to bed, and I suggest you do the same because Kate's invited us out on a boat she's hiring." He handed me back my spoon and kissed the top of my head before heading through to his bed.

I smiled, feeling slightly excited. I loved boats, and if we were going around the coast, I knew we would be in for some amazing views and local wildlife.

We were up early. Kate picked us up at the top of our road. "This is Kate, Kate this is my friend Grace,"

She looked to be slightly younger than Bryce, probably still in her twenties, her blonde hair tied in a knot at the back of her head. She wasn't wearing any make-up, and she didn't need to. She had big rosy, red cheeks, which I wasn't sure if it was because she spent most of her time working outside or if she was just shy meeting me for the first time.

"Hi Kate, it's lovely to meet you, and thank you for letting me join you."

"Hi, that's no problem. It just gives me two apprentices that I can get to give me a hand."

"Sounds interesting."

I sat in the back and noticed the occasional glances between the two of them. I hope I wasn't going to be getting in the way, I didn't want to be playing gooseberry, but selfishly I was looking forward to getting out on the boat. I had brought my camera so I could photograph the scenery for a painting or two, and I did like to have some of my pictures adorning the walls of my home.

The boat came with the job and was like a small fishing boat with plenty of room for all her expensive looking equipment and a workbench. I took more pictures than I ever thought I would. Every turn of the boat made a new perspective on a mountain or the way the waves were crashing on the rocks would make for some spectacular pictures. There was a host of wildlife, and seeing Bryce get as excited as he did had Kate and me laughing, which he just shrugged off. I was seeing Bryce in a different light since we arrived. He was a lot more relaxed, and I couldn't remember seeing him this happy in a long time.

We helped Kate too. She had experiments located in different positions around the island, and it was our job to record the data for her as she read out the figures. I hadn't expected to be away as long as we had, but luckily, she had made a big bowl of pasta salad.

"Kate, I'm sorry. If I'd known we were going to be out for most of the day, I would have made sure we brought something." I felt guilty that we hadn't contributed to the lunch.

"Don't worry about it. It was quick and easy to rustle up." She smiled.

"You'll need to come over for dinner then and let us cook for you."

"I'd like that, thank you." She tapped Bryce on the arm. "You didn't tell me you could cook."

"Our Brycie boy makes a mean steak. I'm surprised he never told you he's never usually shy about his accomplishments," I said, laughing, which gained me a sharp stare.

"To be fair, there wasn't much time for talking, "Kate said, not looking up from her plate, but the look on Bryce's face, I had to stifle the laugh, or I think I would have ended up in the water.

His cheeks flushed at the two of us making fun at him. "Mind me never to come on a boat with you two ever again," he said, shaking his head.

"I'm sorry Bryce, you're just so easy to wind up,"

Kate laughed too. "Sorry."

When we arrived back, Daniel was standing waiting for me on the harbour wall. "You made it back safely then?" he took my hand to help me off the boat.

"Daniel, this is Kate," I introduced them.

"Hi Daniel, it's a pleasure to meet you."

Bryce looked at me, a bit confused as to why Daniel was there.

"Daniel has very kindly offered to take me home, so it'll give you two a chance to spend some more time together without me tagging along." I smiled at Bryce and hugged him. "Kate, thank you again for a wonderful day, and I meant what I said about coming for dinner."

"Well, I owe you dinner too, so how about you all come over to mine tomorrow and let me cook?" Daniel offered.

Kate looked at Bryce for approval. "That would be nice, thank you. Can I bring anything?"

"Just yourself. It'll be good to have some company."

"I know what you mean," said Kate.

I understood what she meant. It could get quite lonely staying here by yourself if you didn't go out and meet people.

"Right, that's settled then. I'll arrange with Grace, and I'll see you all tomorrow."

We said goodbye and left Kate and Bryce together with the boat and the rest of the day to themselves.

"What would you like to do?" asked Daniel as we headed for his car.

"I would love to get home, get the heating cranked up, and relax."

"Sounds good to me." He smiled over at me.

It was good to be home. Daniel made a coffee and a tea, for me and we got cuddled up on the couch with the throw over us.

"I'm going to miss this when you're back home, being able to meet up and spend some time together," he said kissing the side of my head.

“Why don’t you come down for a couple of days? There’s plenty of room,” I offered.

“Do you think we’re ready for that?”

I turned to look up at him. “Only if you think you can put up with me twenty-four hours a day.”

He placed his hand under my chin, tilting my head up so he could kiss me. “I think I could manage that.”

Chapter Twenty-Four

I hooked up my camera to my laptop, and we had a look through at some of the pictures I had taken. Daniel had liked a few, so I copied them and emailed them over.

"I can't believe how talented you are. I take a picture, and it just looks ordinary, but you've managed to capture so much more. How will you decide which ones to paint?" Daniel asked.

"A feeling. If something speaks to me, I might sketch something first then think about the colours." I loved talking about this with him.

"Can I see some of your sketches?" he asked.

"Sure." I went through to the room and brought my A3 sketchbook through along with a pencil. I could never separate the two.

Daniel flicked through the drawings of my time here. The views, houses, flowers, anything which caught my eye was ready to paint at a later date.

"These are amazing."

"Maybe you'll let me draw you some time."

He blushed slightly. "I don't think I could do that. I'd be a bit self-conscious,"

I giggled. "It's okay; you don't need to take your clothes off. Here." I sat him round to face me and picked up my book. I made some preliminary shapes and angles before building up the picture of the man sitting before me. If nothing else, it gave me an excuse to sit and stare at him.

"Don't move. I want to get a couple of pictures first. I might turn you into a painting."

"So, do I get to see?"

I turned the page around for him to have a look.

"Grace. The detail wow, I never knew I could look so good." He smiled, unable to take his eyes off it.

I took another couple of pictures of the sketch for later, signed G.G, and put the date at the bottom right corner before tearing the page out and giving it to him.

"I couldn't." He put his hands up to protest.

"Please." I tried again to give it to him.

"You give me so much, and I don't give you anything." He looked at me with those big, deep dark eyes.

"You give me more than you know." I put my book down on the table and moved closer to him.

I pressed my hands on to his thighs as I pushed myself forward. My lips skimmed over the top of his. His hands moved up my arms as his mouth opened, waiting for my lips to return to his. My lips touched him swiftly before I pulled back, which had him moving towards me. I tried to do it again, but he had had enough of the teasing. His hands went up to my face holding it in place, ready for his mouth to join with mine.

I wasn't going to pull back again. I was enjoying how it was making me feel. I pulled Daniel's jumper up his body, and he helped to remove it. I wanted to get closer to him. I kissed down the side of his neck as he let out a breath. I moved to sit on top of him, feeling him beneath me.

"Grace." He pulled my hips closer to him, and my head fell back as he kissed my neck, his hand at the back of my head, holding me in place.

I dropped a hand to his belt. "I want you,"

His head fell back onto the couch with a sigh as his hands held onto mine.

"Grace, believe me, I want you just as much. I can't be with you like that. Not yet."

I sat back on the couch beside him, I wasn't sure what just happened, but the rejection hit me harder than I thought it would.

He wrapped me in his arms with the covers. "I want us to be sure this is what we want." He kissed the side of my head. "Talk to me."

"I don't think there's much to say." I did feel a little stupid.

He held me tighter. "I'm sorry for letting things go as far as they did. I'm not pushing you away. I want to spend as much time as I can with you. I want to get to know you."

I looked up at him. "Still want to come down to mine?"

"Of course." He kissed me, and I cuddled back into his chest.

I'm not sure if it was the sea air or just being wrapped in Daniel's arms, but I had fallen asleep, and looking at the expression on Bryce's face as he stood over me, I knew Daniel had succumbed too.

"Alright, sleeping beauty,"

Daniel had felt his presence too and moved to sit up, which, in turn, moved me. "What time is it?" I asked groggily.

"Well, the big hand is on the three, and the little hand is on the nine." He laughed; his arms folded across his chest.

"Quarter past nine, are you kidding?" I ran my hands through my hair and stood up.

"I should go," Daniel said, standing.

"What have you two been doing to get this tired?" it was Bryce's turn to get his own back for me teasing him earlier.

Daniel just laughed as he put his jumper back on, but for some reason, I went into total panic mode.

"Nothing, it must have been the sea air and…"

Daniel leaned into me. "I think he's trying to wind you up."

"And succeeding nicely." Bryce laughed as he sat on the chair next to the fire.

"But I do need to go. Bryce, always a pleasure."

"Catch you later."

"I'll see you out." I walked him to his car. "I'm sorry for earlier and for falling asleep."

"It was perfect." He leaned in to kiss me. "I'll see you tomorrow for dinner, seven, okay?"

"Looking forward to it." I kissed him again. "I don't know what I'm going to do now though that I'm wide awake."

"I'll message you when I get home. Night."

I kissed him again before making my way to open the gates. He rolled down his window for one last kiss before he disappeared into the night.

"You two look good together." Bryce smiled.

I sat back on the couch and pulled the cover over my legs.

"How do you think Gabriel is going to take the news?" he was looking serious now.

I didn't answer straight away. There was only so much I could tell Bryce about what was happening with Gabriel. "I'm not sure if there's anything to tell.

Gabriel doesn't know if he'll be staying around, and with Daniel, it's me that'll be going home." I sighed and let my head fall back against the couch. How could I tell him that Gabriel and I had already decided that we were no longer going to be together?

"That's a dilemma only you can figure out, but they are both nice guys, and both love you. You can see that. Just don't string them along for too long, or you risk losing both of them."

"Wise words. How about you and Kate? Did you have a nice day?" I asked, smiling again.

His face lit up at the mere mention of Kate. "We did. I helped Kate take all her things back home. It's quite a set up she's got over there with all her computers and microscopes and charts. She made dinner, and we talked. It was good."

"I can feel a 'but' coming on."

"Same thing as you. I need to go home, but Kate will be here for another eight months. Then who knows where she might end up?" it was his turn to sigh.

"What are we like? Maybe we're both looking into this way too much. We should just be enjoying the time we've got together, and we can decide later what happens."

"I like that, but unlike you, I haven't had any sleep, and I'm knackered, so I'm away to bed. Don't stay up too late." He kissed the top of my head before going through to his room.

I was starving. I hadn't had anything to eat since the pasta salad on the boat. I made some boiled eggs mashed up in a cup with toast.

I hadn't heard the phone beep, but the little blue light was flashing away, trying to get my attention that I had a new message.

"Thank you again for my picture. I don't think anyone has ever done anything like that for me before."

"It was a pleasure. I'm glad you like it."

"I do. I also liked cuddling up with you earlier."

"I liked that too. Maybe you'll let me sketch you when you're not wearing so much." I smiled, wondering how he would respond.

"I could take my jumper off."

"And maybe your shirt?"

"I think I could handle that. What do I get to remove from you?"

I giggled at the thought.

"How about everything you take off, I'll take off too?"

"Sounds fair."

"You'll need to come down to my studio."

"When?"

"How about next week sometime?"

"I've got next Wednesday free. I could leave Tuesday night, stay Wednesday and leave Thursday morning?"

"I would love that."

I could feel the excitement building inside me.

"I'll look forward to it. Will there be time for us to do some other stuff?"

"Like…?"

"Like allowing me to kiss you, touch you."

"I'll make time!" damn right, there would be time, and maybe I could get him to relax his thinking a bit and be more intimate.

"I'll see you tomorrow."

"Night Daniel x."

"Night x."

I sat back, holding the phone to my mouth. I was beginning to feel something for Daniel.

I thought about what Bryce had said about Gabriel. Although we had agreed that our relationship had ended, I didn't want to rub his nose in it with Daniel, but I did want him to come down for a visit. Who knows, maybe Daniel and Gabriel would be able to get on with each other, for me at least.

Chapter Twenty-Five

Bryce went over to pick up Kate before getting me at the gate. I had already packed some wine, and beer and Bryce had agreed with some persuasion to give Daniel some of our ice-cream.

"Hi, come in." Daniel welcomed us at the door.

"Hey." I blushed as I walked past him. He looked incredible in his suit. It fitted into his body perfectly, and he had opted not to wear a tie but instead leave a couple of buttons open, which was just enough to send my emotions over the edge.

"Hey, you."

I hadn't brought much for going out with, but there was always room for a little black dress. It had made Bryce look twice when I walked out of the bedroom, so I was hoping it was going to have the same effect on Daniel.

"Have you given Daniel his surprise yet?" asked Bryce.

"There's more?" said Daniel laughing.

I produced the small cool bag and handed it to him.

"What's this?" he looked nervous. "No way! Is that Lucas?"

"It is indeed." I laughed.

"I would come and hug you, but not until I've had a taste." He took a spoon out from the drawer.

"Am I missing something here?" asked Kate.

Before anyone could answer, Daniel had produced another spoon for her to use. Bryce and I watched as they dived into the box of different flavoured ice-cream.

"That is amazing!" Kate said, putting her hand up to her mouth.

"I used to try and make it over at least once a week." Confessed Daniel.

"Where do you get it?" asked Kate.

"It's a family-run ice-cream shop in Musselburgh, near where we stay. It has the best ice-cream." Bryce informed her.

"Maybe you'll need to take me there sometime." Kate looked at Bryce, and I was wondering if we should excuse ourselves.

Daniel must have been thinking the same. "Drinks! What's everyone having?"

"I'm on the lemonade, I'm afraid, designated driver."

"Bryce?"

"I'll have a beer, thanks."

"Kate?"

"I'll have a glass of white wine, please."

Daniel played barman, and we all went through to the dining room and took our seats, Daniel and I sitting opposite Kate and Bryce. The table was large, and solid with enough chairs around it for another two couples. I couldn't help wondering why a single person would need such a large table, but maybe it was so he could invite people over.

Daniel had made scallops and black pudding to start, langoustines, and salmon in a strawberry and champagne sauce with vegetables and a cranachan to finish.

"Daniel, that was a delight," said Kate, and we all had to agree, there were no leftovers, especially after Bryce had extras. Every plate was empty.

Bryce and Kate went through to the lounge while Daniel and I got the table cleared.

As soon as they left the room, Daniel pulled me in his arms as his lips pressed gently against mine. I melted straight away, draping my arms over his shoulders.

"I've been waiting to do that since you came through the door," he said before kissing me again.

"Remember, there are other people in the house."

"Damn! Whose idea was it to invite them?" he smirked.

I placed my hand on his chest. "I could always sleepover," I suggested.

He smiled. "I would want nothing more, but I'm a traditional kind of guy, and I think I would wait for that."

"Really? Because your hands and mouth are saying something completely different." I kissed him again.

"I never said it would be easy." He smiled as his hands moved up and down the side of my body.

"We should get this place tidied up and head through," I suggested.

"Another five minutes?" he pleaded.

I smirked. “Are you sure you’re going to be able to wait?”

“It’s a nice thought at the moment.”

I pulled back. “Right, Mr Nice thought, you take the glasses, and I’ll take the plates.”

When we joined Bryce and Kate, it looked like they had been enjoying the time to themselves too, sitting close to each other on the couch and Bryce’s arm draped over Kate’s shoulder.

The room was modern with two large couches facing each other. Certainly plenty of room to cuddle up on.

“Dishes washed and put away?” Bryce teased.

Daniel handed Bryce another beer and poured Kate a glass of wine before coming to join me on the couch opposite.

“Grace and I were talking, and I’m going to come down for a visit next week, leave on Tuesday night and come back on Thursday morning if you wanted to come with me Kate, we could share the driving?” he offered.

“That’s a great idea,” I said, looking at Bryce.

“Yeah.” Bryce looked at Kate. “I could take the day off, and I could show you the sights.”

Kate smiled. “If you don’t mind, Daniel?”

“That’s settled then.”

I put my hand on Daniel’s leg and smiled at him. That was a lovely thing to do for Bryce.

We talked until the early hours, and I was struggling to stay awake. “Sorry guys, I’m going to have to make a move, or I’ll have us in a ditch going home.”

“Are you sure you’re okay to drive?” asked Daniel. “I’ll be fine.” I smiled.

“I’m going to stay at Kate’s tonight if you want to come with us?” suggested Bryce. Daniel looked at me for approval.

“I would like that.” I smiled.

“I can give you a lift back in the morning. I’ve got a few things to do tomorrow,” offered Kate.

“We better get going then.”

We dropped Bryce and Kate off, and it was Daniel’s turn to open and close the gates.

We walked into the house, and I shuddered. Even leaving the heating on low, the house was still a bit chilly.

Daniel wrapped his arms around me. “I can warm you up.”

"What about waiting, or have you abandoned that thought already?" I teased.

"I can find other ways to keep you warm."

I turned the heating up slightly, took Daniel's hand, and led him through to my room. I kicked my heels off as Daniel held my waist.

"I know we've only known each other a few days, but I think I'm falling in love with you," he said, looking at me intently.

"I'm enjoying being with you too." I ran my fingers through the back of his hair, and he was kissing me again.

I had gone through to the bathroom to change into my shorts and top combo. When I came back through, Daniel was already in bed. His top was removed, exposing his toned body beneath. It wasn't as muscly as Gabriel, but I wasn't sure if anyone on earth could match his physique. There was a patch of dark hair across his chest and a dark line escaping under the sheet. The covers were pulled back ready for me to enter. As soon as I climbed in, Daniel's hands pulled me into his body and kissed me. "Warm enough?"

I smiled. "I am. How are you coping?" I ran a foot up his bare leg.

"You're making it very difficult for me." He laughed. "But I'm still going to do this properly." He kissed me, and I turned around, his arms still holding me as we fell asleep.

"Grace." I opened my eyes to see Daniel standing dressed in front of me. "Sorry. I need to go. Kate will be here soon."

I rubbed my eyes open. "Have you had something to eat?"

"No, it's fine. It's still early; go back to sleep." He kissed me before leaving. I heard the door close as he left, and I smiled to myself.

It didn't take long before I heard the door opening and closing again and my bedroom door opening, hoping it was Daniel deciding to come back to bed.

Bryce got in beside me. "Oh, you're nice and warm. It's freezing outside. I've turned the heating up. I cuddled into him without opening my eyes.

"Good night?" I asked.

"The best."

I opened an eye and looked at him. "Present company excluded." He laughed.

"That's what I like to hear. Is Kate still wanting to come down next week?"

"Yes, probably more so now."

I laughed. "How could she resist?"

"How are you feeling about going home?"

I shrugged my shoulders. "It'll be nice to get home. I'll miss Daniel."

"And Gabriel?"

"Argh! Why does everything have to be so complicated?" I moaned.

"I think it's called being an adult."

"But I don't want to be an adult!" I mimicked a little girl's voice.

Bryce laughed. "What am I going to do with you?"

"Let me fall asleep like this."

"Anything for you, Gracie Baby."

I was sitting in the kitchen with the phone on the table in front of me. "I think you have to pick it up for it to work." Joked Bryce.

I scowled at him. "I'm trying to phone Gabriel to tell him we're coming home."

"Don't envy you that conversation. Are you going to tell him about Daniel?"

"I think one revelation at a time."

"What are you going to do if Amelia is still creating havoc?"

That was the million-dollar question. "We need to get home regardless."

"I'll leave you to it. I'm away for a run." He kissed the top of my head, put his earbuds in, grabbed his bottle from the fridge, and he was off, leaving me staring at the phone and wishing Gabriel would phone me instead and tell me everything was okay for me to come home.

"How many times do I need to tell you not to phone me?" he sounded angry, but then he laughed, and I knew everything was going to be alright.

"Hi, Gabe."

"What's up?"

"I need to talk to you about something."

"Sounds serious."

"Bryce and I are coming home tomorrow."

The silence on the other end of the phone had me looking at it to make sure the line hadn't gone dead.

"Gabriel?"

"I'm still here. Grace, I'm not sure that's such a good idea. I have no idea where or what Amelia is up to."

"I know, but Bryce needs to get home for work, and I would like to get back to my things again, and I want to sort through my paintings."

"I can't allow that. If Bryce needs to come home, then fine, I'll ask someone to come to stay with you."

"I wasn't asking Gabriel." It sounded curter than I wanted.

"I take it there's nothing I can say to change your mind?" he asked sounding concerned.

"Minds made up, I'm afraid."

"When can I expect you back?" he asked, sounding resigned to the idea. "Tomorrow some time,"

"Okay. If there's nothing I can say that will dissuade you, then I'll see you tomorrow."

"Bye, Gabriel."

"Bye, Grace."

I put the phone on the table and let out a sigh. If that revelation had him concerned and disappointed that I was coming home, the conversation about Daniel was only going to be worse.

Chapter Twenty-Six

Bryce was at Kate's, and I was making my way over the croft land to spend my last night with Daniel. If I was going to have to tell Gabriel about Daniel, it was only fair that I tell Daniel about Gabriel. It was the second conversation today that I wasn't looking forward to having. It could blow everything up before we've even had a chance to start.

"Hey, you," Daniel answered the door, leaning in for a kiss as payment for me to cross his threshold.

"Hey." I pulled back, walking past him and taking my coat off.

"Everything okay?" he asked in the same tone of voice Gabriel had given me earlier.

I put my hand on his arm. "I'm fine, but I do need to talk to you."

"Sounds serious."

It was giving me those déjà vu feelings, only this time I was talking to Daniel. "Not really." I smiled. "I just want to be honest with you, that's all."

"Please don't tell me you have a husband and four kids back home." He looked worried.

I laughed. "No, nothing like that."

He put his arms around me and held me tighter than usual before we sat on the couch.

"It's nothing. I just wanted you to know that before I came up, I was in a relationship with someone."

Daniel stood up and walked over to the window.

"We broke up, before Bryce and I came up. It's just when you come down there's a chance you'll meet him, and I don't want there to be any awkwardness between us all."

Daniel never said anything. Great! I thought all I had to do was come down and tell him about Gabriel, and everything would be fine. How wrong could I be?

He turned around. His hands pushed down, into the pockets of his jeans. "I'm not sure what to say."

"I'm not leaving you. I just wanted to be honest."

He scrunched his mouth, and I knew I should stop talking because I was only making this worse.

"Do you love him?"

Bloody hell, he was bringing out his big guns!

"I did love him, and I'll probably always have feelings for him, but it was never going to work between us."

"Did you make love to him?"

"Daniel."

"I thought you wanted to be honest."

He had a point, I suppose. I wasn't ready for this line of questioning. "I did."

He blew a sigh from his mouth and crossed his arms in front of him. "I don't believe this," he muttered under his breath.

I stood up. "Are you a virgin?" I asked angrily. It was like I had gone behind his back or something, and I didn't even know him when I met Gabriel.

"No."

"But you thought I should be, is that it?"

"I didn't mean that. I hate that I want to wait to be with you, and this guy has already had you."

"And how many women have you slept with?" I mirrored his pose with my arms folded across my chest.

"How long has it been since you split up?"

He was hitting these questions out of the park! "Before I came up. That's why I'm here."

"I'm the rebound?"

"No! I never thought about you like that." I sat back down. "Things were happening that was putting our lives at risk because of us being together. I left so he could sort it out."

He came and sat on the couch opposite.

"What about when you go back? Does he think if he sorts it out, whatever *it* was, that you'll go back to him?"

"No. As I said, it was never going to work between us."

"Does he know about me?"

"No. I was going to tell Gabriel when I get home. I didn't want to do it over the phone." He ran his hand through the stubble on his face.

"Well, I suppose I should feel grateful that you came here to tell me in person." He accused.

"Please, Daniel. I just wanted you to know, in case you were in each other's company."

"I'm only going to be down for two nights; is he over at your house every day? Please tell me he doesn't stay with you." He leaned forward, his arms resting on his legs.

"He stays next door."

He chuckled. "Of course he does. How long have you two been neighbours?"

"Not long."

"How long have you been going out?"

"Not long." I hoped this interrogation was nearly over; all it seemed to be missing was a lamp in my face and hooked up to a lie detector.

"How do I know you're not going to go back to him or find someone else the minute my backs turned? You seem to fall in love very easily and very quickly."

"Not fair!" I stood up and went over to the window. I could feel the tears begin to well up in my eyes, and I didn't want him to see that. The last thing I wanted was his sympathy if he even felt anything for me at this point.

"Grace, I'm sorry. Please come and sit back down."

"I'm twenty-nine, and I'm not in a full-time relationship and haven't been for years apart from a couple of drunken nights with Bryce." I turned around, the tears streaming down my face. "So, I fell in love with a man who helped me when I was hurt, and it just so happened he lived next door."

I took a breath and held onto myself for comfort. "Then we split up, and I come up here, to a place I haven't been in years, and you turn up at my door, and as much as I didn't want to feel anything for you, I did and here we are. Maybe I was wrong about you." I shook my head, wiped at my face, and went for the door. I needed to get as far away from here as quickly as possible.

He was up off the couch and grabbed my arm with one hand as the other slammed the door shut in front of me.

"I'm sorry." He wrapped his arms around me, but I wasn't sure how I felt.

"I think I should leave." I pushed him back.

"No!"

"I wasn't asking your permission!"

"I don't care what you were doing. I'm not letting you go until we sort this out. I'm sorry." He put his back against the door.

I put my hands on my hips. "Daniel, please. Just let me go."

"No! Do you think you're the only one who's hurting? I was engaged, a baby on the way. Life was perfect. The night before our wedding she told me she had been seeing someone else. I tried to tell her that I would always be there for the baby, but she told me it wasn't mine. I was scared of letting you in, and I wanted to wait because I want to make sure this time when I fall in love with someone, they wanted me."

It was his turn for the tears to start. He wiped at his face and stood aside from the door and opened it. "I love you, Grace, and I'm sorry if I hurt you, but you know why this all meant so much to me. If you want to go, I'll understand."

I couldn't move. I wanted Daniel more than I had before. I walked forward and closed the door as he grabbed hold of me, and I held him just as tight. The last thing I wanted was to walk out that door. I had everything I wanted right here.

He took my hand and led me through to his bedroom. "I want to hold you."

We lay on his bed, cuddled together as he kissed me tenderly.

"I love you, Grace." I woke up as his fingers stroked through my hair.

"Sorry, I must have fallen asleep,"

"It's okay. I did too. I get too relaxed when I lie holding you in my arms."

"Were you watching me sleep?"

"You are so peaceful and beautiful to watch."

"Creepy." I smiled.

"It's not creepy."

"A bit." I was teasing him.

He moved over on top of me, holding my hands to the bed. "Tell me it's not creepy." He was laughing.

I squealed. "I'm sorry, I'm sorry. Okay, not creepy." I pushed my head up, catching his mouth with mine.

"What am I going to do with you, Miss Grimes?" he asked, smiling down at me.

"Anything you like, Mr Nicolson."

He smiled. "You're killing me." He let his head fall onto my chest and released my arms.

The sky was giving up its light, and Daniel closed the curtains, turning on the small lamp on the side table.

"I can't wait until the light night's start to come in again," Daniel said, coming to sit next to me.

"I don't know. I like the dark nights. You come home from work, crank the heating, and get cuddled up on the couch. It doesn't matter what the weather's doing outside because I'm nice and snug." I wiggled into his side to make the point.

"But in the summer. Heat, long nights to stay outside and have barbeques, have friends over."

"Too hot to sleep at night, wasps, and flies."

"Eat more ice cream and wear less going to bed. I can't say I'm seeing a downside here." He laughed.

"Okay, so some things are better in the summer, but I still like the winter. Snow falling."

"Ankles breaking!"

"I slipped off the curb, not on the ice," I confirmed.

"Was the pavement wet?"

"Yes, but you get rain in the summer too."

"Not cold, slippery rain."

I thought our family was good at arguing!

"Where were you living again? Anyway, I don't care what the weather is like or what time of year it is as long as I get to spend it with you," I said, looking up at him.

"I couldn't agree more. What time are you leaving tomorrow?"

"I think we're going to leave early, so we miss rush hour back home."

"How early?"

"About six."

"That is early. I was going to come up to say goodbye."

"How about I text you when we're leaving, and you can run out to the car?" I offered.

"I would like that." He kissed the top of my head. "I don't know what I'm going to do without you. I've got used to having you around."

I linked my fingers through his. "It won't be long until you're down."

"I know, but it's only a couple of nights then I need to leave you again."

“Believe me. After a couple of nights, you’ll be dying to get home!” I laughed.

“I wish I could spend every night with you like this.”

“Be careful what you wish for. I might take you up on that idea.” I sat up, facing him.

He ran his fingers down the side of my face. “I couldn’t think of anything I would rather do.”

Chapter Twenty-Seven

I had packed the car with way more going home than we had brought up with us. I sent Daniel a text to say we were leaving. Kate had come over to say goodbye while I was checking we hadn't forgotten anything and making sure I had switched everything off. I stood in the kitchen and smiled. At least this time, I knew I would be back again soon. All the pain had gone, and my memories were full of laughter and fun.

I locked the door and drove the car up the narrow track. Bryce and Kate were waiting at the top gate for me. I gave Kate a wave knowing how she was feeling.

"Okay?" I asked Bryce when we were on our way.

"Yeah. I never thought I would feel like that about someone other than you."

I put my hand on his leg. "I'm happy for you, Bryce. Kate is a lucky girl."

"Do you mean that?" he asked.

I turned my head quickly to look at him. "Absolutely! You're such a nice guy, Bryce. You deserve someone who loves you as much as Kate does."

He put his hand over the top of mine. "That's why I love you, Gracie Baby. You always know the right things to say."

We drove in silence until we got to Daniel's house. I parked the car on the road, and he was already waiting for us.

I threw my arms around his neck, and he held me just as tight.

"I can't believe you're leaving." He kissed me. "Phone me when you get home, have a safe journey, and don't forget about me." He smiled as he pushed the hair away from my face.

"How could I?" we kissed again. "I need to go." I got back in the car and wound the window down.

"Bryce, make sure she takes her time."

"Will do. You do the same for me next week."

"See you then." I got one last kiss before he stood back.

I looked in my mirror, switched the indicator on, and pulled away, taking one last look at Daniel. I put my hand up to wave, and we were gone.

"Are you okay?" it was Bryce's turn to ask me. I looked at him and smiled. "I will be."

We had made good time, and before we knew it, we were down at Dalwhinnie and changing places after having something to eat.

"I'm glad to be driving again, Jackie Stewart!" he said, laughing at me.

"You forget I've been in a car with you before." I smirked at him.

"Motorway driving is completely different. There are lanes to pass in for a start!"

I smiled. It had been good getting behind the wheel of the car again and on my favourite road. It was perfect even if I did have Bryce holding on at some points.

It was lunchtime when I turned the car into my driveway. It was nice to be back in familiar surroundings again. Bryce gave me a hand to bring my things in, including some shopping essentials we had stopped for on the way back. I waved to Bryce and closed the door.

The house was warm. Gabriel must have come over and put the heating on for me. I went through to the kitchen with the shopping seeing a large bouquet on the island with a card.

Grace, a few things in the fridge for your return. G x

I opened the fridge to see what he had put in. All the essentials were there and a bottle of prosecco. I smiled. I would phone him later to thank him and invite him over for dinner. I still needed to tell him about Daniel. That, however, was a conversation for another day. Right now, all I wanted was to get everything away, the washing machine on and something to eat, then a long hot shower and into my pyjamas.

I had ticked all the boxes, and I sat cuddled up on the couch watching some mindless reality television programme. It was all my mind could deal with right now. I had also managed to open Gabriel's bottle of prosecco, my second glass waiting patiently for me.

I had phoned Daniel when I got home, and Niven and Nic, and that left one. Gabriel.

I turned the phone over and over in my hands, trying to pluck up the courage to phone him. It had been hard enough telling him I was coming home, but now I had to let him know I had met someone else.

"Hi, you're back. Everything okay?" He answered the phone, sounding happier than the last time we spoke.

"Back safe and sound. Thank you for the flowers and the food and prosecco."

"I thought you might like that."

"On to my second glass already. Would you like to come over for dinner tomorrow?" I asked.

"Yes, that sounds nice. What time?" He said, the happiness gone from his voice.

"How about seven?"

"Okay, I'll see you at seven. Bye, Grace."

"Bye." I hung up the phone. He probably expected me to invite him over tonight or to spend the day tomorrow, but we had agreed, and there had to be boundaries. That's what I was telling myself anyway.

For now, all I wanted to do was finish this glass of wine and head off to bed with a good book.

I woke early. It was a habit I had picked up in Skye and brought home. There were things I wanted to do, and I didn't want to be lying in bed all day.

I made myself a bacon sandwich and sat at the island, watching a couple of birds in the back garden before heading into my studio. I felt instantly at peace and ready to create. I moved all the paintings from Skye into one corner of the room and looked through my camera for inspiration.

The first picture up was the sketch I did of Daniel. I couldn't stop looking at it. I hooked up the camera to my laptop, turned the music up, and after selecting a canvas and some paints, I was ready to begin.

I sat there for most of the day, adding a bit of colour here or shade there. All for it to come together into the image I was looking at on the laptop. Hopefully, it would have some of his personality coming through also.

The alarm on my phone beeped, and I had to run down the stairs to turn the cooker on for Gabriel coming over. I had about an hour before I had to put everything else on, and at that point, I could run for a shower and change before he arrived. That was the idea anyway.

Everything had gone to plan, and although I could have spent the rest of the evening and night on my painting of Daniel, I had to get ready for Gabriel.

"Hey," he said as he walked in, kissing me on the cheek.

Oh, he did smell good, and how could I forget how good looking he was. He certainly wasn't making it easy for me.

"I brought you another prosecco." He placed it on the bunker.

"Thanks. Dinners ready if you want to take a seat." I dashed back to the kitchen, plating everything up before leaving an array of chicken dinner to be consumed.

"This looks amazing, Grace. I've certainly missed your cooking." He smiled, taking a napkin and placing it over his knee.

I felt like I was staring too much and looked away quickly, taking a quick sip from my glass. Why did Gabriel always have this effect on me? I was just glad Daniel wasn't here to see this.

"So, tell me all about it then. What was it like being back?"

"Yeah, it was great. I had forgotten how much I love the place."

"Sounds like you could have stayed longer."

"I could have in an instant, but Bryce needed to come back, and I wanted to come home and get back to work on my paintings."

"I missed you. I know we said we weren't going to take this any further, but I just wanted you to know how I felt." He twirled the glass stem between his fingers.

I sat back and thought about what Bryce had said. I couldn't lead him on any longer. "Gabe, there's something I need to talk to you about."

He sat back in his chair.

"When I left, I didn't think I would ever find anyone like you again. You loved me so much, and I was happy, extremely happy." I was rambling, and I didn't even know what I was talking about anymore.

"You've met someone else?" he asked, staring at me. I felt like those blue eyes of his were staring straight into my soul.

I nodded my head. "I'm sorry, Gabriel. I never meant for it to happen that quick."

His gaze had broken away from mine, and he was looking down at his plate. "Does he love you?" he was looking at me again.

"Yes, he does."

"Do you love him?"

"I think I'm beginning to."

He nodded his head. “I’m pleased for you.” He placed his napkin on the table. “I should go.” He went to stand up.

“No, please stay. Finish your dinner.”

“I don’t think I can, Grace. I knew it was going to happen. I just wasn’t prepared for it to be so soon.” He stood up, and I did too.

I put my hand on his arm. “Please don’t go like this.”

He hugged me, and I felt completely safe in his arms, but that was the problem. When I wasn’t in his arms, I was open to all sorts of attacks, and I couldn’t live like that.

“I’ll give you a call later.” He left me standing in the kitchen.

It had gone so much worse than I had expected it would. I knew Gabriel was going to be upset, I just never realised how much. I hadn’t even told him that Daniel would be coming down next week.

The tears were streaming down my face, and I sat back down at the table. I had made such a mess of this. Gabriel was never going to forgive me, and I felt at that moment, I had lost him forever.

Chapter Twenty-Eight

Sleep wasn't whisking me away tonight as I lay staring at the ceiling. Not a new thing for me, but not having someone to cuddle into was playing a part. That and Gabriel's reaction to me telling him about Daniel wasn't helping either. Guilty conscience or something like that. I could have probably handled the whole thing a lot better, and I knew I was going to have to sort it out before Daniel came down.

Daniel had phoned before I went to bed, and although he kept asking if I was alright, I don't think I convinced him I was, leaving him with a sense that something was up. I didn't tell him what had unfolded with Gabriel. There was no point putting them at odds before they had even had a chance to meet.

I decided to leave my bed for a night when I was tired enough to sleep in it or when someone was sharing it, instead opting for a night with my paintings. I sat at the easel and put a sheet of paper on. There were a few small photos I had taken of the wildflowers, but I chose a picture of the flowers Bryce had picked and put in a glass for me to paint. The watercolours brought the flowers to life, and the glass sparkled with the water inside.

I sat back, looking at my latest creation, and smiled. I never thought my paintings were good enough for others to enjoy, but for me, they did bring me a lot of pleasure as I sat there smiling.

I sat on the island, swinging my feet and looking into my garden. I never liked it when I wasn't speaking to people, or in this case, when they weren't talking to me. I should go over. If he shouts, then I take it and walk away; at least it will all be out in the open.

I put my trainers on and scuffed my feet as I walked over to his house. I knocked on the door and waited. His car was in the drive, so I knew he was home. My arms were wrapped tightly around my body, ready to fend off any attack that might come my way.

The door opened, and I jumped. "Grace?"

"Can I come in?"

"I'm not sure if that would be a good idea." He never moved.

"I wasn't asking if it would be a good idea if I came in. I was asking if I could come in." I should have just walked away, but I hated us being like this with each other, and I needed to get it sorted.

He stood back from the door. "You better come in then."

I walked into the house and went through to his kitchen. It was a little less cluttered than mine was, minimalistic, is how you would describe it. Only essential items for a kitchen on display, then I remembered what it was like before I left.

"Can I get you something to drink?" he leaned up against the bunker with his ankles crossed in front of him.

He wasn't going to make this easy for me. I pulled the sleeves of my jumper over my hands in my uneasy, nervous way. I noticed he wasn't wearing any socks and he was looking a little bit unkempt since the last time I saw him.

"Water please,"

He poured me a glass, made himself a coffee, and resumed his position at the bunker. Well, here goes nothing, I thought to myself and took a deep breath before speaking.

"I wanted to apologise for last night. I know I sprung the news on you, but I thought we could talk about it." I waited, anticipating the worst.

"I don't see what's to discuss. You've met someone else, and I need to deal with that." His hands were gripping the bunker beside him so hard I thought he would be pulling away chunks his knuckles were so white.

"You don't need to be so matter of fact about it. I didn't mean to hurt you, but if I remember rightly, I was going away because you had decided it would be safer for me! You decided we couldn't be together!" I shouted at him.

"I didn't know it was going to be this hard, okay!" he shouted back at me, pushing himself away from the bunker.

"Well, what did you think? That I was going to go away, and what? You were going to forget all about me, or I was going to come back and beg you to take me back."

"That's not fair, Grace. I love you. Even if nothing had happened with Amelia, I was still breaking the rules. I was never going to be able to stay here with you how I would like to be."

"Then if you knew you were never going to be able to stay, why did you allow me to fall in love with you?"

He jumped on top of the bunker; the earlier anger gone from both of us. "I didn't know how I was going to feel about you, and after your accident, I was in the hospital with you. I fell in love with you, Grace. I didn't mean to; it just happened. Could I have kept my distance? Probably, but I didn't want to. I wanted you. I wanted to see what it was like to love a human and have a human love me back."

"You make it sound like a science experiment." I took a drink and jumped on to the island opposite.

"It was never that. It was real, and although I knew I would have to face the consequences of my actions at some point, all the time, I was trying to work out a way for us to be together. That was until Amelia turned up."

"Amelia. Where is she? You never said if you caught her."

"I don't know which makes this worse. I should have realised what was happening with Amelia right away, and I missed it, and now I can't find her."

"You're a rubbish angel." I smirked.

"Archangel!"

"Even worse, you're the boss. You should have known better."

He ran his hands through his hair. "You're right. I should have had this whole thing sorted by now, and instead, all I can do is think about you,"

He jumped off the bunker and came to stand in between my legs. He brushed the hair away from my face. "I'm sorry about last night. I am glad you're happy. At least now when I go away, I'll know there's someone to look after you,"

"Thanks, Gabriel. I don't want to fight, with you. I couldn't stand the thought of not being able to talk to you."

"I promise as long as I'm here, we'll still be able to talk to one another. How could I be this close and not?" He kissed my forehead.

"You do know I'm always going to love you?" I ran my fingers over the day-old stubble on his face.

He turned his head, kissing my hand. "I could never stop loving you. You will always hold a special place in my heart Gracie Baby." He smiled and squeezed his arms around me while snuggling into the base of my neck.

I squealed and pushed him away, laughing. "Are we good?"

"We're good."

He left me sitting on the island and went back to sitting on his bunker which, was probably safer for both of us.

"I'm not sure if this is a good time, but I invited him down next week. I would like you to meet him."

"I don't know, Grace."

"Please, I think you'd get on well with him."

"If it pleases you, then I'll be on my best behaviour. Is he driving down?"

"Yes. Oh, I never told you Bryce met someone, so she's coming down at the same time."

"Was there something in the water?" he took a drink of his coffee. "What's his name?"

"Daniel."

"Was he not the minister who healed your ankle?"

"One and the same." I took a sip of water, trying to steady my nerves. I felt like I was being interrogated, by my parents, after coming in late.

"A bit of a coincidence that he just turned up at your door like that." He looked at me accusingly.

"A bit of a coincidence, the man who takes me to the hospital ends up living next door and turns out to be an archangel!"

"Okay, you win." He laughed. "I think I would like to meet him. I need to make sure he's going to be good enough for you."

"Of course. I wouldn't want your archangel senses to miss anything," I teased.

"Don't push it, Grace!"

I laughed and put my hand up to my mouth to try and stifle it. "I'm sorry."

I could see his knuckles go white again, but this time I knew he was trying to stop himself from coming over to me and kissing me just as he would when we were teasing one another.

"I should probably get going." I jumped off the island. Gabriel came to stand next to me.

"So, I'll see you soon then?" he asked.

"Try and keep me away." I smirked at him before walking towards the door. I stopped and turned. "Oh, and the next time I see you, I want something done about this." I pointed up and down him.

"I thought you liked it a bit rough," he said, rubbing his hand over his chin smirking.

Yeah, I needed to get out of there. I blew the air out of my mouth and rolled my eyes at the ceiling. I turned and made for the door, hearing him laughing behind me. “If only your angel skills were as good,” I shouted through from the front door.

“Archangel! Bye, Gracie Baby.”

Chapter Twenty-Nine

Daniel phoned every morning before I got out of bed; and every night before I went to sleep. We had sent texts to each other throughout the day or sent pictures of what we were up to or if there was something we wanted to share. Today he was driving down with Kate, and I couldn't wait to see him, even if I did feel a little bit nervous.

I couldn't help wondering if there would still be the same connection between us. I know we had spoken to each other every day, but it was going to be different having him here where I could spend time with him before rushing off to do something else.

Bryce was due over soon. He was going to collect Kate and take her home. We thought it might be a bit much to give him directions to Bryce's house then up to mine. I hoped it wasn't going to be too awkward for Kate and Daniel sharing a car. It was a long way to keep the conversation going.

I saw the headlights sweep into the street. I ran through to the lounge to see if it was Bryce. I had been up and down to the window at least twenty times in the last half hour alone. The car parked in my driveway, but it wasn't Bryce.

I opened the door.

"Hey, you." Daniel got out of the car.

I couldn't contain myself any longer and ran at him. He picked me up and spun me around.

"How did you get down so quickly?" I asked once my feet were back on the ground again.

"I couldn't wait any longer, and Kate sent me a message saying she had finished up early, so we decided just to leave."

I looked over at Kate. "Bryce isn't here yet. I thought it was his car when I saw the lights."

"That's okay I sent him a message as we were coming into the street. He said he was just leaving."

"He'll be here shortly then. Come in just now, and we can empty the car when Bryce gets here." They followed me into the house. "Can I get you a drink of something?"

"I'm fine, thanks." Daniel still hadn't taken his hand away from me yet.

"Not for me either, but could I use your bathroom?" asked Kate.

I showed her through to the small bathroom downstairs.

I took up my position in Daniel's arms when I got back into the kitchen.

"I missed you." His mouth moved close to mine, but the front door opened as Bryce called out. "Save that thought."

"Hey, Bryce."

"Where is she?" I think he was just as desperate to see Kate as I was to see Daniel.

"I thought that was your voice." Kate came out of the bathroom behind him.

Bryce turned around and picked her up, kissing her. She squealed, which made me laugh.

"Come on, let's get your bags and get you home." He took her hand and led her back to the car.

Daniel and I went too.

I closed the door, and Daniel dropped the bags he was carrying. He pinned me up against the door, his mouth pressing against mine while his hands cupped my head in place.

"I've thought about this since you left," he whispered before kissing me again.

"I'm so glad you're here." I held on to him, thinking at any minute, my legs were going to give way. I had forgotten how good he felt.

"Will we put all this away?" he asked.

"I don't want to move."

He laughed. "I'm sure we could find a more comfortable place to do this." He had a point there.

I showed him up the stair. "This is the bathroom, then there are three bedrooms, that one I use for my studio, and this one is mine." I stopped at the door.

"Maybe it would be better if I took one of the other rooms," he suggested, and I felt my heart drop.

"I thought you would want to share my bed," I asked, more than a little disappointed.

"I would love to, but I don't want to get too tempted."

"We've slept in the same bed before."

Daniel sighed and put his hand on my arm. "I know, and it took every bit of restraint not to grab hold of you and make love to you. I told you I want to do this right."

"You can have this room. It has an en-suite," I showed him in and stood back so he could bring in his things.

He placed his bags on the bed, then came back to stand in front of me.

"I know it's not what you wanted, but I'm sure we can still have some fun." He tickled my waist as his arms closed around me.

I couldn't help but laugh. "You'll just need to stop me when I go too far," I whispered, brushing my lips over the top of his.

"Too far, Grace." He laughed.

"Really? That was too far?" I asked, looking perplexed.

He smiled. "No." His mouth pressed against mine.

I kissed down the side of his neck. "This?"

"No."

I pulled his shirt up his body and kissed his chest. "This?"

"Grace."

I let my fingers run down the muscles on his chest and abdomen before reaching his belt. "This?"

His hands grabbed both sides of my head. His fingers spread out through my hair as his mouth pushed against mine. He walked me backwards until my back was touching the wall. His tongue, feeling over mine. He grabbed hold of my arms, holding me against the wall. He pulled back and smiled. "This?"

"Point made." I sighed and rested my head on his.

"It's not a game, Grace. When we do make love, I want us to be sure of what our future will be. I don't just want to have sex with you and then move on to the next person. I want to be sure you want to spend the rest of your life with me."

"I've never done this before, so you might need to be patient with me, and honestly, you will need to tell me when I go too far because I'd have you stripped and tied up quicker than a turkey at Christmas." I laughed.

He laughed and hugged me tight against his body. "I can see I'm going to have problems with you."

I made us dinner, and we sat cuddled up on the couch.

"I love your house and what you've done with it. It's very you. I love the pictures you have dotted around. We'll need to get some of us for you to put up."

"I would love that. Something to remember when you're not here."

His hand moved down my arm. "I want to ask you something. If this becomes more and you think I'm irresistible and can't stand to be without me and can't wait any longer to have me in your bed."

I laughed. "Yeah, that could be a long wait." He gave me one of his looks, and I put my hand up. "Sorry, continue."

"Anyway. If that did happen, would you want to leave here and come and stay in Skye, or would you want me to come and stay here?" he asked, looking serious.

"I have no idea. I love Skye, and I love being there. This is my home and all my friends are here. I know I should be saying wherever you are, that's where I'll be, but at this point, I don't think I could move full time to Skye to be with you," I looked at him, wondering what he was thinking.

He sat for a moment before speaking. "This is why I don't want to make love to you yet because there are still too many uncertainties to work out."

"I do know one thing. I love it that you're here, I love when we're together, and I know how much I hated being away from you. I know it was only a few days, but I missed you." I tried to be honest with him.

"I feel like that too." He kissed the side of my head. "I was just wondering if I needed to ask for a transfer back down here."

I shot him a look. "You would do that?" I asked, sitting up.

He sighed. "If it meant I got to see you every day, then yes, I would,"

"You could move in here." I took his hand in mine. "I would love to have you here all the time."

"Let's not get too ahead of ourselves. How about we keep our options open, and we see how we are while I'm here, and if I don't have you dying to get rid of me, or if I can't wait to get back home, then we can discuss it further."

"I don't think I'll be dying to get rid of you."

"You never know. I might annoy you, and that would be it, over!" He made an explosion noise and flicked his hands open.

"You'll just have to make sure not to annoy me then!" I stood up and looked back at him before going into the kitchen.

He followed me over, wrapping his arms around my stomach and kissing the top of my shoulder. "Annoying you yet?"

I finished pouring the water from the fridge. "Not yet." I tapped his arm.

He let me go and jumped up onto the island. "What do you have planned for us to do tomorrow?"

"I didn't have anything planned. I'm a kind of fly by the seat of my pants kind of girl, "I laughed. "I mean, there's no point in taking you to see the sights because you lived here you've probably seen more than your fair share already."

"How about you let me experience what you like to do?"

I looked at him, not understanding what he was meaning.

"If you wanted to go for a walk, say, where would you go?"

I smiled. "Vogrie."

"Right, so take me there."

"It's not Edinburgh Castle." I scrunched my face up.

"I've seen the Crown Jewels and the Stone of Destiny, but I haven't seen Grace Grimes walking in Vogrie."

I smiled at him. "Okay, I know a few places we could go." I walked over to him, placed my hands on his legs, and stretched up on my toes to kiss him.

The knock at the door just another interruption to us being together. Maybe moving to Skye would be a better move!

"Hey, is this an okay time?" Gabriel stood at the door.

"Perfect. Come in." He walked behind me into the kitchen, where Daniel was still sitting on the island. I coughed slightly to get his attention.

He jumped off the island and came round to meet Gabriel.

"Daniel, I'd like you to meet Gabriel, Gabriel, this is Daniel." The two of them shook hands staring at one another. Well, that wasn't too bad, I had half been expecting a face-to-face prize fight weigh-in, but this was much more civilised.

"Just like the angel." Daniel laughed.

"Yes, just like the angel." Gabriel gave me a side glance. "Wasn't it Daniel that Gabriel came to, to explain the vision of the ram and the goat?"

"Yes, it was, Daniel 8:16, you know the Bible."

"I had a good teacher." He smirked.

I had to roll my eyes at that one. Well, at least they had something in common, I suppose.

"Can I get you a coffee?"

"No, thanks, Grace. I was wondering if tomorrow night you would like me to put on a barbeque, invite Nic and Niven over. It would give everyone the chance to meet Daniel and Kate?"

I looked at Daniel.

"That would be great." Beamed Daniel.

"We're going out during the day if you want to do it here?" I offered.

"Sounds like a plan. I'll get in touch with everyone. Anyway, Daniel, it was a pleasure to meet you; enjoy your day tomorrow. Grace." He shook Daniel's hand and left, closing the door behind him.

"Are you sure that's okay? I mean, you're only down for a couple of nights?"

"I would love to meet all your friends. Gabriel seems nice."

"He is."

"Is that all I'm getting?"

I nodded my head. "That's all."

Chapter Thirty

I sat on the island waiting for the bacon and sausages to cook while I thought about what Daniel had said about him coming to stay here or me going to stay there. If the relationship developed, then that was a decision needing some attention.

I jumped down and turned the food, hoping I wouldn't need to wake him as I set the table. I was looking forward to going for a walk, it had been a while since I had been to Vogrie, and it was on these kinds of days that I especially liked it when it was frosty outside.

"Hey, you." Daniel walked in, wearing a pair of jeans and a T-shirt.

I had no idea how someone could look that good when they were just out of bed. "Morning. I hope you're hungry."

"Starving." He took hold of my arm as I walked past him, puling me back into another embrace and another kiss.

"It's going to burn," I said, struggling to get away.

"Let it burn."

"You won't be saying that when your tummy's grumbling later." I laughed.

He let me go, and I finished the breakfast taking plates over to the table. "Can I get you a coffee?"

"I'll get it. You've got enough to do."

"Sit down, and I'll bring it over." I smiled at him.

I poured a mug of fresh coffee and took it over to him. "Thanks, you not having one?" he said, taking a sip.

"Can't stand the stuff." I took the orange juice from the fridge and gave it a shake before joining Daniel at the table.

"Why, if you hate coffee, do you have an expensive coffee maker?"

"Because everyone I know loves coffee and I want them to have the best when they come over." I smiled.

"I'm sure they would be just as happy with instant."

"Okay, so what would you prefer? If I handed you a cup of instant or a cup of that, what would you choose?"

"Yeah, okay, but it's because it tastes delicious. If you had handed me instant, I would still drink it."

"It's okay, I'm not going to take it off you," I said, taking another bite of breakfast.

"Just as well. This breakfast is amazing, by the way. It's usually just a plate of cereal or some toast."

"I only have this now and again, usually if Bryce is staying over."

"You two are close?" he asked.

"Yeah, he's a great guy and friend."

"Did you ever go out? You said you had spent a few drunken nights with him," he asked, picking up his coffee.

"We never went out."

"He seems happy with Kate. I was asking her what she was thinking about them being together." He used a piece of toast to mop up the last of some egg yolk that had oozed onto his plate.

"And?" I sat forward, waiting to hear the rest of that story.

"Private conversation."

"No way," I said incredulously.

He sat back, laughing, and wiping his mouth on a napkin.

"I think she likes him too, but I think they are having the same issue as us as to where they're going to spend their time."

"If Bryce has fallen in love with her, he will follow her anywhere?" I sighed.

"Jealous?"

"Of losing my friend, yes."

"He probably feels the same way about you," he said, sitting back in his seat.

I shrugged my shoulders. "I can't wait for you to meet everyone tonight."

"Yes, I'm looking forward to it and to seeing Niven and Darcy again. They are such a nice couple and very funny if I remember rightly."

I laughed. "Yeah, they are. They crack me up, and they are just perfect for each other."

"I wonder if your friends will think the same about us."

"How could they think anything else?" I laughed. "Finished?"

"Yes, thank you. It was lovely. Ready to go?"

"I'll just load the dishwasher."

I drove down towards Woodburn and turned right at the lights, then took another right heading for Pathhead. The roads were pretty quiet, and we made it there within ten minutes. I parked the car, put my hat and gloves on, and locked it before walking over to the woods.

"Have you been here before?" I asked.

"No, this is my first time."

"I love it. I used to come here all the time with my dad."

"You haven't told me much about him." He took my hand in his as we walked.

"I think you would have liked him. He was so funny we would walk around here and come up with all this nonsense about the squirrels and the animals and make names up for them. He could be serious too, we could have many a discussion on the state of world politics, but it was cars he loved the most. He would tell me about all these new cars and the engines, and I would listen, but I don't think I was a good student. We would go to art galleries together, and we went to see a couple of operas together." I had to swallow the lump that was forming at the back of my throat.

"He sounds like an amazing man, and it looks like he produced an amazing daughter." He pulled my arm around his back and pressed me against his side as we walked.

We stopped at the small bridge over the stream. I let go. "Find a stick."

"What?"

"Pooh sticks. Find a stick." It was something we always did when we were walking around.

He picked up a stick that he could have used to play baseball with.

I bent over laughing. "Have you never seen or read Winnie the Pooh?"

He just looked at me, which had me laughing harder.

I held up my small, finger length stick.

He threw his back down and found a more suitable one.

"Right, hold it out at arm's length, then when I count down, we drop it at the same time, okay?"

I wasn't sure if he got what I was showing him, but he went along with it anyway. "Three, two, one." We dropped our sticks into the stream, and I moved him to the other side so we could see whose stick was first to come through.

"I won!" he shouted enthusiastically. As my stick finally emerged from the dark recesses of the bridge.

"Beginner's luck," I shook my head astounded.

"Sore loser?"

"No!"

He tickled my waist, and I squealed, trying to get away from him, but he was too quick and too strong for me.

"Okay. You win." I laughed.

He kept hold of me, his face moving closer to mine as his mouth opened slightly to come together with mine. That was the only thing wrong with being outside in the winter. There were too many hats, scarves, and gloves to get through.

A breeze rustled the fallen dried leaves on the ground, sending them scurrying down the path in front of us.

We continued to walk around, and we were lucky enough to see a deer, two squirrels, and a whole host of birds.

"I can see why you love it here," he said.

I scuffed my feet through the dried, crunchy leaves. We passed under a horse chestnut tree with all the seed pods lying on the ground.

"Tell me you've played conkers?" I asked him as I searched around the base of the tree for one of the dark-coloured seeds.

"I've seen them but never played them."

I picked up a few and put them in my pocket. "Bryce and Nic will sort them out tonight and give you a game. Watch out for Niven; she's a hustler!" I laughed.

We got back in the car, and I pulled off my hat and gloves. Daniel took my hand in his and kissed it. "Thank you."

"What for?"

"For allowing me to share your memories."

I squeezed his hand. "Anytime."

We stopped in at the supermarket on the way back to pick up some things for the barbeque. Daniel was unloading the car when my door opened in front of me.

"Hey. I wasn't expecting you here so soon," I said, surprised to see Gabriel.

"It's okay. I'm not staying. I was putting some things in your fridge for later."

"Hey, Gabriel, give me a hand, would you? I think she's bought half the shop," Daniel said, as he walked past carrying two crates of beer.

I walked into the house and took my coat off while Gabriel and Daniel emptied the car. Daniel was last in and closed the door.

"I thought I said I would do the barbeque?" Gabriel said, dumping another bag of food on the island.

"I know, but I thought I would rustle up a couple of things to go along with it."

"You didn't think I would make enough," he said, crossing his arms in front of his chest.

"No, I just thought that I would maybe make some pasta and a salad to go along with what you make," I said uneasily.

Daniel pulled a packet of chicken and one of steak from the bag, holding them up for Gabriel to see.

"Right, well, that was for Niven because she likes a spicy sriracha dressing on hers," I tried dismally to explain.

"Daniel, open the fridge." Ordered Gabriel.

"Wow!" Daniel said, looking at me. "I think you need to apologise." He smirked.

There was chicken, steak, prawns, burgers, sausages. You name it Gabriel, had prepared it.

"Sorry, Gabriel."

He came over to me and kissed the top of my head. "Put what you got in the freezer, and it'll do another day."

"Can I at least make a salad?" I huffed.

"You can, and I'll even let you put some crisps and dips in bowls."

Daniel giggled beside us, and I knew then that Gabriel was winding me up.

"I hate you, Gabriel," I said scrunching up my face.

Gabriel and Daniel laughed as they began to unload the shopping.

"Why docs hc wind you up so easily?" Daniel asked after Gabriel had left.

"It's not just, Gabriel, I'm like that with everyone. I think people are far more intelligent than I am, so when they tell me things, I believe them. I don't get how people say things to make themselves look better, or in this case, to make fun of me." I shrugged my shoulders.

"Don't do that. Don't put yourself down."

"Come here. I want to show you something I've been working on." I took hold of his hand and led him up the stairs.

"I was wondering when I was going to see the famous studio."

I put my hand over his eyes and opened the door. I took a deep breath before dropping my hand allowing him to view my painting of him on my easel. "Open them."

I stood fidgeting beside him.

"Grace, don't ever think you're less than anyone else. You are the most amazing person I think I've ever met."

"Do you like it?"

"I love it. It's incredible." He turned and held me against his body.

"I haven't finished it yet, but as soon as I do, it's yours."

"Thank you."

I pulled back slightly. "Are you crying?" I wiped a tear away from his face.

"Nobody has ever done something like that for me before."

"Well, I'm going to keep on doing things like this for you!" It was my turn to squeeze him slightly.

"How long do we have before everyone arrives?"

"Why, what do you have in mind?" I teased.

Chapter Thirty-One

Gabriel came back over and started the barbeque for people arriving, and I got drinks and glasses set up as well as bowls and cutlery and plates.

"Mind and light the patio heater," I called over to him.

Daniel was enjoying spending time with Gabriel. He didn't know he was an archangel; I think it was their common interest.

Bryce and Kate were the first to arrive.

"Hey. What have you two been up to today?" I asked.

"I'll let Kate tell you, and I'll go and grab a beer," he said, pointing outside.

"Nice time?" I asked Kate.

"Yeah, it was good. I've never been to Edinburgh before."

"Where is it you come from again?"

"Oban. If we wanted to go into town shopping, we went to Glasgow."

"I see. Did Bryce take you shopping?" I asked while filling bowls with nuts and crisps.

"No," she smiled.

I laughed. "Hiking up Arthur's Seat?"

"Yes!" she laughed with me. "I thought I was fit, but Bryce took me right to the top. I honestly thought I was going to die."

The door went. "Excuse me a minute.

"Hey." Niven walked in, giving me a big hug.

She was holding onto Charlie's hand as he stood quietly beside her. I picked him up and gave him a big kiss on the cheek. "He loves his, Auntie Grace's kisses." I laughed at his giggles.

"Hey, Grace." Darcy kissed me on the cheek as he came in with everything needed to entertain and change two young children.

"Hi, Darcy. And who's this big girl?"

"Violet."

"Violet, I'm sure you get bigger every time I see you," I said, which made her laugh. "Come in. Let me introduce you to Kate, Kate these are our friends Darcy and Niven and Charlie and Violet." There were handshakes and kisses and hugs all around.

"Daddy, can we draw?" asked Violet, in the cutest voice imaginable.

"Daddy is going to see Uncle Bryce, but mummy and auntie Grace and Kate would love to draw with you," he said in a high-pitched voice as he backed away with his hands up, mouthing the words 'I'm sorry' to Niven.

Kate and I were laughing so hard.

"You do know he'll pay for that later!" she said, looking stern, and I fully believed what she said. She put some books and pencils on the coffee table, and the kids sat on the floor. "So, Bryce." Niven poured herself a glass of prosecco.

Kate smiled. I could tell she was feeling just a little bit nervous.

"You can pour one for each of us," I told Niv. "He took her hiking." I smirked.

"Arthur Seat?"

"Yes, indeed," I said.

"Did she make it to the top? Did you make it to the top?" Niv asked Kate.

"Just, but yes, I made it," Kate said, smiling.

"You passed the test." Niven held up her glass. "To Kate." Kate and I did the same and took a drink.

"What test?" Kate asked.

"Bryce has this thing where if he meets someone he likes, he wants them to love the same things, so he's got these wee tests that help him decide," Niven explained.

"Sounds a bit weird," Kate said, scrunching up her face.

"It totally is. Bryce isn't as confident as he makes out." Niven teased.

"Don't think of it as him being weird; it means he likes you," I said, smiling at her.

"What if I'd failed?" she asked.

Niven and I looked at each other. "Mussels." We laughed. Niven screwed up her face.

"That would have been your next test. Bryce has more than one to give you as many chances as possible," I told her.

She took a drink of her prosecco. "So, have you two?"

"Scared of heights." Niven sighed.

"Hate mussels!" I sighed. "Honestly, you have made that man very happy today." Bryce came into the kitchen, and Niven and I burst out laughing.

"You told her?" he asked, looking disappointed and already knowing the answer. He went to stand next to Kate and kissed her on the top of her head.

"I like mussels too, just in case you were wondering, "Kate looked at him and put her hand up to cup his face.

Bryce leaned over and kissed her, which had Niven and I looking at each other smiling. "See, told you it wasn't weird," Bryce said, turning to us.

"No, it is a bit weird." Kate smiled at him.

Bryce kissed her again. "Give me a shout when Nic gets here." He went back out into the garden.

I was wondering how Daniel was getting on outside with the boys when he walked into the kitchen. Gabriel had sent him to collect a sauce from the fridge. Now it was my turn to be in the hot seat.

"Daniel this is Niven, Niven, Daniel."

Daniel went over to Niv and gave her a big hug. "Nice to see you again. I was catching up with your husband. Is that Charlie? He's like a proper wee boy now."

"You too, yes, I know. I can't believe you never noticed Grace at the Christening, which would have made for a better story," she joked.

Daniel got the sauce from the fridge. "I think this story was pretty good." He gave me a wink and went back outside.

"He is gorgeous. I'm so jealous!" She exclaimed.

"I thought you would be. I remember how I thought I was going to have to prise you off him at the Christening," I teased.

"Hardly," she said, looking a little perturbed. "Okay, only a little then."

We were all laughing when the door went again. "I'll get it." Shouted Niven as she ran for the door. "Nic!" They hugged each other at the door.

"Wow! I'm beginning to like how this kitchen is full of beautiful women." Nic said, blowing the air from his mouth.

"Nic, this is Kate, Kate, this is Nic," I introduced them.

Nic went straight over, took Kate's hand, and kissed the back of it. "Pleased to meet you."

Niven and I were laughing so loud, Bryce came bursting in. "I thought I told you to give me a shout when he got here," he asked, staring at us.

"Bryce!" the two hugged each other.

"Keep your hands off." Bryce joked.

"I wouldn't dream of it." He laughed.

Bryce put his arm around Kate. "I think the food's nearly ready if you want to come outside."

We all sat down outside, the heaters keeping the frosty air at bay for the time being anyway.

"Gabriel, this is amazing," I said, taking another bite of the marinated steak.

"I had some help from Daniel. You've got yourself a bit of a chef there," he praised.

"Lucky girl." Niven teased beside me.

Once we finished eating, we all went back inside. Niven and Darcy slumped on the couch. Bryce, Kate, and Nic headed for the kitchen and more drinks. I had a sleepy Charlie in my arms and sat down on the couch opposite. Daniel sat next to me while Violet had Gabriel sitting on the floor, finishing off a drawing.

"That looks good on you." Niven nodded towards Charlie.

"How could he not; he's so cute!" I exclaimed in a high-pitched voice.

"I think you better watch Daniel, Grace, might want one of her own." Darcy laughed.

"Grace can have whatever she wants," Daniel said, putting his hand on my leg.

"Well, she can have those two," smiled Niven.

"I think we can manage to make our own." Daniel announced confidently.

This time it was me that looked at Daniel. I could have taken him right there on the couch had it not been for all the other people, but it was such a lovely thing to say.

"Should we give you two some space?" asked Darcy.

Daniel just looked at me and smiled.

"How about a game?" Nic shouted over.

"No!" there's little people here," I said, turning my head.

"Yeah, I don't think twister and tequila shots would be suitable," smirked Gabriel.

"If I remember rightly, you weren't too bad at it." Teased Niven.

"You lot are crazy!" commented Daniel.

"You haven't seen the half of it." I patted the back of his hand.

"There's more?" he asked.

"Much, much more!" Darcy said, shaking his head. We all laughed, and Daniel looked a little worried.

"Well, if all you old people don't mind, we're going to head down to The Hole. Show Kate the local sights." Nic downed the drink he had in his hand.

"Thanks for this. It was very nice to meet you all," said Kate.

"If you have Kate here for seven, Bryce," Daniel called over.

"Will do. She might be home by then," said Bryce helping her on with her coat.

"I think you're going to be doing all the driving tomorrow," I said, looking at Daniel.

"I think you could be right."

Nic, Bryce, and Kate left.

"Look, auntie Grace." Violet held up the picture she and Gabriel had drawn.

"Wow! That is incredible. I think you're going to have to come over to my studio sometime."

"Can I?" she asked, looking at her mum and dad.

"I think Auntie Grace does summer sleepovers." Niven looked at Darcy.

"Yes, seven weeks of summer, painting retreat for under-fives." Darcy looked back at Niven and kissed her.

"What are you two like?" I asked, shocked.

"You can come over anytime you like," I said to Violet, who started to yawn and wipe at her eyes.

"I think that's our cue to leave." Darcy sat forward.

Charlie had fallen asleep, so Daniel picked him up, careful not to wake him.

"I'll give you a hand out to the car." We waved from the door.

"I'm going to head over too." Gabriel moved me to the side so he could get past. "I'll come over tomorrow and help you clear up," he offered.

"It's fine. You did the cooking. I'll do the clearing up."

"You sure?"

"Absolutely. I think once I get rid of this one, I'll just be heading back to bed for a while anyway," I said, bumping against Daniel's side.

"Right, I'll see you both again. Daniel, it was nice meeting you."

"You too. I might take you up on that offer," he said, shaking Gabriel's hand.

"Please do."

As soon as the door closed, I turned to Daniel. "What offer?"

"I was wondering how long it was going to take you to ask about that." He smirked.

"Just interested."

"He was giving me a few ideas for ways to connect with the community. He offered to send a couple of his employees up to work with me."

I looked at him and smiled, knowing Gabriel's employees were angels. "That was good of him," I offered.

"What are we going to do about that?" Daniel looked in at the kitchen. I switched the light off and took Daniel's hand.

I stopped outside Daniel's door. "Do you have to sleep here tonight?"

He brushed the hair back from my face. "You don't make it easy for me."

"I promise I'll put a big jumper on and my long pyjama bottoms." I smiled.

He sighed. "I suppose I could spend the night in your bed."

"You made that sound really bad," I said, looking at him sternly.

He moved closer to me. His mouth was open ready to join with mine.

"Do you know I am pretty tired? Maybe you should sleep here?" I joked.

He pushed me up against the wall, his hands holding my wrists next to my head. "How tired?" he asked before his mouth pressed firmly against mine.

"Not that tired." He kissed me again. "Wide awake." I smiled at him. He took my hand and walked me to my room.

Chapter Thirty-Two

Daniel had left early. Bryce had dropped Kate off, and we said our goodbyes, again. Bryce had asked me if we could go up in a couple of weeks for a long weekend, which I agreed to, and it seemed to please Daniel, knowing it wasn't going to be too long before we could see each other again.

I had gone back to bed when Daniel left, but sleep took a while in coming. I couldn't stop thinking of our time together, all of it. From the minute he arrived until the minute he left, and our last night cuddled together. We had been good and hadn't taken things too far, but it did leave me wanting so much more.

I wondered how long he would make us wait. He said he wanted us to be sure this was what we both wanted before we took things further. I have to say I was pretty damn sure last night! Anyway, for now, I was going to have to find something to take my mind off him, and maybe us not being together for a couple of weeks was a good thing. It would give us space, and I wouldn't feel like I was going to rip his clothes off if he looked at me the wrong way!

I had been pottering about all day, tidying up from the night before. There was tons of food left, some of which I put in the freezer and some I thought could do for dinner. It did cross my mind about asking Gabriel over to join me. I tied up a black bin bag, unlocked the patio door, and went outside. It was freezing, and I only had my strappy vest top on. The dark had come quickly, and the sky was clear, showing off the magnificent night sky with all the sparkly diamond stars. I couldn't help standing for a moment to admire the sight.

It was the bottles falling over that startled me to what was happening next door. I put the bag in the bucket and walked over to the fence, looking through the slits. Gabriel was sitting on the top step at his door. There were bottles around him, and he was swigging back another.

"Gabriel?"

There was no reply.

"Is everything okay?" I had never seen him like this before.

"I'm fine," he said, taking another drink and not looking at me.

I shivered. "Gabe!" I shouted again, but there was still no reply forthcoming. I walked over to the shoulder height fence and began to climb over it.

"What are you doing?" he asked angrily.

I jumped down on the other side, walked over to where he was sitting, and stood there with my arms crossed. "Well?"

"It's fine, go home."

"What so you can sit here hoping to get drunk, which I know you can't, or freeze to death, which I'm not sure if you can do that either!" I shouted.

He laughed into himself. "You don't know what you're talking about!"

"Well, obviously, if you don't talk to me and tell me what's going on, how can I help?" I was angry at what was happening here.

"You can't help if you're the problem." He turned away from me, picked up the empty bottles, and threw them in for recycling. He went to walk into the house, his hand resting on the door handle. "Go home, Grace." He walked into the house and closed the door.

I stormed in after him. "Really! I'm the problem! Well, I'm sorry I never asked for any of this, and you are just as much to blame as I am for what's happened between us. Or is that it? You've had enough; do you want out, Gabriel? The angry tears were blinding my vision.

"You don't know anything," he spat back vehemently. "After everything we've been through, you think I've had enough, you think I want to walk away?" he shook his head.

"Then what, what do you want?" I pleaded with him.

"I want you!" he shouted back immediately.

I stood for a minute as the shock of hearing him say how he was feeling hung in the air.

I walked over to where he was standing. My hands grabbing at his face as my mouth found his. He squeezed his hands around my body. There was something almost primeval to our kiss. The frenzy of our emotions had bubbled to the surface as we clawed at each other. Wanting to feel something anything but the pain we were both feeling right now. We were quickly discarding clothes from our bodies, and each time apart meant coming together was harder, forceful. There was no time for soft, gentle kisses or loving words, this was lustful passion, and there was no time for anything else.

He pushed me up against the wall, his fingers interlocked with mine against the wall as he continued to kiss me. "Gabe." His name, escaping in a breath.

"I want you, Grace." His hands moved to my body, pulling me into him.

I ran my hand down his chest. Only to stop at the top of his shorts, tapping his stomach with the tips of my fingers. I rested my head on his chest.

Gabriel pushed the palms of his hands into the wall, his body still close to mine, and I didn't want him to move away just yet, but I knew the time was coming for me to pull away from him.

"Gabriel."

His hands fell to my shoulders, my breathing becoming normal again. "I'm sorry," he whispered.

"Talk to me." I ran my fingers through his hair. We moved away from the wall.

"I was jealous," he admitted.

"Of what?"

"I see how you are with Daniel. Hearing him talk about having kids with you." He began picking up his clothes from the pile on the floor.

"I'm sorry, maybe it was too soon to have everyone over."

"No, I'm glad you did. It was nice meeting Daniel, and he is a very nice guy, and I'm happy for you, Grace," he said, trying to smile.

I watched him as he pulled on his jeans and sat at the table.

"I know I'm never going to be able to stay. I'm never going to be able to give you what you want or what you need, but I want you so much it hurts."

I began to dress. "I'll speak to you tomorrow," I said, walking past, leaving him sitting alone.

"Wait. Don't leave like this." He stood behind me, his hand holding the door closed.

I could feel his breath on my neck, and I wanted to turn around and melt into that body of his, to have him make love to me again, but then what? We would be back in the same position as we were now.

I pushed him back slightly and turned around. "I love you, Gabriel, but you're right; you can't give me everything I want."

He took a step back, his hands pushing down into the pockets of his jeans as if he was trying to stop himself from grabbing hold of me again. His jaw clenched tightly, and I could see how hard this was for him, and I didn't want to add to that.

I smiled. "You're the bravest, most caring, funny, incredible, cutest damn archangel I have ever met, and I will never stop loving you. I hope we can still be friends and that you'll be staying around for a long time yet, but this can't happen. I'm sorry." A few stray tears ran down my cheek, and I wiped them away.

He put his hand behind my head and kissed my forehead before letting his head lean against mine, just for a moment before letting me go.

"I'm here if you ever need me or if you ever want to talk," I said before leaving him standing at the door.

I clambered back over the fence and into the house, closing the patio door behind me. I stood there with my back against the door before sliding down the door and sitting against it. I wrapped my arms around my knees and just sat there.

I didn't feel angry, I wasn't going to start crying, and I didn't feel disappointed or confused. The problem was I wasn't feeling anything. I was completely numb. How could I let myself get caught up again? Was I ever going to be able to let him go?

For the first time, I began to think that maybe Gabriel leaving was the only way I was ever going to move forward in my life. I tilted my head back, so it was resting on the cool of the glass. The only problem I had was I could never let him go. Regardless of how I felt about Daniel, Gabriel had a pull on me that I was never going to escape.

Everything had been perfect with Gabriel, and then it wasn't, now everything is perfect with Daniel was this relationship going to fail too? I was beginning to see a pattern emerging.

I sighed. What did I want? I thought about my paintings, and I knew in that instant that whether I was with Gabriel or Daniel or neither of them, I needed to do something for me, something that brings me joy.

I smiled and went up to my studio. The painting of Daniel was still on the easel. I stood looking at it for a while. Not because it was Daniel, but because it was an exceptional painting. I had never looked at my work like that before. It was just something I enjoyed doing, but now I was looking at the colours, the detail, and I was impressed with what I saw.

Maybe I *could* make a career out of this. I decided that tomorrow morning, I was going to phone around a few places and see how I could start displaying my work. I removed the painting of Daniel and took a large canvas I had bought. I wasn't sure what I was going to do with it that was until now. I attached it to the wall, as it was far too big for my easel, mixed some paints, and started to put down some shapes.

I felt consumed at that moment. Everything else had faded away, leaving me in my bubble of perfected bliss. Nothing could touch me, nothing could come close to me when I was in control, and I was creating something that five minutes before had never existed in this world!

Chapter Thirty-Three

For the next week and a half, I lived and breathed my painting. Before I began in the morning, I would come in and sit on the floor with my back against the wall, looking at what I had created and feeling amazed that I could have achieved something so spectacular. I had also been busy trying to find someone to display my work, and I had an interview set up for later on that day with a gallery in Edinburgh.

When I looked at their website, I didn't think I should even bother to call them. It seemed very posh, and the paintings they were selling were incredible and way above anything I could even imagine paying for a piece of art. However, the constant niggling that I should go for it was too hard to refuse, and the woman said she was looking for new talent to display. I was to take a few of my paintings for her to have a look at, and I photographed my work in progress so she could see what I was developing. It still needed some work, but it would give her an idea of what I was capable of doing.

I hadn't told anyone. There was nothing worse than people asking if you had managed to sell any of your work or find somewhere to exhibit them and having to tell them you hadn't. That crushing disappointment of failure that cripples everything inside. No. In this case, I wanted to see if I could do it first, then I would tell everyone, and if it didn't work out, then no one would be any the wiser.

I packed a few paintings in the car, including the one of Daniel, and set off into town. I had dressed for the occasion too in a trouser suit, which I kept for interviews or weddings, and a top I had recently bought for going out with Niven. It wasn't what I would wear normally, but this was important to me, and I wanted to make a good impression. I had even dried and straightened my hair, rather than going for the easier tied up option.

"Hi, I have an appointment with Katerina," I said to the man at reception. I read his nametag—Jazper. I wondered if he changed the S for a Z or if his parents were trying to make him as unique as possible! He looked like he was just out of school, probably his first job, with one of those stupid haircuts you see all the young people with, shaved at the sides and back and this mound on top forever falling into their eyes. He was probably only getting away with it because he was working in an art gallery!

"And your name?" he asked, probably knowing exactly who I was.

"Grimes, Grace Grimes." I rolled my eyes when he looked away to check his computer.

Strike one!

"If you would just like to take a seat, Katerina will be out shortly."

I smiled and went over to the leather couch. I placed the paintings at the side so they wouldn't fall over. Luckily, I had bought a bag to carry the canvasses in on a trip to the States years ago, and it was finally coming in useful.

"Grace." The lady standing before me was very tall and slender with incredibly sharp-looking features. She looked a bit like an old schoolmistress you would see in old black and white films. There was also a bit of an accent that I couldn't place and wondered for a second if it was real or if she was putting it on to give herself more prominence.

I stood. "Hi, yes, I'm Grace."

Jazper sniggered. Strike two! But I couldn't resist a sly look over Katerina's shoulder to make sure he understood not to start with me.

"If you'd like to come through."

I followed her into a large office with a large desk at the far end and windows down the left-hand side, and a continuous long table along the other wall.

"If you could display your paintings along this wall and we can take a look," she said, standing back and clasping her hands in front of her.

I smiled. It was better than speaking because something which had come so naturally to me for most of my life was now proving to be a challenge.

I arranged the paintings along the wall, and after shuffling around a couple, I stood back. Proud of my achievement.

Katerina looked at me and began to walk down the row of paintings like the Queen inspecting the troops. I could hardly breathe. Some she looked at closer some I felt she didn't look at, at all. Then she turned with such speed that I took a breath and stood up straight, thinking it was my turn to be inspected.

"Grace, darling." She smiled and put her hand out, pointing to my paintings. "These are exquisite. I don't know why you've been hiding away for so long with talent like this."

I still didn't trust myself to say anything.

"I think I could make you a star, my child. Leave it with me, I'll get all the top critics, dealers, and buyers to come and see your work. "She was speaking while walking over to her desk. She pressed a button on her phone and waited.

"Yes, Katerina." Jazper's voice echoed through the intercom.

"I want you to get in contact with everyone I need to put on the greatest show ever. You know what to do and who to call," she instructed him.

"Yes, straight away," he said. I wondered if they were related. Maybe that's why he got such a prestigious job this early on in his career.

"We need more pieces if we're really going to make this an evening to remember and maybe one main piece. Is that something you have?" She asked.

I took a breath this time to calm any nerves before I spoke. "Yes, I have more pieces at home, and I have a lot of photographic work too. I'm not sure if it's a focal point, but I'm working on this at the moment. It's not finished, but you can get the idea." I handed her my phone, showing her the picture of my work in progress.

"Perfect!" she clasped her hands together at her face and smiled. Do you think you can finish it in a couple of weeks?" she asked, looking straight through me.

"Yes, that won't be a problem."

"Excellent! Then that will be our star feature."

I left her office and gave Jazper a smirk as I walked past him. I had just batted this meeting out of the park!

I got in the car, and with my music turned up, I was on my way home, feeling like I had just won the lottery. I was laughing and smiling and singing along to my music. I had finally achieved what I had always wanted to.

I slumped onto my bed and began to dial Daniel.

"Hey, you."

"Guess what?" so much for me trying to play it cool.

"What?"

"I had an interview today with a gallery in Edinburgh, and in a couple of weeks, there will be an exhibition with my name on it!" I squealed with excitement.

"No way? I'm so proud of you."

"I still can't believe it. Will you be able to come? I'd like you to be there."

"I wouldn't miss it for the world. Will you still be coming up with Bryce?"

I had forgotten about that. How was I going to finish my painting, arrange the rest, and go up to Skye?

"Grace?"

I would work around it. "Yes, I'll still be up." I could maybe do some work from there, especially my photographs.

"You sure? I don't want to take you away from your work."

"No, you're fine. It'll be nice to get a break before all the crazy starts."

"I like the sound of that."

"Me too. I can't wait to see you again. I miss you."

"I miss you too. So, what are you going to do to celebrate? Are all the gang coming over?"

"I haven't told anyone yet. You were the first person I called."

"I am honoured."

"I don't think I'll have everyone over. I've got a lot of work to do."

"Well, you better get back to it, and I'll speak to you tonight."

"Okay, I love you."

"Love you too."

I hung up the phone and got changed into my work clothes. I stood looking at my painting with a new purpose. If I was going to finish this, then I needed to get on with it, but I also didn't want to rush it and make a mistake.

My phone buzzed, and I switched off my music to answer it. "Hey."

"Hey. You still speaking?" asked Gabriel.

"Of course."

"Then come and open your door. I've been standing here for ten minutes trying to get your attention."

"I'll be straight down." I opened the door. "Hey, sorry about that."

"I'll forgive you. I hear congratulations are in order, and I brought some champagne," he said, holding up the bottle.

"How did you know?"

"Daniel phoned."

"Of course, he did."

"So, can I come in?" he asked, looking at me.

Was it rude to say no? I was enjoying what I was doing. "Of course." I stood to the side as Gabriel came in.

"Don't sound too happy about it."

I laughed. "I'm sorry. Thank you for coming; it was very thoughtful." I followed him through to the kitchen and took out a couple of glasses while he opened the bottle.

"To Miss Grace Grimes, the best painter this side of the Esk!" he raised his glass before clinking it against mine and taking a drink.

There was one thing about Gabriel, everything he bought was the best of the best, and this champagne was no exception.

"Thank you for coming over; it was a lovely surprise," I said, taking another sip of my drink.

"I'm glad you like it. I wasn't sure if you were still talking to me though, I haven't seen or heard from you for over a week." He looked down at the glass he was holding in both hands.

"I'm sorry, I decided I was going to try and do something with my paintings, and I think I just got carried away." The last time I had seen Gabriel, we had probably allowed our emotions to get the better of us, and I didn't want to keep ending up in that situation, but I had honestly got caught up in my work.

"You think?" he laughed. "It's okay. I know how you are when you're painting. I wish you had told me your good news yourself."

There had to be a limit to the number of times you could apologise in one conversation. "I'd like it if you could come to the exhibit." I smiled, hoping to make it up to him.

"You're forgiven! I would love to come. I suppose I better let you get back to it." He stood up.

I went over to him, kissed him on the cheek, and hugged him. "Thank you again for the champagne."

"Don't be a stranger."

"I won't, I promise. Mind, I'm going up to Skye with Bryce this weekend."

"Of course. I had forgotten about that. Please be careful; we still haven't found Amelia yet."

"I will be."

Gabriel left, and I went back up to the studio with the bottle of champagne and glass in tow. Well, I wasn't going to waste it.

My night-time routine was always to speak to Daniel before I went to bed, regardless of the time.

"Hey, you. I love our night-time chats."

It was nice that we had the technology nowadays to see the person we were talking to. It made me feel closer to him. He was lying on his bed, and I wished he was lying in mine.

"You told Gabriel."

"I did. Am I in trouble?"

"No, it was a nice thought."

"Did he bring you flowers?"

"Champagne." I held up the glass for him to see.

"Nice. Much left?"

"Not really? It was lovely. The only thing missing was you."

"I can't wait to see you on Friday."

"Me too. I hate when we're apart."

"I know. We can talk about it when you come up."

I sighed and closed my eyes.

"What was that for?"

"I'm just a bit tired, and I've got so much work to do."

"I'll let you go."

"No." I opened my eyes and touched his face on my phone. "I love you."

"That's twice you've said that today."

"I know it's taken me some time, but I do mean it."

"I like hearing you say it. I was wondering if you were ever going to say it,"

"I wanted to make sure first."

"And now you are."

"Now, I am."

"I love you, Grace. Now go and get some work done!"

I rolled onto my back and stared at the ceiling. I was falling in love with Daniel, but I also knew I didn't just want to see him every couple of weeks, especially now that I was going to be busy with my art. I sighed again, wondering why everything had to be so complicated. I closed my eyes, just for a minute.

Chapter Thirty-Four

Bryce and I decided to travel up on Thursday night rather than waiting until Friday morning. There was no point in waiting, and there would be less traffic. We were going to have to be a bit more careful as all the deer would be coming down from the mountains as the snow was covering their usual feeding ground. The other thing we weren't so sure about was whether the snow gates would even be open. The weather was definitely on the turn, and it wouldn't be the first time I had to stop and turn around as the road ahead was closed.

On this occasion, we were fine, and the snow poles were still clearly visible at the side of the roads, so no scary drive this time.

"It looks a bit eerie in the dark," commented Bryce. "Yeah, I wouldn't want to break down, that's for sure."

"Don't go out on the moors!" he said, putting on a bad Yorkshire accent.

I looked at him and shook my head. "No."

"No? I thought it was pretty good."

"Not even close."

"It was a little bit. You do it."

I laughed. "You have noticed I'm driving in the dark here?"

"Do it." He turned in his seat, so he was facing me.

"Don't stray from the path," I tried, my Yorkshire accent sounding more like the hunchback of Notre Dame than anything else.

Bryce turned back around, returning to the position he was in before.

"What? That was way better than yours."

"I'm not even going to bother to entertain that with a response."

I couldn't stop laughing.

A bright set of headlights shone from a car behind us. He was too close, and any earlier fun left us instantly. I wasn't going that fast, and there was a long straight stretch coming up, so I kept driving until we got around the curve, and I slowed down and indicated for the person to pass us. He didn't do it straight away, and I could feel Bryce begin to tense in the seat beside me. Luckily the car passed us and zoomed ahead.

I let out a breath.

"That was a close one." Laughed Bryce.

"Yeah, too close. Put some music on and stop distracting me." I squeezed his thigh laughing.

Once we had put all our things in the house and having a quick rest, I dropped him off at Kate's, and I drove down to Portree, parking in Daniel's driveway.

I stood at his door. It was still dark, and the frost had covered everything like a light dusting of icing sugar. I had my arms wrapped around me to keep what heat was left inside.

The door opened. "Can I help you?" came a sleepy-looking Daniel. "I hope so."

"Hey, you." He took my arm, pulled me inside, and pushed me up against the door. His mouth found mine without any difficulty as I melted into his arms.

"Surprised?"

"You can wake me up like this anytime you like," he said, unzipping my coat and helping me to remove it. "I'm going back to bed if you want to join me?" he said, continuing to kiss me.

"I would love to." I kicked my shoes off and took his hand as I followed him through to the bedroom.

His body pressed against mine as his arms held me tightly. "I can't believe you're here."

"Bryce left his work early and suggested it would be a nice surprise for you and Kate. I couldn't disagree with him."

"What about your work?"

"I've been working around the clock, and I've got my pictures downloaded to pick which ones I want to use while I'm here." I kissed him. "Anyway, I'm not here to discuss work." I ran my fingers through the hair at the back of his head as my mouth opened against his.

"I don't care why you're here. I'm just glad that you are," Daniel said, pulling my top over my head, as it got discarded along with his T-shirt, which he pulled off, at the side of the bed. "I want to feel your skin next to mine."

It wasn't like him to be this forward in initiating things. We had come close on many an occasion, but he was always the one to slow things down or stop them altogether. I couldn't say I wasn't enjoying him being more in control, but there was something that wasn't quite clicking, and I couldn't tell what it was.

His hands were holding me and moving me, ready for his mouth to kiss me. "Daniel, we should stop."

"And what if I don't want to?" his hands went to my jeans and began to unbutton them.

"Daniel. Stop!" It wasn't like him. He was usually so gentle and loving, but this wasn't passion; what he was doing had a spitefulness to it. "Daniel, no!" I said as I tried to push him away again.

"What? It's not like you to want to stop." He smirked as he struggled against me, pushing me onto the bed. The more I tried to fight him off, the more he was enjoying it. He was acting like a completely different person.

I wasn't sure what was happening. I had a feeling like a blanket being placed over my head ever since I walked into the house. Dark, heavy as if all hope had faded. All I could see was how bad things were. I needed to get out of here; maybe it was the place the atmosphere was thick around me.

"Daniel, please. Let me go!" I was scared, and I needed to get away, but he was lying on top of me, and I couldn't move him.

"Please, Daniel." He mimicked my voice. "You're like a nippy little puppy going on and on and on, wanting everything you can get, but not giving anything in return. Well, I've had enough of it and your teasing. I'm going to take what you've been dangling in front of me since the first time we met."

"No! It wasn't like that."

"Then what was it like enlighten me, please. I can't wait to hear it."

I continued to struggle against him, but as soon as I thought I had an arm free or was able to move, he was just as quick, pinning me back down. All I could think of was Gabriel. He said if I ever needed him, I was to pray, and if God thought I needed him, he would send him. I wasn't sure if it was going to work while he was still on earth, but there was nothing else I could think of doing.

"Go then, run back to Gabriel," he spat as he moved off me, letting me go.

I grabbed my clothes and ran out to the car, locking all the doors before putting my top on. I heard him arguing and wondered if he had someone else inside the house.

Daniel came out the side door, and I didn't think he had seen me still sitting in the driveway. He was shouting at someone inside the house. I was curious as to what was happening, and I couldn't look away. He stepped back, and the person he was shouting at walked out in front of him.

"Amelia!"

Both of them looked towards me, hearing me through the open window. "Grace?"

I shook my head. "No!" I started the car and quickly drove away.

What had I just witnessed? Why was Daniel speaking to Amelia, and why were they shouting like that? Was Daniel in on all of this from the beginning?

My mind had a thousand and one questions running through it, and my eyes were blurring with the tears that were forming in them. Luckily, I knew the road like the back of my hand, and I knew when to brake and change gear and when I could put my foot down. I was nearly at the house when I thought about Bryce.

"Call Bryce."

"I'm sorry, could you repeat that?" came the voice from the car.

"Call my phone." At least this time, it was ringing.

"Come on, come on, pick up." Nothing.

I didn't know what to do. I ran into the house, shouting for Bryce but he wasn't home. I picked up my phone and began to dial Gabriel.

The door crashed open behind me, and Daniel stood in the doorway. "Get out!" I screamed. "I'm going to call the police."

"Don't do that. It won't end well if you do, and I don't want that," he pleaded.

"Really? Because five minutes ago, you were ready to do whatever it took to hurt me."

"I know, please just stop and listen."

"Why are you doing this?" I begged.

"Grace, I'm sorry I never meant for any of this. Just do what she says, and you won't get hurt. It's not you, she's after." He walked over to me.

"Stop! Stay there. Don't come any closer." I had my hands up in front of me like it was going to do any good. "How could you?"

"Grace, please, let me explain,"

"There isn't anything you could say that would make this any better."

"Please."

He held out his hand for me to take, but how could I trust him now? I could never believe another word he said.

"She said you were the key to heaven."

"Really? Daniel, I don't even go to church, let alone be the key to heaven." I shook my head incredulously. I folded my arms in front of me.

"Grace, you don't know how special you are. There's something in your future, I don't know what, but it has them rattled."

"So, what are you meant to do to me?" I asked, looking into his eyes. I put my hand to his face. "How can I ever trust you again?"

"Please, Grace. I will do anything to make this right."

I felt so betrayed and let down.

"Oh, isn't this sweet?" the familiar voice came from behind us.

I moved away from Daniel. "Amelia, I don't think I invited you in."

"That's vampires, my dear, not demons!" she flicked her hand as if to swat away my empty words.

"You're right, but it is a house built on prayer, and you're not welcome here!" I had no idea what I was doing. I had watched the Exorcist a few times, but there was no way I was going to remember the words to cast out a demon.

"She's right, Amelia, you can't stay here," Daniel said, standing in front of me.

"Then why are you here?" she smiled.

He left me and walked over to Amelia. "You need to leave, Amelia; this is over!" A part of me was willing Daniel to finish this once and for all, but I was wrong.

"You're right; this is over!" with one blow across the head, Daniel was now lying in an ever-increasing pool of his blood.

"Daniel!" I screamed, falling to my knees beside him. I grabbed a towel from the bunker, placing it under his head. "Stay with me, Daniel, stay with me. Don't leave me, please don't leave me."

I wasn't sure what happened, but the last thing I remember, I was lying on the floor, staring into Daniel's frightened-looking eyes.

Chapter Thirty-Five

My eyelids fluttered open, but the pain was instant. The noise I made sent shockwaves through my body, alerting every sense that something was wrong. My head hurt; my body hurt. I tried to move, but they had tied my hands behind my back. The rag tied around my mouth was pulled way too tight, and I think whoever had tied it had caught half my hair in the knot.

Amelia! The realisation hit me. She was there when Daniel, Daniel! I tried to look around, but the small slit of light coming from the bottom of the door wasn't enough to see in this dark dungeon I was captive.

I tried to remember what Daniel had said about me being the key to heaven. What if they had the wrong person? Was that the reason Gabriel had found me and tried to get close to me? My head was a swirling mess of questions and pain.

The door swung open, and I had to turn my head away from the bright light.

"She's awake. Grab her arms." The dark silhouettes from the doorway came over to me.

The pain was too much, and I was starting to lose consciousness again. It was then that I saw Bryce and Kate tied up in the corner. I tried to struggle to get to them. Bryce's eyes were closed, and I wasn't even sure if he was still alive. Amelia must have gone over to Kate's, trying to tie up all loose ends. I was just glad she was here and not at home with Nic, Darcy, Niven, and the kids.

This time when I regained consciousness, I had been tied to a chair. Each wrist and ankle tied to the arms and legs. I still had the rag in my mouth, and I wondered if that would need to be cut out, considering how much hair they had managed to encapsulate. It was going to be a bit like getting a piece of chewing gum cut out when I was a kid. A cord had also been placed around my neck, which made it difficult for me to move my head. There was one thing, I wasn't going to get out of this unless someone came to rescue me.

The room was dark except some sort of candle or torch arrangement placed further back, which was throwing up strange ghostly shadow figures that danced over the walls like some eighteenth-century ball.

I saw Daniel out of the corner of my eye. He was kneeling with his arms tied behind him and a rag tied around his mouth. His face covered in blood from the earlier head wound, but I couldn't remember how the rest of his face had become as bruised as it was. The horror on his face, his beautiful dark eyes, staring at what was unfolding in front of him. He was breathing hard, trying to shout through the cloth around his mouth. I closed my eyes. I wasn't sure how I was feeling about him at this moment in time. Hopefully, I would get a chance to work that out later. Whatever was going to happen, I had no way of stopping it. All I could do was hope and pray that I wasn't going to endure too much pain and suffering and find peace in a happy place until this nightmare was over.

"Ah, there she is, my darling Grace." Amelia stood beside me. Her features were looking sharper than usual, like something was trying to burst through from under her skin.

I tried not to look, and I tried not to struggle. I wasn't going to give her the satisfaction.

A man appeared beside her. He looked to be about the same age, but he was more frightening than Amelia. His irises were diamond-shaped, and I could see flames burning inside them. His hair was pulled tight in a small ponytail at the back of his head. There was something appealing and also hypnotising about his rugged looks.

"Grace, let me introduce myself. I'm Oliver, and I'm here to make you suffer more than you could ever imagine!" he smiled, looking at Amelia. Just relax and don't fight, it will only delay the inevitable, and who knows, I might enjoy it." He was polite like Amelia, but I could tell he was the one who was running the show here.

Where was Gabriel? Why wasn't he here helping me? He was probably the only person who could save us now. All I had to do was find something inside, find that place where I knew everything would work out. I would feel the pain, but I wouldn't let it show. It was my life, after all, and I was going to decide my final moments.

"Gabriel," I thought in my head. *"I'm sorry you were too late to help me. I did love you. I knew we could never be together, but what time we did spend together was amazing. Maybe I'll see you again in another life."*

Oliver produced a knife from behind his back, and before I had the chance to worry about what he was going to do with it, he had it dug deep into my body. I realised instantly there was no happy place on earth that was going to take the pain of this away. I screamed through the gag in my mouth while Amelia laughed and clasped her hands together as her excitement built.

I heard Daniel make a noise beside me as he struggled to get to me, but Amelia was quick and swiped him across the face with the back of her hand. He hit the floor hard, and I wanted to tell him to stop, that it didn't matter anymore. I was dying, and time was running out too fast to hold grudges. It was over. My eyes flickered, and I felt the cord dig into my neck as my head dropped forward.

A gust of wind blew across me, and I lifted my head to see Gabriel and another angel standing beside him. Their beautiful strong wings on display for all to see. Gabriel's body looked different, bigger, stronger. He looked a bit like a Roman centurion with his body armour and sword. He flew across the room, and I couldn't keep my eyes open any longer. If I could just stay alive.

The pain and the inevitable loss of blood was making staying awake virtually impossible and I tried to fight it for as long as I could. The sounds of steel crashing against steel or stone, words I didn't recognise being shouted from either side of me. The flapping of wings and the draught it was causing to circulate around and over me. The whole thing sounded horrible.

The squeals of anguish echoed in the room as I was cut free. Seeing in time Gabriel's wing come out in front of him, and with a quick slashing action, Oliver's throat was slit in a spray of black blood.

"Grace, I've got you," Daniel said, his hands pulling at the rag in my mouth.

He lifted me off the chair and carried me away. I tried to focus my eyes on him as he wiped at my face.

"Stay with me, Grace. It's nearly over," he continued to repeat.

"Daniel! Get her out of here!" I heard Gabriel shout.

Hopefully, far away from what was happening here. He picked me up again, and we were back in darkness.

"I think you've gone far enough." It was a voice I didn't recognise.

"Get out of my way," Daniel shouted at the man.

I opened my eyes, wondering who or what was trying to get me now.

It was the man in the white suit I had seen everywhere. Was he in on this whole thing too, or was he here to help? I had never mentioned him to Gabriel, I never thought I needed to, but here he was again.

I couldn't make out any more than that. I dropped to the ground; the air knocked out of my lungs in one deep guttural sigh.

"Grace." A familiar voice broke into my dream state. I could feel him gently holding my head as he lifted my hand in his, kissing it gently.

"Gabriel?"

My head lolled from side to side, I didn't have the energy to keep it up any longer, and it was becoming more and more of a struggle to concentrate on the words that were being spoken.

"We need to get her to a hospital and now!" I could feel myself being carried again.

Chapter Thirty-Six

It was the rain battering off the window that woke me from my slumber. The large window was like a framed picture of the sea loch and the road into Portree. I recognised the view. I had spent many days in the local hospital visiting my elderly relatives. I never thought for one minute that I was going to be one of its patients.

Unlike the last time I woke up in the hospital with a room full of people, there was no one here this time. I tried to move, everything seemed to be working, and I did a quick check over to make sure. There was a large tube in my side which I took to be a drain, there wasn't anything pouring out of it, which I was glad about, but what did I know? I had seen enough of my blood to last me a lifetime.

There was a bunch of white roses on the unit, and I wondered if Gabriel had been in to visit. I picked up the card.

Grace, My love always G x

I smiled and put the card back into the small white envelope.

I wondered if Bryce and Daniel had been in too. I tried to sit up, and that's when the pain came back, rapidly shooting through my body likc a warm knife through butter.

A nurse came running in, my monitors going crazy beside me.

"Grace. You're okay, you're in the hospital," she tried to speak to me softly, trying to calm me down.

"Pain!" was the only word I could muster.

"Where about is it?" she asked.

"Everywhere, I moved," I said, screwing my eyes closed.

She flicked about with some dials on the machines that surrounded my bed, and the pain began to ease. I took some deep breaths, and it began to dissipate.

"Is that better? On a scale of one to ten, ten being the worst, where would you say your pain is now?"

I thought about it. "Maybe a five."

"Great. That seems to be working. Don't move, and I'll adjust the bed so you can sit up." She was a lovely looking woman. Small, but I don't think she was going to stand for any trouble.

"Has there been anyone here?" I asked, feeling a little on the lonely side.

"A lot of men." She laughed.

"Are they okay? They were a bit banged up the last time I saw them." I studied her face looking for any signs of bad news.

She smiled and put her hand on my arm. "They're all okay. I had to throw them out to give you some rest. I have a contact number if you'd like me to call them? Or I can keep them away for a while longer?" she smiled.

I laughed. "That would be great, but I know what my lot are like; you'd be better give them a call."

"There's a button here if you need anything, push it, and I'll come through." She left, closing the door behind her.

It didn't take long before I heard a rabble outside my room and a nurse giving them orders before she allowed them back in, which made me giggle.

"There she is." Bryce was first in the door, his arm in a sling. He came over to the bed and kissed my cheek before standing back to let the next one in for a cuddle.

"Hey, Grace." Gabriel kissed me and held on to my hand. "I can't leave you alone for five minutes before you're getting into trouble."

"Stop leaving me then," I chastised with a roll of my eyes and a shake of my head followed by a smile so he would know I was only teasing him.

"This is my brother Michael." He stood back but hadn't let go of my hand. I didn't know if he ever would again.

"Hi, Michael." I looked between the two. Michael was bigger built than Gabriel; his long blonde hair tied neatly at the nape of his neck.

"Hi, Grace, it's nice to be able to put a face to the name. I've heard a lot about you." He smiled, and my heart skipped a beat, which was dangerous, considering all the monitors capturing everything my body was doing.

"Where's Kate?"

Bryce smiled. "She's fine. I told her to stay at home and rest today."

When Gabriel didn't move away, I knew I was going to have to ask. "What happened to Daniel?"

The looks darted over the top of my bed, unsure who was going to speak first. "Gabriel, where is he?" I demanded.

"He's at home. He didn't know if he'd be welcome," he answered.

"Well, he isn't!" I snapped.

"Grace, as much as I'd like you to walk away from Daniel forever, this wasn't his fault.

Amelia was too powerful for him; there was nothing he could do," he tried to explain.

"I have to agree with Gabriel. He feels terrible about what happened. I went to see him this morning, and he's in some state." Bryce gripped the rail at the side of my bed.

"I'm going to go and get him. I think you two need to talk." Gabriel left before I could refuse.

"Tell me what happened to you," I asked, turning to him. "The last thing I remember was seeing you tied up in the cell. I didn't know if you were alive or dead." I wiped at a stray tear that had managed to break through my steel exterior.

"It was nothing, I had just arrived at Kate's, the door went, and I opened it, and that was it. I woke in the cell tied up and not in a nice way." Bryce could turn any situation sexual.

I rolled my eyes.

He smiled at my reaction. "I saw them throw you in. I couldn't move to get you. I just kept praying that someone would find us,"

I didn't think he knew about Gabriel and Michael, and I wasn't going to make him any the wiser.

"It was Michael who found us and got us out of there before the police came."

"How did you explain all this?" I asked, looking at me and his arm.

"We told them about Amelia and Oliver her accomplice in all this. They're trying to find them, but I can't see them hanging around." Bryce explained.

Michael moved uneasily beside the bed, and I smiled, more to reassure him that his secret was safe with me.

The room door opened, and Gabriel walked in first, followed by Daniel. His face was a mess. All I wanted to do was jump out of bed and throw my arms around him, but I still couldn't help wondering why he had been an accomplice to Amelia's reign of terror.

"Hey, you," he said, walking over to the bed.

"Hey. Could you three give us a minute? I'd like to have a quick word with Daniel if that's okay."

They left the room without any argument.

"What happened, why Amelia?" I asked, unable to get my head around what had happened.

"She needed someone close to you, and I fitted the bill perfectly."

"But why couldn't you just tell her no?" I needed to know why he would turn against me like that.

"I shouldn't have been as susceptible as I was, but I had become depressed, and nothing seemed to be working out for me. It was part of the reason I moved up here in the first place. The way Gabriel described it; I was the perfect person for her to manipulate. I had no idea what I was doing, Grace. When we first met, and when I was down at yours, it was like my head was clear. Everything was great, but when I got home, I couldn't think. I was watching, shouting, pleading for you to run away, but I had no control over what was happening to me."

I held my hand out for him to take. If Gabriel said he didn't know what was happening, then maybe I should believe him.

"I'm glad you're okay," I said, squeezing his hand in mine. His gaze remained on the bed.

"I'm sorry for what I did to you. I'm sorry for hurting you." He was struggling to hold his composure.

"You were used by Amelia and hurt as much as the rest of us."

"I wasn't hurt as much as you," he mumbled.

"I'm fine, and this will all heal in time," I looked over my body.

"I'm sorry, Grace. I don't deserve your forgiveness." He looked at me this time, his eyes welling with tears.

"But you have it. I don't know what I'd do without you." I smiled teasingly at him.

"What?" he looked at the door. "Do you want me to get someone?"

I shook my head. "No, I want you to come closer."

"Grace, I'm not sure if…"

"I want to kiss you."

After taking another look at the door, he leaned forward. I put my hand to his face and kissed his mouth, trying not to hurt him. His bruised face and his bottom lip were cut and swollen.

He winced back. “You’ll need to be gentle with me,” he said before trying again. This time he didn’t pull away.

“What happens now?” He was sitting on the bed, in front of me, holding my hand. His face looked like a weight had been removed.

“I have no idea. Hopefully, this will heal. I’ll stay at the house for a couple of days then head home. It’ll be good to have some time to myself. “

“Hopefully, not too much time alone. I’m glad you’re staying.”

I giggled. “No, not all the time on my own, but it’ll be good to relax and get some work done.”

“What about Gabriel and Michael?” he asked, nodding his head towards the door.

“I think they might stay for a couple of days and then go home, but I have no idea. I only know what I want.”

“I like a woman who knows her own mind. Especially one that includes me in her plans.” He leaned in again, kissing me.

“What’s going on here?” Bryce, Gabriel, and Michael stormed into the room. Daniel looked at me, smiling.

“Sorry, we had to come back in before the nurse came back and threw us out again,” Bryce admitted.

“Well, try to behave then,” I said, rolling my eyes at them.

“We were discussing our plans.” Bryce came over to the bed. “I’ll need to go home on Monday as we planned. I can’t keep taking time off work. Hopefully, by then, you’ll be discharged. Maybe Daniel can pray for healing for you again.” He smiled at Daniel putting a hand on his shoulder.

I looked at Gabriel, who seemed more interested in his feet than anything else that was happening around him.

“What about you two?” I asked, looking between Gabriel and Michael. There was still an awkward silence, and it was all feeling a bit uncomfortable.

“I’m going to go home and catch a shower, is there anything you’d like me to bring in for you?” Daniel asked.

“I think I’m fine, thanks. I’ll message if I think of anything.” He kissed me before leaving.

“Right spill!” I said, looking around the room. You could have cut the tension in here with a knife.

“I’m going to get going too. I told Kate I wouldn’t be too long.” Bryce made his excuse to leave.

"Would you mind if I got a lift back with you?" asked Michael. "I hope you don't mind us staying at your house."

"No, I'd be annoyed if you weren't staying there."

Michael and Bryce left, leaving Gabriel and me alone to talk. "Your turn. What's with the sulking?" I asked, smiling.

"I'm sorry, Grace. This whole thing could have turned out so much worse than it did."

"But it didn't! What is with you men today? Stop taking the blame for something that had nothing to do with you." He tilted his head slightly.

"Okay, so it might have had a little to do with you." I giggled.

"I never meant for any of this."

"I know that." I squeezed his hand. "What did you tell Daniel?"

"It's okay. Daniel only remembers the parts we allowed him to," Gabriel said.

"Is this part of your compelling thing?" I smirked. "How does he think we escaped?"

"Sort of, he remembers us being there, just in a different situation," he explained.

"So, what are your plans? Are you and Michael going to stick around for a while or do you need to get back too?" I asked.

He laughed and swayed back on his heels. "Well, someone has to look out for you, always getting into trouble,"

I laughed with him. "I hope you'll stay here until I get out of the hospital, at least."

"You just want someone to play games with."

"Of course, you know how bored I get lying around all the time."

"I'm going to get going too and let you get some rest. Is there anything you need before I go?"

"Just one thing."

He looked at me quizzically. "A hug?"

"I think I can manage that." He leaned over and wrapped his arms around me. Squeezing me, just a little, to make me squeal. I wasn't worried about the pain anymore. I was just glad I had all my boys safely with me again.

Chapter Thirty-Seven

My hospital stay had been bearable. Gabriel had come in to play games and keep me company while Michael helped Daniel with his ministry. At night Daniel came in, and we would spend time talking, and if I was lucky, he would smuggle in some food.

When I was able to leave, my boys made my first few days as comfortable as possible, but I just wanted things to get back to normal again. I had started painting again, and with Gabriel fussing over me, I was healing physically. Mentally I was still waking during the night in sweat fuelled nightmares of Amelia and Oliver. The whole thing could have ended up with a completely different outcome, which left me scared and anxious.

I had thought I would relish the idea of being on my own, but I found the walls of fear closing around me if I was on my own, even for an hour. Daniel helped me by letting me speak to him. I told him about my fears, and he listened. I could tell the whole thing had affected him too. He still blamed himself, the way his head would fall when I was explaining a dream or if I was crying on the floor for no apparent reason.

I know there had been secret talks between the boys. What would be best for me? The thing was, if I didn't know what I wanted, then I had no idea how they were going to figure it out. It was Daniel who had broached the subject of me going home first. I had been face-timing Niven and I just felt lighter. I was laughing again, and Nic had called a few times or sent funny messages. I had played it off, saying how I couldn't be away from my boys, but the fact was I didn't want to leave.

The eerie quiet that filled me with panic was also the same thing that I had come to enjoy. I knew at home there would be bangs and cars driving in and out of the street, people shouting, and just the general noises of a faster pace of life, and I wasn't ready. Anytime someone tried to have *that* conversation, I was quick to walk away or change the subject. I knew at some point; I was going to have to decide my future.

We were all sitting at the table, Bryce was going home in the morning, and I had decided to go with him. It was just, I hadn't told anyone yet, and that included Daniel. I still loved him, but there was something that wasn't clicking. The trust I once had, was damaged and I wasn't sure if that feeling would ever go away. I needed to get back though for my exhibition. It was the one thing that brought me joy, the one thing that I could get excited over.

"So, I was thinking. I might catch a lift home with Bryce tomorrow." I blurted out. The looks between the four men had me sitting back angrily.

"I think that's a great idea," said Kate. "You'll be wanting to get back for the exhibition?"

The looks she got from around the table, you would have thought she had just said it would be better if I had died!

"Thanks, Kate."

"I'm not sure if that's entirely a good idea. I'm sure if you phoned the gallery, they could push the date in the circumstances." Offered Gabriel.

"We don't need to worry about Oliver and Amelia anymore, and I know I've to take it easy, but I can do that at home. It's time." I tried to sound as confident as possible even if everything inside was screaming in opposition.

"Are you two coming back?" I asked, looking at Gabriel and Michael.

"I'm going to stay here with Daniel for a bit, help him with his ministry," Michael said, sitting forward.

"I'll come home with you two," said Gabriel, he did not look happy, but this was my decision.

Daniel was being his usual quiet self, which was annoying me more than usual.

"I'm staying at Kate's tonight. I'll be over in the morning." Bryce said as he and Kate stood up to leave.

"If you don't mind, Grace, Gabriel, and I have some things to go over before he leaves tomorrow. We'll be back later." They both kissed and hugged me before leaving.

I stood at the sink filling it with hot water and soapy bubbles.

"Can I help?" asked Daniel. He was standing in the doorframe with his hands pushed down in his pockets.

"The tea towel is hanging up if you want to dry?" I said continuing washing the dishes. He picked up a plate and began to dry it. "Are you sure you're ready for this?"

I turned to face him. "I need to try. I can't stay here with you all wrapping me in cotton wool all the time."

"What about us?" he leaned against the bunker.

"What about us? Everything's fine, isn't it?" I knew it wasn't. Ever since the morning, I had arrived to surprise him, and the way he tried to force himself on me had me pulling away from him or making excuses not to be alone with him.

"Is that what you think? I've felt you writhe away when I try to get close to you, and now with you leaving, it feels like you're running away from me." He threw the dishtowel down.

There was nothing else in the sink, nothing else to distract me.

"Talk to me," he said tenderly.

"I'm fine. I'm still a bit sore, that's all." I lied.

He shook his head. "Stop!"

I dried my hands on the towel and backed away from him. The fear was building inside of me, and I could feel the emotion building inside too.

"Yeah, there's nothing wrong right enough! Look at the state of you." He ran his hands through his hair. "You need to talk to me, shout at me, but for your sanity and mine, can we get it over with?"

I stood watching him, and I could feel my body shaking. "I'm scared. You scared me," I blurted out.

It looked like I had just punched him. The colour drained from his face. I don't think I could have said anything else that would have hurt as much as that had.

"Grace, I'm so sorry." He folded his arms in front of him and looked at his feet as he tried to compose himself. "Do you want me to go?"

I shook my head.

"What can I do to make this up to you?" he asked.

"I need to be able to trust you again," I answered honestly.

He nodded his head. "Can I hold you?"

Now it was my turn to feel as uneasy as he looked. "Wait there, let me come to you."

He dropped his arms to his sides.

I walked over to him slowly. I leaned into him, resting my head on his chest. I brought my hands up and placed them on his waist. I looked up at him. "You can hold me now."

His hands ran up and down my arms as he kissed the top of my head. "Is this, okay?"

I brought my hands around his back, pressing my palms into him, he followed my direction, and it was all feeling weird, but I wasn't shaking. I was the one making the decisions, and it seemed to be working.

"Can I kiss you?" he rested his head on mine.

I moved my head up to catch his mouth. He was gentle, and it felt nice, not forced. His hand moved to the back of my head, and I panicked. I pulled back way quicker than I had intended.

"Sorry." He put his hand in his pockets and stood there looking at me like a frightened little boy.

I smiled and shook my head. "No, it was me." I laughed nervously.

"No, I tried to go too fast," he admitted.

I put my hand out to him, and it was his turn to recoil.

"I don't want to hurt you again, and I hate that I scare you. I've never been that person," he tried to explain.

"I know."

"I wasn't sure what took over me, but I don't want this to be our story."

"This is wrong. Amelia has come between us, and I can't believe she's still controlling things even when she isn't here." I put my hand on Daniel's face and kissed him. I moved his hands around me. "I still want to be with you," I said as I kissed down the side of his neck.

He picked me up and put me on the table, standing in-between my legs. "I want you more than anything, but I still want us to wait before I make love to you."

"As long as you still want to, then I suppose I can wait." I smiled at him.

Gabriel and Michael came back in we were still kissing each other. "You two at it again?" teased Michael.

We laughed into each other.

"I should go. Drop-in before you leave tomorrow?" he asked.

"I will."

I stood looking at the stars with my hand resting on the gate. I had left the boys to say their goodbyes. His car drove past and stopped. I got into the passenger seat, wanting our goodbye to be a bit more private.

"I wish you didn't have to go." My hand was resting on his leg.

"We talked about this. I want to do everything right by you." He wrapped his arm around my waist and pulled me as close as he could before allowing me to share one of his long, slow, sensual kisses.

I lay in bed that night, wanting nothing more than to be in Daniel's arms. I had considered going down to his house to surprise him, but our surprises had a way of backfiring lately.

I packed the last of my things and had a final look around the room to make sure I hadn't left anything.

"You ready?" asked Gabriel popping his head around the door. "Yeah, I'll be out in a minute."

It seemed like I was always leaving somewhere. I couldn't wait until Daniel was back down with me.

I watched the scenery whizz along. I smiled when I saw Daniel waiting at his gate for us. "I'm going to miss you, Miss Grimes."

"I'm going to miss you too. Message me all the time, and I'll see you on Friday for the show."

"I wouldn't miss it for the world. I've got someone to cover me on Sunday, so I'm looking forward to spending some time alone with you."

"I'm looking forward to it already," I said, kissing him.

"We need to get going if you want to miss the traffic at the other end," Gabriel said with his head hanging out the window.

"I suppose it's time," I said, giving Daniel another kiss before getting in the car.

The journey went quickly, with Gabriel and Bryce keeping me from getting bored. I hadn't thought I would be as pleased to be home as I was. The boys had offered to stay, but after dinner, I was glad to be able to go for a shower and get into my pyjamas.

There was only one person I wanted to talk to, and that was Daniel.

"Hey, you." His usual greeting when he saw me.

Seeing his face made me miss him even more. I was lying on top of my bed with the phone propped up at the side of me. It was my way of making it seem like he was lying next to me.

"Hey, I wish you were here."

"I wish I was there too. Where are you?"

"Bed."

"Are you there yourself?"

"Just me."

"Good, I can talk dirty to you then without anyone hearing." He laughed.

"Daniel!" I exclaimed, knowing he wouldn't. He was being good, and I was finding it a nice change.

"I do wish I was there holding you."

"I would like that. Only four more sleeps, and then you'll be here."

"Four sleeps sound like a lifetime without you."

"I love you."

"I love you too. Now go and let me get my beauty sleep. I don't want to look all tired and dishevelled when I see you again."

I smiled. "Night, Daniel."

"Night, Grace."

Chapter Thirty-Eight

The champagne was flowing, the gallery was full to capacity, and I had been waxed, plucked, plumped, and every other thing to get me into a formal dress and heels. It was a long way from my strappy top and shorts; the long flowing dress, with a thigh-length split up the side, was a tight fit around my chest, showing way more than I would normally. That, coupled with my four-inch heels, I was surprised if anyone would recognise me.

I never thought this day was going to arrive, and I never thought I was going to get everything done on time, but it all worked out nicely. The large painting was collected by the gallery and hung in the centre of the space. It looked impressive. The man in the picture facing away, and his head hanging down, but on his back were two of the most magnificent wings the world had ever seen. I was so pleased with it, and Katerina couldn't stop gushing over it.

I stood holding the wall up near the back of the room. It was giving me a clear vantage point to suss out the feel of the clients. So far, everyone seemed to be enjoying the champagne and canapés, my paintings were coming a close second, and I could feel the excuses and smiles for the end running through my head as my friends said how sorry they were that it hadn't been the success I had hoped. My gut felt like it was going to twist itself into a pretzel, and the onslaught of tears warned to keep themselves at bay until I got home and locked the door behind me.

Jazper had been here most of the afternoon, and it was him and Katerina that had decided on where to put the different pictures. Every time Katerina asked him to do something for her, he would give me a pout or a smirk, and every time I wanted to punch the little prick in the mouth! Now he was here in some flamboyant suit that didn't fit in with the ambiance of the room in the slightest. I sighed and looked away; it wasn't his damn pictures that were on display!

Daniel had arrived at lunchtime the day before as a surprise. I think Gabriel and Niven had been on the phone as my nerves got the better of me, the closer the exhibition got. We spent the rest of Thursday enjoying being back together again, even if he had insisted on sleeping in one of the spare bedrooms.

"Hey, you." He put his hand on my waist and kissed my cheek. I couldn't manage a reply.

"Your paintings look amazing. I'm so proud of you." Daniel slipped his hand around to my back. His fingers, pressing me closer to his body. "So how long do we have to stay?"

I looked at him with a shocked smile.

"That's better, now go and mingle." He slapped my bum before walking away nonchalantly.

I took a deep breath and, scanning the room, found Katerina. Her hair pulled way too tight that I thought she would have problems blinking, her make-up too thick, and her clothes too revealing for her age. Mutton dressed as lamb sprung to mind. I walked over, lifting a glass of champagne from a tray that was being expertly balanced by a girl half my age.

"Katerina."

"Grace." She kissed both my cheeks. "Everyone let me introduce the fabulous new artist we're displaying tonight, Grace Grimes."

"Hi, I hope you're all enjoying the evening?" I smiled at each of them.

"This is Marcus Healy, Teddy Cunningham, Paul Jamieson, and Edgar Peter," I shook each of their hands, in turn, feeling like I was meeting royalty.

"You're a very talented young lady; I can see a bright future for you," Edgar commented. He had a warm smile and such a kind way about him which made me relax and enjoy the conversation we were having.

Paul turned to the painting of the woman. She was lying on the pavement with her throat slit and the feather in the gutter.

"I love this. Tell me, was the feather the murder weapon?" He asked, intrigued.

"Oh, now that would be telling. I mean, how could a feather possibly make an incision that deep?" I flirted slightly, touching his arm.

The rest of the crowd laughed.

"I think she's got you there, old man." Teddy slapped Paul on the back, chuckling.

"I love your painting of the angel. I have to say I haven't seen anything so real for a long time. You must allow me to pick your brains about it later?" asked Marcus.

"I'm sorry, I have some more people for Grace to meet." Interrupted Katerina as she ushered me away against a backdrop of disgruntled sighs and pleadings.

"You couldn't have come over at a better time, your paintings are selling fast, and I've had requests for another showing of your work and also for some private pieces. I have to say, Grace," she said, leaning closer. "You come with a fine-looking entourage."

My eyes went to where she was looking, and there standing in different poses were Daniel, Gabriel, Michael, Bryce, Nic, Darcy, Niven, and Kate. All the men were looking like they could be the next James Bond while Niven and Kate were certainly passing for one of his girls. I couldn't help but try to contain my giggle, wondering which one she had her eye on.

After listening to an array of compliments from different critics, buyers, and artists, Katerina excused us to a quieter spot.

"I think tonight has been a wonderful success. I want you to enjoy the rest of the night with your friends, and we'll meet again next week." She hugged me briefly. In fact, there was hardly any touching, not like one of Bryce's hugs.

"Katerina, I was thinking of moving the painting of the angel into the back. It doesn't seem to be gaining much attention and…"

I could feel my hand grip the stem of my champagne glass, ready at any minute to grab him by the throat and take him outside.

Katerina expertly jumped in without letting him finish. "That's because it's already sold to Marcus Healy for three times its original price, and he's taking it to New York next week as part of his collection to go on shown at Insatiable, which is the only place to be seen. I think that will be all tonight. I'll see you Monday morning Jazper."

She rolled her eyes, and it was me who took a deep breath as I felt for the first time like I belonged here, not to mention seeing Jazper sulk his way to the front door. He'll learn, I thought to myself with just a little bit of a smirk on my lips.

"Oh, there's Cassandra. Here take this." Katerina handed me her empty champagne flute as some other high flyer caught her eye.

I handed it on to one of the waitresses.

"You lot can't stand together like this. You're putting people off looking at my pictures," I said, pointing a finger from around my glass.

"Of course, no one's looking at those perfect boobs!" teased Niven.

I laughed, and any anxieties leftover were gone in that instant.

A cheque would be arriving within the next couple of days for all the paintings that had sold. Katerina was going to hold onto the ones that hadn't sold for another event she was already planning.

By the time Daniel and I got back to the house, I was desperate to get my heels off and into something a bit more—me.

"Come through to the kitchen. I've got a surprise for you," Daniel whispered into my ear.

"Can I take my shoes off and get changed first?" I huffed.

"Five minutes."

I followed him into the kitchen. He switched the fairy lights on to reveal an enormous bouquet of red and white roses and a small turquoise box sitting on the island. I looked at Daniel.

"Open it." He leaned against the opposite bunker, his hands holding on and a smile that was turning me on, way more than it should have done.

My hands were shaking ever so slightly. I opened the lid, and there, sitting proudly on a satin pillow, was a Tiffany's pear-shaped, single cut diamond ring. I couldn't stop looking at it; it was the most beautiful thing I had ever seen.

"Do you like it?"

I had almost forgotten that Daniel was there. I looked up. "It's beautiful."

He walked over, took the ring from the box, and got down on one knee in front of me. "Miss Grace Grimes, would you do me the honour of being my wife?"

How had I managed to be this lucky? Was I going to wake up having had some cruel trick of a dream played on me?

"Grace."

"Sorry, yes, yes, I'll marry you!" he slipped the ring on my finger, and I threw my arms around his neck while his arms encased me into his body.

"I love you, Grace!"

"Can I take my shoes off now?" I laughed.

My shoes and dress were lying in a heap along with Daniel's suit. I couldn't keep my hands off him or him me, but for all the passion, something was missing. We had an understanding that for all the kissing and touching, we didn't want to go against our promise to one another that we'd wait. I went into the bathroom to change into my pyjamas while Daniel changed in the room.

When I came out, he was lying back on the bed; his T-shirt and shorts combo had me smiling. Maybe we did have some things in common. The pillows propped up at his back, and his ankles crossed. A bottle of champagne and two glasses had magically appeared.

"Where did that come from?" I asked, looking towards the champagne. "The fridge!" he laughed. "I've put a DVD on."

I sat next to him on the bed, and he handed me a glass. "To my very talented, super sexy fiancée." He kissed me.

I took a drink, placed it on the bedside unit, and cuddled into Daniel's body. I laid my hand on his chest, still admiring the ring in its very subtle platinum setting.

"I love my ring."

"I love you wearing it." He kissed the top of my head.

Chapter Thirty-Nine

"Do you think we've got enough beer?" I asked for at least the tenth time that day.

"You've got enough beer for the whole street, let alone a few friends. Stop worrying; everything is going to be fine." Daniel tried to calm my nerves, but I just wanted everything to be perfect.

It wasn't every day you got engaged, and I wanted everyone to know how happy I was. I opened the fridge to check the food. "Maybe I should make a chicken?"

"You've cooked two already!" he pushed the door of the fridge closed. "Do you know the story in the Bible of the feeding of the five thousand? Peter goes up to Jesus and asks how are we going to feed all these people? Jesus looks at him and says, don't worry about it, Grace Grimes is here, there'll be enough to feed everyone, including leftovers for tomorrow!" he laughed.

"There's plenty of food?" I screwed my face up.

"There's plenty of food! Now, how about you crack us open a couple of those beers before everyone gets here?" he leaned in and kissed me, and for that instant, I felt better. Then there was the knock at the door, and I looked at Daniel in a state of panic.

"Open the door."

I took a deep breath and opened the door.

"Hi, congratulations!" Screamed Niven, grabbing me like she hadn't seen me in months.

"Niven, I just saw you the other night."

"I know, but I missed you."

"A little help here?" Darcy asked, struggling with the kids and a changing bag and a bag with more drink in and flowers!

Daniel helped Darcy with his things while Niven and I continued our chat.

It wasn't long before Bryce, Kate, and Nic came in, and the music got cranked up, then last, but not least Gabriel and Michael came over. You would have thought they would have been first staying next door but always one to make an entrance.

The men had all congregated around the barbeque like some primitive hunter-gatherer caveman ritual.

"Look at them, Darcy will hardly go near the kitchen to make dinner, but the minute you mention barbeque he's on with the apron thinks he's Gordon Ramsey!" she laughed, taking a drink from her glass.

Kate came and joined us.

"Have you decided on anything for the wedding yet?" asked Niven excitedly.

"Not so much. You'll both be my bridesmaids, of course!"

"Of course, I mean who else is going to be able to organise everything to your high expectations?" smirked Niven.

"Not that high!"

"And that's why I'm going to be your bridesmaid!"

I would be quite happy getting married in a pair of shorts and a top, but knowing Niven, she was going to have everything perfect right down to the last-minute detail.

"That's very kind of you to ask me," said Kate.

I laughed. "I know, but Bryce couldn't carry off the dress, so you'll need to stand in his place."

She laughed. "I'll try my best." She went to join Bryce and Nic at the barbeque. The three of them were becoming inseparable. I was glad, I just wished Nic could find someone too.

Niven had gone off to the bathroom with Charlie, which gave me time to sit and spend some time looking at my future husband. He was integrating well with my friends, and I'd caught him swinging Violet around a few times or holding her while Darcy had something to eat. He was going to be a great dad someday.

It wasn't something I had given much thought to, but then again, I hadn't expected to get married either. Was this me finally growing up? An involuntary shudder ran through my body, which made me smile. No, I was too young to be a grown-up!

I couldn't help looking at Gabriel and wonder what could have been. It was good that we were still friends after everything that had happened. My mind wandered, and I thought about what I would do to him. I would certainly take my time taking his tie off, opening every button while my lips would skiff over his body. He turned around and looked at me and smiled and I wondered if he could read my mind.

I looked away quickly, trying to find something else to distract me.

"You okay there? You're looking a bit flustered," said Bryce, dropping into the seat next to me.

"Me, no, why?" I put the back of my hand up to my cheeks to feel the hot flush of embarrassment.

He laughed, and I could tell I was making this worse.

He leaned in. "What were you thinking of doing to him that has your cheeks redder than that top your wearing?"

I must be like an open book!

"Stop!" I gave him one of my looks, and he put his arm around me and kissed the top of my head.

"I remember when I used to make your cheeks flush like that."

I put my hand on his leg. "And who was to say it wasn't you I was thinking about?" I smiled up at him.

"Ouch! I hope in this case that its Daniel, that's making you blush. Still not putting out?" he looked over to the group of men.

"We both decided we'd wait, something you were never very good at if I remember rightly!" I said, tapping him with the back of my hand.

"I couldn't keep my hands off you, so he's either not that into you, or you are killing him!"

I laughed. "Why do you think the wedding is only a couple of months away?"

"I see. I did wonder why you were doing this as quickly. Now I know. In that case, I'll lay off the fact that Daniel's not that into you but give the man a break you don't need to look so hot!" he kissed my head again before re-joining the group.

Niven was on her way back and passed Charlie, to Bryce who looked like a fish out of water before Gabriel saved him.

I couldn't stop watching him lift Charlie into the air and then back down where he was blowing raspberries on his tummy. Charlie was screaming in delight, which had that infectious laugh ripple through everyone there.

"Now what I could do with that!" Niven commented, looking over at Gabriel.
"Niv!" I declared in shock at what she had just said.

Gabriel looked over laughing, and I was sure he knew what we were discussing.

"Having said that, that fiancé of yours is a close second and I'm not even going to start on Michael," she said, looking over longingly at the men surrounding the barbeque.

"Niv honestly. What am I going to do with you?"

"I can't believe you're waiting until you're married before bumping uglies." She laughed.

"It's called self-control."

"It's called a waste!" she said, shaking her head.

I laughed. I couldn't argue there.

"Who do you think will be better, Gabriel or Daniel? Because I wouldn't mind taking either of those models for a test drive!"

I nearly choked on my beer with that comment. "Niv, I don't know how Darcy manages to leave the house." I laughed.

"I allow him out now and again, and you never answered my question."

I sighed beside her. "I don't think you can compare the two. They are both nice and,"

"And hit all the right buttons?"

"Exactly!"

"Nice. Well, I'm very happy for you. Oh, here he comes." Gabriel had put Charlie down, and he ran over to us. Niven put her arms out to scoop him up, but he bypassed her and came to me. "I see how it is, just remember who feeds you."

"Auntie Gracie will feed you." I lifted him up, gave him a big kiss, and sat him on my knee before he cuddled in.

"You're a big sook." She tickled his tummy.

"How are things with you and Darcy, baby number three planned yet?"

"You know how he likes his spreadsheets. I'm not sure if I want anymore."

"Really? I thought you wanted lots of babies?"

"I did until I had to start carrying them and then squeezing them out. I would have more if Darcy could take over, I don't know. I would also like to get our bed back at some point. We spent a fortune buying beds, and furniture and carpets and decorating rooms, and we wake up in the morning, and there are two people in-between us, and they never lie the same way we are so there's never any covers."

"And no sex, by the sounds of it."

"Our parents are great at taking them so we can spend some time together, but it does take a lot of work. I know I joke, but I don't know what I would do without him." She looked over at Darcy with a tear in her eye.

"Look at you, miss soppy," I teased.

"I know this is all getting too serious. I'm going for more wine. Can I get you another beer?" She asked without waiting for a reply.

I gently stroked Charlie's hair.

"Are you wanting one?" Daniel asked, coming to sit next to me.

"Only if they're as good as this one." I smiled over at him.

"Maybe we could just keep him."

"I think Niven and Darcy would have something to say about that, and anyway, it might be fun trying," I teased.

"You have a point there."

"Do you want kids? I was watching you earlier with Violet," I asked, probing for more information.

"I suppose I've always wanted to have a wife and kids. A proper family. Feels like I'm at least halfway there." He leaned over and kissed me.

"It does look good on you; maybe it's something we could talk about?" I held his hand and smiled.

"I've run out. Can I get you a beer?" He was now the second person to leave me in tears.

Any more of this and I'll be getting a reputation.

I boxed up the food that was leftover and put it in the fridge while Daniel filled the dishwasher.

"How about we leave the rest until the morning?" I suggested. All I wanted to do was get into bed and relax.

At least Daniel had moved into my room and my bed. We hadn't made love, but it was nice being able to cuddle into him and talk to him. It wouldn't be long before he had to go back up to Skye for his work, so I wanted to spend as much time as I could with him just now.

Daniel was lying beside me; his arm draped over my waist. "I can't believe I need to go home soon. I could stay like this forever and never miss going back." He kissed my shoulder.

"I used to think I'd never leave Skye when I was a child," I said, reminiscing.

"I wish I had a place to go to like that when I was a child," he confided.

"You must have had places that you went with your parents." I realised I had never heard him talk about his family.

Daniel brought his arm away from my waist and turned on to his back. "I never had the childhood you did, Grace." The melancholy in his voice was apparent.

I sat up on my elbow, my fingers running over his body. "You've never told me about it." It was nice to know I wasn't the only one who wasn't good at opening up.

He took a breath before continuing with his story.

"I envy the memories you have growing up. My dad thought it was a good idea to use my mum and me as a way to relieve stress, especially if he had been to the pub or out gambling."

"When did you leave home?" I asked.

"I didn't leave." He took my hand and put it to his mouth. "I was removed when my dad attacked my mum and me. I had been out with a couple of friends on our bikes, and I knew something was wrong as soon as I came in. My mum was sitting in the kitchen at one end of the table, my dad at the other. They had been arguing about something or nothing, but it wasn't when he was shouting that you needed to watch; it was when he went silent. He was intimidating.

When I came in, I don't know I must have done something because he grabbed a bottle of whiskey off the table and proceeded to smash it against the bunker. I can remember my mum jumping up from the table, glass, and whiskey flying everywhere, but as his hand came back over from the bunker, he smashed it across my face. My mum went white at the sight of all the blood. My skin was hanging off my face." He ran his fingers along the scar on his jaw. "Then everything was quiet. I remember kneeling on the floor, trying to hold my face together, and he walked past me, dropping the bottle at my side." He wiped at the tears in his eyes.

I sat up, holding his face in my hands. "It's okay, you don't need to go on," I kissed him on the forehead, on both cheeks anywhere his face was wet, on his chin on his mouth. I held him tight, and he did the same with me.

"He killed her, Grace. He killed my mum, and I didn't stop him." He broke down completely. I held him as his body jerked along with his cries. The pain of remembering that day was too much for him.

He wiped his face. "I went to stay with my mum's auntie, she was lovely, but she was older and didn't have enough to look after me as well as herself, so we used to get handouts from the local church. I don't know what we would have done without them; they were lovely. They would try and get some fresh vegetables so my auntie could make soup, and they always tried to put in a packet of crisps or a small bar of chocolate for me. I can remember getting a colouring book and pencils and new pyjamas and slippers one Christmas."

"Is that why you decided to become a minister?" I asked.

"Partly. Other things happened that I had to sort out, but I liked the idea of being able to help people when they needed it."

"What happened to your dad?"

"He died in prison. All those years of drinking to excess finally caught up with him." He pushed himself off the bed. "I'm going to go and wash."

I watched him in the mirror as he bent over the sink and splashed water on his face, "Hey, you," he said coyly; as he got back into bed.

"You, okay?"

He pulled me close, holding me. "I've never been better. My life was pretty horrible growing up, but I promised myself that it wasn't going to define me but make me stronger. I never thought for one minute; I would find anyone like you. I'm not going to let you go; you do know that? I don't care what we argue about or what we might need to sort out. I'm always going to be there for you." He kissed me, and I believed every word. "You've shown me what love means, and I can't wait to spend the rest of my life with you."

I leaned over the top of him, kissing him. "I promise you that I will never do anything but love you."

He moved me over on to my back, smiling. "I'm going to hold you to that!"

Chapter Forty

We had the best time while Daniel was back home, but all too soon, it was time for him to head back. At least he had decided to come back down and live here once we were married. I hated having to watch him go. It always felt like I was losing a piece of myself every time his car drove away from me.

Katerina had been on the phone nearly every day since the exhibition offering me other opportunities to meet and expand my portfolio. I was busier than I could have ever imagined, which was good because it took my mind off Daniel not being there, but I also had a wedding to plan. Niven and Kate had been great, and all I had to do was confirm things with Daniel and phone the people back that needed numbers or what food the caterer was making.

The one thing I did have to do myself was buy my dress. I had been putting it off, offering excuses when there wasn't any, and I wasn't even sure why. Kate had come back down, and Niven had left Darcy to babysit. We were meeting Bryce, Nic, and Gabriel at the shop. I wanted to get a male perspective as to what I was going to wear, hoping that Daniel would agree.

"Don't look too happy." Niven shook her head, exasperated by my lacking enthusiasm.

We walked into the dress shop, and I felt sick. It was every girl's dream to find the perfect man, to get married and of course pick out *the* dress, but seeing the lace, rushing, bling, strapless, sleeves, fairy tale princess, fish tale dresses had my mind spinning, and all I wanted was just to run and escape.

"Hi, my name is Olivia, and I'm going to be helping you today to find that perfect dress," she said, smiling with a passion I was sadly lacking. She was definitely a girly girl. Her make-up and nails were perfect, and she had a lovely tight-fitting wrap around dress on which showed off her figure perfectly.

"I hope you've got a pair of jeans and a top back there because auld grumpy puss won't be happy in anything else!" Niven teased.

Olivia laughed. "Dresses, not your thing?" she asked.

"I don't mind. I'm just not sure what to even look at. There are so many," I answered her honestly.

"That's where I come in. Now, before we start, let's get some champagne." Olivia came back through with another girl. "This is Jessica, my assistant."

Jessica looked to be around the same age as us and wasn't nearly as formal looking as Olivia, but what she lacked in style she certainly made up for in looks. She opened and poured the champagne for us as Bryce, Nic, and Gabriel walked in.

"Just in time." Smiled Nic, picking up a glass of champagne.

"Have we missed anything?" asked Bryce as he hugged me then snuggled in beside Kate.

"How are you feeling?" Gabriel took my hands in his.

I sighed, and he hugged me. "I'm here for you," he whispered so only I could hear him.

"Right, so introductions, I'm Olivia, this is my assistant Jessica."

"I'm Grace, the bride."

"I'm Niven. Her bridesmaid and best friend."

"I'm Kate, the other bridesmaid."

"I'm Gabriel."

"I'm Bryce."

"And I'm Nic."

"Leaving the best to last." Smiled, Jessica.

I gave Nic a quick look. Bryce and Nic could pick up women anywhere!

"Great. Now shall we get started?" Jessica asked, the excitement building in her voice.

I sighed.

"What are you like?" Niven teased.

I walked through to the changing rooms with Olivia and Jessica.

"Now, because you're not very sure what kind of dress you want, I'm going to put you in a few different things so we can get an idea of the style and the material, then we can focus on that type of dress and hopefully find the one that's right for you."

I must have tried on about forty dresses, walking back and forward, so the rest of the crew could give their opinions. There were tears, wows, laughs, and some tumbleweed moments of complete silence. I was finding this excruciating. I felt like a roll of beef, and in some of the dresses, I looked like it too.

I sat on the small stool placed against the wall in the changing room. It was turning into a nightmare, and all I wanted to do was escape. I knew it wasn't going to be the dream experience Niven and Kate had promised it would be. I wiped at the tears that were running down my face.

Jessica walked back in, and I tried in vain to wipe the tears away.

"Oh, I'm sorry this isn't what you expected." She produced a box of tissues for me to use. "Can I get someone for you?"

I nodded my head. "Could you ask Gabriel to come through?" I asked, looking at her through puffy red eyes.

She left the changing room, and Gabriel walked in. He didn't even speak but picked me up off the stool before sitting on the floor, holding me into his chest. I cried into the tissue.

"I've got you. Just say the word, and I'll have you out of here, quicker than you could ever imagine," he said, kissing the top of my head.

"I don't think Niven would ever forgive you."

"Archangel, remember, I can handle Niven."

I shook my head. "No, you can't." I tried to laugh.

"No, you're right, but I could sneak us out the back."

It made me laugh, but the laughter quickly turned to tears again.

"I'm never going to find a dress, and everyone has their own opinions of what I should be wearing, and I look like a side of beef."

Gabriel laughed and played with my hair.

"You're laughing at me."

"I am, and I'm sorry, but you're hysterical." He moved me, so I was facing him. He wiped at my face with some tissues. "It's just a dress. A dress that you are going to look amazing in because Daniel deserves for you to look amazing. Am I right?"

I nodded my head.

Gabriel held up my hand. "Look at that ring. He managed to pick out a perfect ring for you, and now you need to find the perfect dress to blow his mind when he turns round to see you walking down the aisle."

"But what if I can't find it?" I huffed.

"Do you trust me?"

I sighed. "What archangels have a special power of finding the perfect wedding dress?"

He laughed as he stood up and placed me in front of the mirror. "No! What do you think archangels do? I'm going to go and get Jessica to help you." He kissed my neck and left.

Jessica came in with another of the 'I think you are going to love this' dresses. I kept my eyes closed until it was on, and everything was in place.

"What do you think?" she asked.

I opened my eyes and looked in the mirror. The dress was gorgeous, and it fitted me perfectly. I turned to the sides, and they gave me a mirror so I could see the back. It was everything I wanted it to be.

"I love it. I don't know if I want everyone to see it." I couldn't stop smiling.

"I'm sure they'll love it." Olivia gushed.

I walked through. Everyone was chattering away until I walked in. The silence descending on the crowd.

"Can we see it, with a veil?" asked Niven, standing.

"Of course." Olivia looked to Jessica, telling her which one to bring.

Jessica attached the veil, and Niven smiled. "That's the one. What do you think?"

"I love it," I smiled. "So?"

Kate came over. "You look amazing."

Bryce and Nic started laughing at each other as the tears were streaming down their faces. They both got up and came over and gave me a hug.

I looked at Gabriel, who was sitting forward, his arms resting on his legs. "Gabriel?"

Everyone looked at him, waiting for his opinion.

He stood up and came over to me. "You look beautiful." He ran his fingers down the side of my face.

"Do you two want some space?" asked Niven.

"Yeah, I think I'd like that," I said, looking into Gabriel's eyes. We walked through to the changing room closing the curtain behind us.

"You look just like an angel."

"Well, you'd know." I smiled up at him.

He leaned forward. "Can I kiss you?"

I nodded my head.

His mouth joined with mine. "Daniel is a lucky man." He wrapped his arms around me and just stood holding me. I held onto him; this was turning into one of those special moments of my life.

“I know this is a big ask, but would you walk me down the aisle on my wedding day?” I asked, looking into his eyes.

“It would be an honour.” He kissed me again before holding me.

We all went out for lunch after my ordeal and Bryce, called Daniel so he could join us for a little bit of the day at least.

“Hope you all have a lovely day and I’ll see you all when I come down for the wedding. Grace, I’ll speak to you later. I love you.”

“Love you too!”

“Awe. Right beat it, Daniel, we’re all starving here.” Niven joked. We all shouted bye before ordering another round of drinks.

Chapter Forty-One

The preparations for the wedding had gone smoothly. Everything was completed and ticked off the list.

I sat on my bed with the pillows propped up behind me. My wedding dress hung on the wardrobe door. Daniel had asked me to marry him, and I had said yes. It was Gabriel I had been in love with, but we were never going to be together. We would never get married or have children, and anytime I did get close, I came under attack by those wanting to hurt Gabriel.

The rain couldn't have been coming down any harder. I rolled onto my stomach and rested my head on my arms. In just a matter of hours, I was going to be walking down the aisle with Gabriel at my side, and Daniel would be standing waiting for me to marry him. I smiled to myself. Why did I always make everything so complicated? I was happy, wasn't I? I needed to know for sure was I making the right decision?

I got up from my bed and looked out the window. The rain was battering down hard.

Typical. The weather had been great, all week and the night before my wedding the rain was torrential. Hopefully, it wouldn't be like that tomorrow. I was bored. Maybe if I made a run for it, I could be over at Gabriel's, but then what? What were all these crazy ideas floating around my head? I had tried to sit and paint, but even that was proving too difficult for me to concentrate. And then there was the feather.

The night Gabriel had stayed over. The one stray feather left lying on his pillow. I had picked it up, not knowing how sharp it was and cutting the back of my hand as I ran it over my skin. There was still so much about Gabriel I didn't know, and I wasn't sure anymore if I wanted to.

Tonight was my last night of freedom, that's what people said about the night before your wedding, wasn't it, but how free? I laughed. What was I doing? I ran downstairs and put my trainers on and ran next door to Gabriel's.

"Grace. What?" he looked at me both with shock on his face and a smile that I knew I had made the right decision.

"Can I come in?" I still had my pyjamas on. It wasn't like me to do anything so impulsive and not take a moment to think it through. At least I had managed a pair of trainers.

"Yes, quick, come in." He closed the door. "So, drooned rat or droochit? That's what you Scots say, isn't it? Which one are you going for?" he smiled.

I started laughing, knowing he was right. "Yeah, never really thought this one through." I lifted my arms, water dripping from every part of me.

He laughed. "You are crazy, amazing, but crazy."

I stopped laughing. "Is that what you think?" the water still running from my hair and down my face.

"What, that you're crazy? Yes, that's exactly what I think," he joked.

"Don't play games with me." I was serious, and I needed him to be too. "I should get you a towel."

He walked away, leaving me standing in the hall, wondering if I had just made the biggest mistake of my life. "Gabe!" I looked up at him holding the towel.

"What, Grace? What do you want me to say?" he was wringing the towel in his hands as his knuckles turned white under the force.

I walked over and placed a hand on his arm.

"Grace," he whispered.

"Hold me." I kissed his arm.

He brushed the wet hair away from my face. "You look cold. How about we dry you off first?" He gently wiped my face and arms, then patted my hair and head. "I can get you one of my T-shirts and a pair of shorts."

"It's fine. I should probably be getting back. I should think about getting some of that beauty sleep, Niven keeps going on about." I smiled, knowing my time here was over.

He kissed the top of my head as his lips pressed into my wet hair, his hands holding my face. Was he going to kiss me? Was this why I had come over here? My lips parted, ready for his mouth to find mine; his breath was light over my skin before it wasn't. He stood back.

"It's okay, I love you," I kissed his cheek and left.

I was so embarrassed. What was I even thinking? I kicked my trainers off, leaving a pool of water forming beneath them. I walked up the stairs, slower than

I had come down; every step seemed to drain another bit of energy from my body. I stood in my room, the wedding dress, a constant reminder of how lucky I was and how stupid I had been. I picked it up and took it through to the spare room.

When I heard the knock at the door, I wasn't sure if it was something being blown over outside in the rain, but when I heard it again, I ran down the stairs picking up the keys as I went. I didn't want anyone standing out in that for too long.

"Gabe!" he was standing there, the water streaming down his face.

He came in, kicked the door shut, and picked me up, pushing me back against the wall kissing me. I instinctively wrapped my arms around his neck and my legs around his waist.

"You're soaking." Our breathing fast and heavy, our hands forceful over each other's bodies.

"Sorry," he said as his mouth pressed hard against mine. "I want you."

He carried me up the stairs and into my bedroom. I slipped myself from his waist as he pulled me close. His tongue, moving over mine. His hands moved under my top, taking it off while I pulled at his shirt. I wanted him, wanted to feel his body next to mine. I tugged at his belt, opening his jeans and placing my hand inside.

He gasped as my hand moved over him; he pulled his jeans and shorts over his hips before pulling my shorts down.

He moved my hands around his neck. "I like the touch of your skin next to mine." His fingers danced over my back before lifting me gently and placing me on the bed. He made his way down my body, kissing me as he went. His tongue, finding a new way to pleasure me. I ran my fingers through his hair, knowing I wouldn't be able to last much longer.

"Gabe." I grabbed the sheets beside me, but he didn't stop.

He moved on top of me, his hand dropping to adjust himself while pushing inside me. I moved my head up to catch my lips on his before he broke away, a breath escaping with every movement. I ran my fingers through his hair while he bit my shoulder, and his hand grabbed me. My nails ran down the entire length of his body, while every powerful thrust emphasised that this was going to be our last night together.

The passion we were feeling culminating at the moment when we couldn't keep going any longer. I grabbed him as the orgasm gripped every part of me.

He breathed in my ear. “I can’t hold on.”

“I want you to come inside me.” His final thrusts marking the end. We were still holding onto each other as we lay entwined, afraid to let go of each other.

A slight shudder ran over my naked body, and without thinking, his wings enveloped us both. “Gabe!”

“Sorry, I.”

“I like it. You make me feel safe.”

“You should never be afraid of anyone or anything.”

“I wish that were true.”

“It is. I will never let anything bad happen to you ever again.”

“We will never have another night, will we?”

“You’re getting married tomorrow. I can’t take another man’s wife.”

“But you can stay tonight.”

“Just tonight.”

I didn’t want to stay away from him for long. I began to kiss him as he lay on his back, my legs straddling him. I sat up, moving him inside of me. His hands were working their way up my thighs as he sat up, his arms pulling me closer. My hand dropped down his chest; my head fell back as his hands grabbed my shoulders from behind, and he kissed me as my slow but steady motion had him completely transfixed; his hand came up the back of my head, pulling my hair as he went.

“You’re so beautiful,” he whispered.

“I love you.” I began to move quicker.

“Grace.”

My nails dug into his shoulders as I steadied myself, scared I might pass out, but he held me, both of us enjoying the sensation of each other’s bodies.

“I’m never going to forget this or you.”

“If things had been different.”

I wasn’t sure who was going to let go first.

I opened my eyes as the sun streamed through the windows, a perfect day for a wedding. I thought to myself.

He leaned over kissing me, his arm on my stomach, pulling me into his body.

“You should have wakened me.” I smiled.

“You looked so peaceful I didn’t want to disturb you.”

I sat up and turned around, the covers falling from my body, my hand on his face, my lips pressing against his. His fingers rand down my back.

"I should go and let you get ready."

"Is that what you want?"

"It's what we agreed. I can't give you what Daniel can."

"We were good together." I laughed, kicking his leg playfully.

"We were, weren't we?" He laughed, putting his arms around me and pulling me back down. We lay holding onto each other just for a few more moments before we had to let go forever and get on with our lives.

Niven and the kids were first to arrive, by which time I was up, showered, and underwear on with my favourite red kimono wrapped around me. Gabriel had made us breakfast. I had said I'd be too nervous to eat anything but, as usual, he knew best, and the glass of champagne was a lovely touch.

"Here, she is. How are you feeling? Well, at least you're showered. When is Kate due to arrive? Darcy is picking up the flowers as we speak." Niven said, bursting into the house.

I glanced at Gabriel and smirked.

"Niven." Gabriel put his hands on her shoulders. "We're right on schedule. You planned everything down to the last minute. Now how about a glass of champagne?"

It looked like Gabriel was hypnotising her.

"A glass of champagne sounds good." She nodded her head. I poured a glass and handed it to her.

"Drink!" I ordered her.

She drank the full glass. "I think I need another one," she said, handing me the glass back.

"I think you do." I refilled the glass and handed it back to her. This time she took a sip. The door went, and Gabriel went to answer it.

"I don't think you were this nervous on your wedding day." I smiled at her.

"I just want everything to be perfect for you, Gracie." She smiled.

I gave her a hug. "It will be, but I want you to enjoy it too, so relax."

My house exploded with people. I wasn't sure how they had all managed to arrive at once, but the chance for me having some quiet time was over. My hair and face were being worked on as Darcy and Niven got the kids dressed. Kate was first to finish getting her hair and make-up done and appeared in her dress.

A silence descended on the room as everyone turned to look at her. Bryce went over to her. "You look beautiful."

"Thank you."

Niven and I had a quick awe moment before we were back to it. “You should go and get your dress on too,” I said to Niven.

“Will you be, okay?” she asked with all seriousness.

“I think I’ll be fine, now go.” I shook my head at her.

My hair and make-up finished; I took another sip of champagne as Niven walked into the room. A hush fell as it had previously with Kate, and I did wonder if I was going to have the same reaction when I entered the church.

“You look amazing; how dare you upstage me on my wedding day,” I joked with her before giving her a hug.

“Gabriel. You need to go home, get showered, and changed.” Niven was back ordering everyone around, and he wasn’t going to argue with her.

I followed him through to the door as the rabble continued behind us. Gabriel opened the door, and I took a deep breath, ready to say goodbye to my lover before he returned as my friend, ready to take me to the church.

He looked at me with those blue eyes, and it took all my strength not to throw myself at him.

His hand slipped into my kimono at my waist, and I was sure I was blushing in his arms. It was like everyone in the house had disappeared, and it was just us. I could feel my kimono lift away from my body and hoped no one was watching us.

I smiled up at him as his hand cupped my face, and he leaned in to kiss me. It was the last time I was going to feel his lips on mine, the last time I would taste him, but something had changed. The tingly sensation that always coursed through my body when he touched me had gone. I was getting married to Daniel, and I couldn’t wait to be in his arms, kissing him.

“Auntie Gracie.”

That was enough for Gabriel to stand back as Charlie ran through in his little kilt and Jacobite shirt. He was just the cutest thing I had ever seen in my whole life. I scooped him up and sat him on my hip.

“I should go.” He ran his fingers down the side of my face, and he walked away.

I stood watching him for a moment, that part of my life over. I smiled, ready for what the day was going to bring. I turned and closed the door.

Chapter Forty-Two
Daniel

The day of my wedding had arrived. The day I was going to put all my past experiences behind me. I had a list of all the things I wanted to do as well as everything I had to do, like turn up to the church on time!

It was going to be the last morning I would wake up on my own, the last morning where Grace wasn't beside me, and the first morning of our new lives together. I stared up at the ceiling, knowing I had to get up and get ready, but something was niggling at the back of my mind, and I could not shake what it was. I prayed and read my Bible before going for a shower.

Nic had offered to put me up the night before the wedding, which was great. I didn't want to stay in a hotel, and since Grace and I were doing everything by the book, this was just another thing ticked off the list.

Nic was already up when I went downstairs.

"Here he is, the man of the hour." Nic stood up as I walked into the kitchen.

"Morning."

"I thought you would have been up hours ago. You have nerves of steel," he said as he poured me a coffee.

"Cheers, mate." I took a drink, and Grace was right; I did like her fresh coffee better. "I don't know about nerves of steel. We'll see how good I am when I'm standing waiting for her to walk down the aisle."

"What's the plan for today then?" Nic asked.

"Breakfast first, then I've got a present for Grace, just a little something for her to wear today, then back here, dressed, and I need to be at the church for two," I explained, taking another drink of my coffee.

"Busy day, but I thought you didn't want to see Grace before the wedding?"

"I know. I might give them to Gabriel to give to her." I turned the cup in my hand.

"I could make breakfast, but I think it would be quite nice to go out, so get your coat," Nic ordered.

I did what he said.

When we arrived at the restaurant, Bryce and Michael were there as well as a couple of my friends Nate and Moore, my best man Greg and our minister for the day my other friend from University Blake.

I looked at Nic. "Did you do this?"

"It was Grace's idea. It was her gift to you." I hugged each of them and sat down with a beer placed in front of me.

"Congratulations, mate." Greg was always there when I needed him. We had met each other at university and had stayed friends for years along with Blake; the three of us had been inseparable. Nate and Moore, I had gone to school with, and we had never lost touch. They were probably the best group of friends any man could have.

"Thanks. It all seems a bit real now." I coughed, feeling the emotion of the day begin to well up inside of me. I took a drink to try and steady the fracture that was starting to appear in the steel exterior.

"Tell us about Grace." Asked Moore. "Is she everything you ever dreamed of?"

"Watch what you're saying now." Joked Bryce, which had everyone laughing.

"Yeah, she's great, talented, fun, caring. I couldn't be happier," I gushed, and I meant every word of it.

"I had the pleasure of meeting her to go over the service, and I can honestly say she is far too good for this man, that's for sure." Blake joked, and everyone laughed. "No, she is one of the nicest people I've ever met. You're a lucky man, my friend."

"Here." Nic brought his phone out to show them a picture.

"She's gorgeous!" exclaimed Nate. "You're punching above your weight there!"

"Wow! There must be something wrong with her if she's marrying you!" joked Moore.

I looked at Bryce and Nic. "See what I have to put up with?"

It was a great morning, and I couldn't have been happier. Nic wasn't drinking, so he had agreed to take me round to Gabriel's to drop off the present I had for Grace.

We stopped across the road seeing as how both Grace's and Gabriel's driveways were full of cars already. I twirled the box round in my hand.

"Can I see?" asked Nic.

I opened the box showing off an elegant pair of diamond and pearl earrings that my mum had worn on her wedding day.

"They are beautiful. Family heirloom?"

"My mums."

Grace's door opened, and Nic and I turned round to see who it was. Gabriel.

Nic went to put his window down to shout over to him. "Wait." I put a hand on his arm, and we continued to watch.

Grace appeared beside him with her red silk kimono hung loosely around her. His hand slipped inside, at her waist, pulling the red silk away to show her stocking covered leg. My eyes dropped. I hated how he was with her.

She smiled up at him before he cupped her face in his hand and kissed her. Not a quick peck on the cheek, either. He let her go when Charlie appeared. She swung him up into her arms, holding him on her hip. His fingers ran down the side of her face before he left her standing at the door, watching him walk away. She turned and closed the door.

I watched Gabriel for a bit. He seemed too happy for someone who was losing the woman of his dreams to another man. What was with that kiss? Was there still something between them?

"I wouldn't worry about that. The two of them are always a bit touchy with each other, but it doesn't mean anything. Grace wouldn't do that to you." Nic tried to reassure me.

"He can't let her go."

"He doesn't need to. Grace made that decision when she started going out with you. If you want, I can run over and give her the earrings?" he offered.

"Thanks, but I think I'll go over to Gabriel's. I need a word."

"Just remember how Grace would feel if you turned up to the wedding with cuts and bruises over you and Gabriel," he said, looking serious.

"I'm not going to hit him." Even if that's all I wanted to do at this point. "I just want to talk to him." I got out of the car.

A man was standing with his hands in his trouser pockets. I had to take a double look.

There weren't many people who could pull off a white suit, especially with silver hair. "Somebody's having a party," he commented, nodding his head across the road to Grace's house.

"It's a wedding. Sorry, I've got somewhere I need to be." I left the man and crossed the road to Gabriel's house.

I wasn't sure what I was going to say to him, but I knew I had to say something. He couldn't keep putting his hands all over my wife like that.

"Daniel. Should you not be getting ready for something?" he joked as he answered the door.

"Can I come in?" I asked. I wasn't in the mood. I needed to know if the woman I was going to marry wanted me as much as I wanted her.

"Sure." He stepped aside, and I walked in.

"I was making a coffee. Can I get you one?" He offered.

"I'm fine, thanks."

"So, what can I do for you?" he asked, taking a drink from his cup.

"I came over to give you these. Would you give them to Grace to wear today? They were my mums." I held up the box for him to see.

"Of course. Is everything alright? You don't seem your usual self or are the nerves starting to kick in?" he smiled.

With that smile, I could see how Grace had fallen for him and all his charm. I wondered if she'd be able to walk away from it.

"Nic and I parked across the road." I paused, trying to find the right words.

"You should have brought him over. I'll go and shout him in." He put his cup down and began to walk away.

"No! I wanted to have a talk with you on our own." Maybe hitting him would be for the best it might get rid of some of this tension that was building up inside of me.

"Okay." He went back to get his coffee.

"It's about Grace. I saw you when you left her house. The way you touch her, and that's not a friend's kiss." I shook my head. "What's going on, Gabriel?"

He looked shocked at what I was saying.

"Daniel, I'm sorry. I love her, I will always love her, but she chose you." He tried to explain.

"Exactly! She chose me, so why are you still kissing her like that?" the temper was building up in my body, and I don't think I had ever been this angry with anyone since my dad.

"There's a connection between us. There are things you will never know between us, but that doesn't mean Grace doesn't want to be with you."

"What about when we're married? Are you still going to be hanging around, confusing her?" I felt I was now fighting for Grace.

"I'm leaving," he exclaimed.

"I find that highly unlikely that you would just leave her, especially when you love her as much as you say you do." I folded my arms in front of me.

"And that's why I'm leaving. I do love, Grace and yes, it's killing me that she's marrying you today. I can't give her the life you can. I can't be there for her like you can." He sounded disappointed.

"Does she know you're leaving?"

"We've talked about it."

"You've not told her, I mean, you didn't tell her, you'll be away by the end of the year, say?" I began to wonder how much Grace knew. Was he stringing her along?

He took a moment to answer. "I haven't said to Grace when I'm going to be leaving because I don't know myself yet. Please don't say anything to her today," he asked.

"I don't think you're in any position to be asking me for favours. Does Grace love you that much that if you told her you were leaving, what, she wouldn't go ahead with the wedding?" I looked at him incredulously. Was he serious?

"It's not like that."

"Then, maybe you better enlighten me to what it is like, or do we get Grace over here to explain it?" the anger was coming to the surface now.

"No! Don't do this to her. She loves me but not in the same way she loves you. She would be devastated if I was to leave. There are still a lot of things she needs to work through in her life, and people leaving her suddenly is one of those things," he was pleading with me, and I didn't want to hear it.

I hated that he knew more about my wife to be than I did. Had I rushed into this too quickly? I didn't know her that well; all I knew was I loved her.

"When was the last time you slept with her?"

He looked down before answering. "Yes, I've made love to her. Is that what you want to hear that I made love to her, and I wish I could have her like that every day of my life? When are you going to realise that it doesn't matter what I think or feel, she chose you!" he shouted back at me.

He never really answered my question, then that look in his eyes, the kiss at the door, and the way he was touching her. I leaned my hands on the island.

"Did you sleep with her when I wasn't here? Were you sneaking over to her house?"

"I'm not listening to this." He went to walk past me, and I grabbed his arm.

"Was it after I asked her to marry me?"

"I suggest you think about what you're doing," he said, looking straight into my eyes.

I wasn't going to be intimidated. "Was it last night?" I wasn't even sure I wanted to know, but I had gone too far to back down.

"Yes! Yes, I made love to her last night, all through the night, and it was incredible." He grabbed hold of my shirt and pushed me against the wall. "It was my name she sighed in the height of her passion,"

All the anger and fight left me, and I was devastated. I had pushed and pushed, and this wasn't what I wanted to hear. I didn't need all the details laid bare.

Gabriel's grip loosened, and he took up his previous position, his back to me as he leaned forward on his hands against the bunker.

I slumped against the wall. I couldn't think, and I was finding it hard enough to breathe at this point. What was I meant to do now, knowing this? Why did I keep pushing him? Was there some weird part of my brain that craved the drama that wanted to feel the pain this was causing?

"What are you going to do?" Gabriel asked.

I stood up and straightened my shirt. I ran a hand through my hair, anything to focus my mind on what was happening here now. The room felt like it was spinning out of control, and I had to make a decision. I was supposed to be getting married in a couple of hours. Everyone was going to be waiting at the church for us to arrive. Grace would be walking into a church full of people, and I wasn't sure if I was going to be standing at the front waiting for her.

Gabriel turned round. "Daniel. Don't leave her."

I shook my head.

"Daniel!"

I raised my hand for him to stop. I needed time to think.

"I'll leave, I'll leave now. There are plenty of people who would jump at the chance to walk her down the aisle. Please," he begged, the emotion building in his voice.

He knew he had messed everything up, and this was his attempt to make things right. "You don't say anything. As far as anyone is concerned, I came here to drop off the earrings for her to wear at our wedding. That's all."

"And the wedding itself?" he crossed his arms in front of his chest.

"You will get dressed, go to Grace, give her the earrings, and you will turn up at the church at two." The emotion had left my voice. I was saying what I needed to at the moment to give me time to think.

"Are you going to be there when she arrives?" he asked.

I began to walk towards the door, stopping, I turned around. "I don't know yet." I left Gabriel standing in the kitchen as I made my way back to the car.

Chapter Forty-Three
Gabriel

The door closed, and it felt like the final nail in my coffin. The room was spinning, and I knew it was all my fault. Why did I have to say those things? I could have just dealt with his comments, and he would have been none the wiser, but he kept pushing, and I don't know why but I wanted him to feel the pain that I was feeling, the hurt that I could no longer be a part of her life. He didn't understand how much I loved Grace and how much she loved me.

It was selfish, and it was not the quality of an angel, let alone an archangel. Even if he decided to walk away, I still wouldn't be able to give her everything she wanted. I would, at some point, need to leave. I had behaved like a man of the world, taking what I wanted, and when it was time to go home, there would be no looking back.

I had come here with the task of protecting, Grace. I had been to earth countless times to defend or give information before, so why had I failed so badly this time? What was it about Grace that had me acting like a complete fool?

I dropped to my knees. How could I have done this to Grace? Was this what love looked like on earth? A horrible, twisted mess of emotion. I leaned forward, resting a hand on the floor in front of me. Please, God, help me. I couldn't stop the tears from flowing or the cries that shook me to my very core. I had never felt anything like this. I had just destroyed two people's lives in an instant.

I had no idea if he was going to turn up to the church or not. How was I meant to take Grace to the church knowing he might not be there waiting for her and that it was all my fault? She would hate me, and she would have every right.

What was I going to do? My head joined my hand on the floor. How could I even return home after this? What kind of example had I been while I was here? I had probably lost all respect in the Heavenly Kingdom. I had been solid in all my years, and I had destroyed it in an instant, and for what? The love of a woman.

A woman I could never really have. It wasn't as if it hadn't happened between angels and humans before creating the Nephilim, the offspring of sons of God and the daughters of men. They couldn't be controlled and were destroyed and removed from this world.

I heard the door open and close, but I couldn't look up. I had sinned against God. There was no hope for me now.

"Gabriel. I'm here for you." Michael was kneeling beside me. I shook my head. "I've ruined everything."

"You made a mistake."

I sat back on my heels; my eyes closed. "I went against everything I was here to do."

"You were here to protect Grace, and you did that."

I looked at him. "I've just destroyed her life."

"No, no, you haven't. As I said, you made a mistake, but that's all." He rested his hand on my shoulder. "Come." He rose to his feet and held his hand out for me to take.

I stood with his help.

"I'll make some coffee. You go and wash your face. I'll be waiting."

Michael was not an archangel you said no to, I had tried it once, and I vowed never to again. I splashed the water on my face and looked in the mirror in front of me. I held on to the sink to steady myself. Who was I?

I dried my face and went back to the kitchen. A cup of coffee was sitting on the island.

Michael was sitting on top of the opposite bunker, holding his cup in his hands. "Well, at least you look like an archangel again," he commented, smirking.

"I don't feel like one," I said, taking a drink.

"Talk to me," tell me exactly what's been going on, and I'll see what I can do to help, but you need to be honest with me, Gabriel. If we want to get this sorted, then you need to tell me everything, don't leave anything out.

"I don't know where to start," I said, shrugging my shoulders.

"Just start somewhere, and we can take it from there."

I jumped up on to the island. If I was going to be here a while, I might as well get comfortable.

"When I first saw her, I thought she was beautiful, but I also knew I had a job to do, and I put all my feelings behind me. Then she ended up in the hospital, and I was taking care of her at home." I shook my head. That was where I crossed the line, and Michael knew it without me having to tell him.

"You fell in love, Gabriel. No one can fault you for that," he tried to reassure me.

"We all feel love for people we come into contact with, and we all know that's as far as we take it. I went further."

"Gabriel, I knew what was going on with you two, but just how far did you take it?"

I took another drink of coffee before I spoke. "I made love to her." I ran my hands through my hair, clasping them at the back of my neck.

Michael sighed. "You're lucky she isn't pregnant. Now that would have been a mess to clear up."

I sat there frozen to the spot.

"Gabriel, please tell me she isn't pregnant?" Michael looked shocked, but that was only a fraction of how I was feeling. I hadn't even thought about it seriously until now.

"I never even thought about that." I took another drink. "She knows what I am. I took her flying one night."

"So basically everything you're not supposed to do, you've done it?" Michael rubbed his hand over his face.

I sat watching him as he tried to figure out how he was going to help me turn this around.

"So, what happened today?" he asked.

"Daniel was out with us, and we had some food and drink. He was as about as excited as I think I've seen anyone, and I get a message to come here urgently. I saw Daniel, getting into Nic's car, and he didn't look as excited, that's for sure."

"He asked if I had ever made love to Grace."

"And you told him?" he shook his head in disbelief. "Why? Why would you do that?"

"He kept pushing me to tell him and then when he asked if I made love to her last night."

"Gabriel, please tell me you didn't?"

"I didn't just tell him I made love to her last night, but that it was all night, and it was my name she was screaming." It sounded ridiculous repeating it back to Michael. I had no idea why I had allowed myself to get so caught up in trying to hurt him.

"This keeps getting better. Why? Do you think if he leaves Grace that she'll come running back to you?"

"I wasn't sure what I thought. I just wanted to hurt Daniel the way he had hurt me!"

"You're not supposed to feel hurt or make anyone else feel pain. Grace fell in love with him because you knew you couldn't be there for her. She was in danger, and she met someone who could love her and give her everything she wants in life. She chose Daniel to marry. Not you!" Michael was angrier than I had seen him in a long time.

"It's different being here. I got completely caught up, and I just wanted for once to experience all that life and earth had to offer."

"So, what's happening with the wedding?" he asked.

"He only said to go ahead as planned and be at the church for two. He doesn't know if he's going to turn up." I closed my eyes. "I don't know if I can go through with this."

"Damn right, you're going through with this! You don't get to make a mess of everything and then run away. You will stay, and you will accept any of the consequences coming to you. If you don't, she'll hate you."

"I think she's going to hate me anyway. As soon as she finds out that I told Daniel, I don't think she'll ever talk to me again."

"Well, that's something you'll have to deal with, but for the moment you do exactly, as Daniel has asked. You get dressed, and you get over there." He was saying all the right things. I just wasn't sure if I could do what he asked.

"I don't know if I can lie to her."

"Try! You knew how important this mission was. You need to do everything you can to make this right." He took a breath in giving himself time to think. "Whatever happens, you need to accept the consequences. I'll speak up for you at home, but here, well, you're on your own."

There was a heaviness in my chest that I had never experienced before. I didn't want to go over to Grace's house, and I didn't want to see Daniel or anyone for that matter ever again.

"Go and get dressed," he ordered me.

"What if he doesn't show up?" I asked, wondering what was going to happen to the mission and whether Michael would need to step in to try and recover this whole sorry mess.

"Leave it to me, and I'll see what I can do. Maybe when you go to get changed, it might be an idea to pray there is only one who can turn this around."

I walked away, leaving Michael in the kitchen. I had made a mistake, but he was right. I had to humble myself and ask for forgiveness and for things to be made right with Daniel and Grace.

As far as I was concerned, I was going to have to leave here and explain what happened.

There was a chance I would have to go home, my archangel status stripped after all these years of committed service. I fell in love with a daughter of man, and I was going to have to face the consequences of my actions. I just wondered if I was going to get out of this with Grace still talking to me or whether I had destroyed any chance of happiness she was due.

Chapter Forty-Four
Grace

I sat on the island in the kitchen. People were busy going back and forward, but for at least the next five minutes, at least I was keeping out of the crazy.

"Right, Miss, I've got plenty of time to get ready. Move your bum!" Niven was in charge today, and it was all going to go like clockwork, or she was going to have something to say about it, and I wasn't going to contradict her. Everyone was doing what she said. I could see that they were all of the same opinion. I smiled. I was glad she had taken control.

The house was full of people, and I couldn't find a damn thing I was looking for.

"Has anyone heard from Gabriel yet?" I asked as I ran upstairs for the twentieth time this morning. I had no idea why everything was scattered all over the house when usually everything was in a set place.

"I'll give him a call." Shouted Niven running in the opposite direction.

I stood in my room, pushed the door shut, and closed my eyes. I took a deep breath and let it out slowly. Why was I so nervous? I couldn't wait to see Daniel and get married. My night with Gabriel was just what I needed to let go. I was one hundred percent committed to Daniel, and I wasn't going to do anything to jeopardise my new life with him. I had thought about phoning him this morning, but we had agreed to meet at the church at two, and that was what I was going to do.

I picked up my phone; a text was different, and I wasn't sure why, but I knew I needed to give myself and Daniel every chance of happiness.

"Hey, you. I hope you enjoyed your surprise. I just wanted to say I love you so much. Can't wait to be your wife and spend the rest of our lives together. Anyway, I better get my dress on! Meet me at the church at two. Love always, G x."

I tapped the phone off my chin, thinking about him smiling when he reads my message.

I unzipped the bag that surrounded my dress. It was gorgeous. It was always my assumption that I'd get married wearing my jeans and a shirt, but after trying all the dresses on, Niven had changed my mind.

"You, okay?" asked Kate. I nodded my head.

"I think it's time to get that on," Niven said, coming into the room. I wiped at a stray tear that had escaped.

"Hey, we'll have none of that. Thank you very much." Niven grabbed a tissue and very carefully wiped it away so as not to spoil my make-up.

"Sorry. I don't know what's wrong with me this morning, "I shook out my arms, trying to get rid of whatever was clinging to me.

"You're about to get married. It's a big step." She held both my arms and looked me squarely in my eyes. "I'm only going to ask you this once. Is this what you want? If not, we stop. We put all this away, and you phone Daniel and tell him you can't do it."

She was so stern I couldn't help but laugh. "Thank you, but I think I'm going to go through with it."

"Well, alrighty then. Let's get this dress on," she said, reaching for the hanger.

I stepped into the dress as Kate and Niven helped me pull it up and fasten it at the back. I stood in front of the mirror and smiled.

"Daniel is going to be blown away," said Kate.

"Do you think?" I asked, looking from side to side.

"Absolutely! I bet he can't wait to see you out of it too!" Niven laughed.

"I think we're both looking forward to that," I teased.

We all laughed as we heard the front door going.

"I bet that's the other man of the hour." Niven stopped at the door. "Now, you are sure you want Daniel and not the hunk downstairs?"

Kate and I burst out laughing.

"Go and get Gabriel!" I pointed at her. I shook my head.

"You look amazing," Kate said with a wide grin.

"Thanks, Kate."

"Gabriel, do you want to come up?" we heard Niven shout from the stairs.

Gabriel stood in the doorway. "Well, what do you think?" I asked. As I stood swishing my dress back and forth.

He coughed, clearing his throat before he spoke. "You look beautiful."

"You can stay," Niven said, patting him on the back.

"How are your nerves, Gabriel? It's a big job making sure she gets down the aisle without falling over." Asked Kate.

"They were fine until I saw her," he said, looking at me.

"Could you give us a minute?" I asked Kate and Niven.

"I'll check on the cars." Niven darted away, closely followed by Kate.

"You look very handsome," I said, touching his jacket.

"Thank you. I knew I would have to be on my A game if I was going to have to walk you down the aisle," he returned the compliment.

"I'm glad you're here," I said, looking up into those sparkling eyes.

"Me too. Daniel's a lucky man." He closed his eyes as a stray tear rolled down his cheek.

"Don't cry; you know it will just start me off," I wiped the tears from his face. "I know this was a lot to ask after everything we've been through, but I couldn't think of anyone else I would rather be here with me."

I wrapped my arms around him. I had my night with Gabriel, but he wasn't going to be there for me the way Daniel was. Today wasn't about Gabriel. It was all about a new life, a fresh start with Daniel. If it had been anyone else, I was marrying today, my heart wouldn't have been in it, but I loved Daniel. It was different with him, I felt like everything fitted into place, and I couldn't wait to begin my life with him.

"Do you honestly think that you would have been able to stop me?" We both laughed as we held on to each other.

"Grace, that's us away. The cars are here." Shouted Niven.

"Okay, see you there," I shouted back as my arms unwrapped themselves from his neck. "I've got something to give you." Gabriel said pulling a box from his pocket.

"You didn't need to do that."

He ignored my hand on his arm. "Open it. It's from Daniel. His mum was given them on her wedding day, and he wanted you to wear them today."

I unwrapped the box, opening it to reveal a pair of diamond and pearl earrings. I went over to the mirror to see what I was doing. "They're lovely."

"Well, they will suit you perfectly then."

There was a knock at the door. "I think that's for us," I said excitedly.

"Come on then, let's get you married."

I couldn't stop smiling all the way to the church. Now, and again I would steal a glance at Gabriel. He looked more nervous than I was. I took his hand in mine and smiled as he smiled back, kissing the back of my hand.

When the car arrived at the church, I felt more nervous than I had all day. I took a deep breath. A man I hadn't seen before spoke to the driver, then opened the back door and leaned in.

"Hi, Grace. I'm Greg, Daniel's friend, and best man. I was saying to the driver to take you for a little drive. Daniel hasn't arrived yet. I'm sure everything will be fine. Gabriel, is it? Can I take your number?" Gabriel and Greg exchanged numbers and pleasantries.

I had let go of Gabriel's hand, and I looked at the flowers laying in my lap. I should have known things weren't going to go as planned today. After last night I was probably being punished. The thought that I was having my cake and eating it came to mind. What was I thinking? I had ruined everything.

"Take me home."

"Grace, honestly, I don't think he'll be that much longer. He's probably just got caught in traffic." Greg tried to explain.

A tear ran down my cheek. I shook my head. "He's not coming." I tried to smile. I had heard that hearts could, literally break and that's exactly how I was feeling.

"Grace, I think we should wait another five minutes, at least," Gabriel suggested.

I took hold of his wrist and looked at his watch. "It's quarter past two. Please. Take me home."

"Hey, you."

I looked up to see Daniel kneeling at the side of the car. I wasn't even sure what to say to him.

He took hold of my hand. "Grace, I'm sorry, I'm late. Please forgive me?" he smiled.

"Are you sure you want this?" I asked. I would rather he said now than standing in front of everyone. At least now, I could drive home.

"I have never been surer of anything in my whole life. Grace Grimes, will you marry me?"

"Yes." I smiled. "Yes, I'll marry you."

Chapter Forty-Five
Grace

I stood at the back of the church, closed my eyes, and took a deep breath. This was how my wedding was supposed to start if Daniel hadn't been running late. If he hadn't turned up when he did, I was going home to lock myself away for the foreseeable future. Luckily that wasn't going to happen, and I waited for Daniel and his best man Greg to get into position. I felt the nerves begin to swish around my stomach, or that could have been the prosecco Niven had been plying me with from the moment she arrived to help me get ready!

"Are you ready?" Gabriel asked.

I smiled. "Yes, I think I am."

There had been a few close calls in getting here, but for once, I knew I had made the right decision. I looked at Gabriel, my archangel, and thought about what could have been. Even after our last night of passion between the two of us, there wasn't any way we were ever going to be together, and Daniel had proved to be everything Gabriel wasn't.

Nate and Niven and Kate and Moore positioned themselves at the door as the music began to play. It was a piece of classical music, from a film that I had loved since the first time I had heard it and it was perfect for today. They began to walk.

Gabriel took my arm, breaking me back into reality. "Ready?"

I nodded.

He kissed the side of my head and smiled as he took a deep breath and began to walk us forward. Everyone turned round to look apart from Daniel. He was standing at the front with Greg. I tried to smile at everyone, but something was wrong. He should have turned round to see me. Was this why he was late in arriving? Was he having second thoughts?

We reached the front, and Gabriel kissed my cheek before taking his seat. I looked at Daniel, who was looking straight ahead. The panic built up inside of me, and I felt that at, any minute my world was about to collapse around me.

"Hey, you," Daniel said as he finally turned and smiled.

"Okay?" I looked at him anxiously.

He took my hand and squeezed it.

Our vows exchanged, and the register signed, the only thing left was the kiss.

"Hey, you." Daniel turned to me, both hands cupping my face perfectly for his mouth to join with mine for the first time as husband and wife.

We smiled at each other as our friends and family around us gave a round of applause.

We walked back down the aisle together, posing for another barrage of photographs, and then we were in the car heading for our reception.

"You look beautiful, Grace," Daniel said, squeezing my hand.

"Thank you and thank you for the loan of the earrings that was such a lovely thing to do today," I said, smiling at him. There was something different about him. He looked confident, pleased with himself almost.

"They weren't a loan. I had thought we could pass them on to our kids someday," he said with a look of hope in his eyes.

"I would like that." It wasn't something we had sat down and discussed, but I knew he wanted to have a family of his own, and I would love to be able to give him that.

"Thank you for this morning too. It was great to see all my friends for brunch, and then your text. If there were any doubts in my mind that you loved me, that text put them all to bed." He leaned over and kissed me. "I love you, Mrs Nicolson."

"I love you too," I said, staring into those deep dark eyes.

We made our way to one of the local castles with private grounds for our reception. We had more photographs taken before everyone arrived from the church, and it was nice to spend some time alone together before everyone started making a fuss.

Daniel took my hand as we had a walk around the marquee.

"I have to say Niven has done a good job," commented Daniel looking impressed.

"Was there any doubt?" I laughed.

From the minute we had announced our engagement Niven went into full wedding planner mode, which was great because if Daniel and I were left to organise it, we would have ended up at the local pub with a takeaway back at ours!

"I still can't believe she managed to get you in a dress." He pulled my hand around his back, which, in turn, pulled me closer into him.

"It was touch and go there for a while, but when I tried this one on, I knew it was the right one. I hope you like it?" I asked, looking at him for approval.

"You look amazing." He stopped walking and leaned into my ear. "As much as I like you wearing it, I can't wait to get you out of it." He kissed down the side of my neck, and I melted into him.

"Hmm," came a cough from beside us.

We smiled at each other before turning around to see who was trying to get our attention.

"I'm sorry to disturb you, Sir, but your guests are starting to arrive in the reception lounge. If you need more time?" the manager asked.

"No, that's okay. We'll be there in a moment."

"Very good, Sir." He turned on his heel and walked back into the castle.

"Is there anything else Sir, will be needing today?" I teased, squeezing his hand.

He chuckled before continuing where he had left off before we were interrupted. "Sir will want you to stick to him like glue for the rest of the day," he said before finishing kissing my neck. His hand had continued to move down my back and was now resting on my bum.

"Yes, Sir!" I quipped before we made our way to meet our guests.

The meal was lovely, the cake cut, and the speeches had passed without too many red faces even if Daniel's friends had tried their hardest to embarrass him. All that was left was what I had been dreading most, the first dance. It wasn't that I didn't want to dance with Daniel. It was the fact that everyone would be standing watching. I was the centre of attention; at least this was the last job of the day.

He spun me around the floor as his smiles, kisses, and quips kept my mind focused on him and nothing else. Everyone else in the room had disappeared, and it was just us enjoying our time together. The music finished, and he bent me back, kissing my neck to the applause of everyone watching. The next song started, and Daniel went to dance with Niven leaving me to dance with Gabriel.

"I am so pleased for you, Grace," he said smiling.

I pulled back slightly, looking into his face, that gorgeous looking, angelic face. "Are you?" I smiled.

"No, but…I'm only joking. Yes, how could I not be? You're happy, and I couldn't want anything else for you." He kissed the top of my head.

"I'm glad you're here. How funny would it be if you brought your wings out?" I laughed.

"Yeah, I think this would go from being a wedding to a funeral in one easy step!" he shook his head. "Trust you to think of something like that."

I shrugged my shoulders. "I don't think Daniel would be too happy either."

Gabriel screwed up his face. "No, I don't think wrapping your new wife in a set of wings would go down very well." I laughed at the thought.

"Right, you two break it up; there are others who want to dance with the bride," Bryce said cutting in.

"Brycie boy." I smirked as I put my arms around him. "Gracie baby." He squeezed me lifting me at the same time.

I squealed. "Bryce!" everyone round about us was laughing too. "So how long are you going to wait before you ask Kate?" I asked slyly.

"I think we're going to give ourselves some time yet," he replied.

"Really, because you're not getting any younger, Mr McKinley." I smirked at him.

"I'm in my prime, I'll have you know." He jutted out his jaw to prove his point.

The song ended, and Nic was pushing Bryce out of the way.

"You look amazing, Grace," he said before kissing me and squeezing me tightly, which made me squeal.

"Honestly, you two!" I laughed.

"I'm so pleased for you. And thankfully, all the crazy has finished." He twirled me under his arm and out to the side, which made me laugh.

"Thank you for allowing me to invite Jessica."

"Of course, I'm pleased you've met someone who makes you happy," I said, smiling back at him.

Jessica was the assistant when I went to buy my wedding dress. She was lovely, and her and Nic had hit it off immediately and had been inseparable ever since.

There was an influx of people all wanting to dance with me, so as soon as the song finished, Nic passed me onto the next person. I wasn't sure where Daniel was at this point, but I kept going, not wanting to disappoint anyone.

I was having the best evening, and everyone else seemed to be enjoying it too. I did wonder where my husband needed to be that was more important than being here with me. I excused my way politely through the crowds of guests that were still congratulating me. I was hugged, kissed, spun around, and even had another marriage proposal, but I thought my cousin's six-year-old son was just a tad too young. I was nearly back at the main reception when I saw Daniel and Gabriel huddled together.

Chapter Forty-Six

Daniel

"There you are." Grace walked over to us, but it was on me she draped her arms, and I couldn't resist kissing her.

I raised an eye at Gabriel. It was petty schoolboy behaviour, but she was mine, and he needed to know that! My arm held her tightly around her waist, but it was too good an opportunity to let my hand wander until it was grasping at her bum.

While I sat back at Nic's getting ready, I received a text from Grace, and that was enough to convince me that I wasn't going to throw what I had with Grace away. It was Gabriel that needed to go, not Grace. I loved her too much to leave her now.

"Gabriel was just telling me how he was about to leave." I shot him a look.

She let go and swung round to face him. "What, you're leaving? Why? What's happened? Daniel, tell him he can't leave, not tonight." She had a handful of my shirt scrunched in her fist.

"Nothing's wrong. We were discussing when to tell you." I slid my hand up and down her arm.

"You're awfully quiet." She directed the fiery question at Gabriel, who hadn't said anything yet.

"You always knew I would need to leave, well, I've been called home. I'm sorry the timing isn't better, but I need to go." He went to touch her, but she pulled away from him. "Grace, please."

She shook her head, fighting back the tears from making an early appearance at our wedding. "You promised you would always be there for me." She spat.

"I'm going to have to pass that on to Daniel, I'm afraid. I really am sorry."

This time she didn't push him away, clinging to his neck. "Will you be back?"

Gabriel looked at me for what he should say. I shook my head behind her.

"No, I won't be back for a very long time."

She let go of him, wiping at her eyes and pushing away the offer of my hand on her back as comfort and support. "Well, it was nice meeting you. I hope you have a safe journey."

Gabriel looked at her. Even I felt sorry for the way she was pushing him away. "Don't do that." Gabriel said looking deeply hurt.

She held her hand out for Gabriel to shake.

"Goodbye, Grace." He walked away, not turning to look at her as he got into the waiting taxi.

We watched him go.

"Hey, you." I put my hand on her back.

"He left." The shock in her voice was evident.

I kissed her shoulder. "I'm sorry this had to happen tonight, but we've got a room full of guests that are going to be wondering where we are." I tried to coax her back to the party, but I could tell she was going to need some time before going back to face everyone.

She walked over to the grand staircase and sat down. "Do you know I always loved a staircase? I'm not sure if it was because of my love of the dramatic or a romantic story end where there was always a final scene on a staircase." She shook her head with a laugh.

I knelt on one knee in front of her holding her hand. "Grace, I made promises to you today that I didn't make lightly. You're my wife now, and I love you more than anything in this world. This is our day, and I won't let anyone ruin it for you or me. Please, come back to me." I waited for her to respond.

Her fingers traced the outline of my face before she sat forward, letting her head rest against mine. "I love you, Daniel. But how long is it going to be before I lose you too?"

"No way are you taking responsibility for him leaving, especially not today." I stood up, pulling her with me. "I've heard you say a hundred times how you can put a smile on your face even though your worlds been crumbling around you, and it's horrible that I'm asking, but I need you to do it again. For the few hours that we have left here tonight. Then when our guests go home, you can crumble. And I know you will, but I'll be there, Grace, picking up every piece and helping you put your life back together again. I love you."

She looked at me, wiped her face, took a deep breath, and smiled. “I’ll hold you to that.”

“We wondered where you two had got to,” Niven asked, looking for us. “Everything okay here?”

“We’re just coming,” Grace said, her voice sounding happy again.

I walked behind Grace and Niven. I hadn’t expected her to come looking for Gabriel and me, but I should have realised. It would have been better for her if Gabriel had just disappeared, but that would have been too easy. She had her chance to say goodbye, and it seemed like as good a time as any for him to go.

I knew she was going to be upset, but I didn’t want to be this close when it happened. I had laid everything on the line; if she had run after Gabriel, who knows what I would have done. I took one last look behind me just to make sure he had definitely left before following my new wife back into our reception.

Chapter Forty-Seven
Daniel

The party had ended, and everyone had gone home. I had given Grace the news that I had booked us a room at the castle, and I was glad I had. I didn't want to take her home, not tonight.

I held her hand as I walked her to our room. I had hoped this would have been a night filled with anticipation, but as she trundled along behind, I wondered if she would even want to be with me tonight.

I used my card to get into the room, pushing the door open for Grace to walk in. "I had them leave a bottle of champagne for us, but if you've had enough, we can take it home."

She walked over to the window and looked out onto the woodland that surrounded us.

She rested against the window sill, her hands holding on tightly. "Would you mind if we took it home with us? We could open it tomorrow."

"Sure." I pulled it out of the ice bucket, leaving it on the small table. I went into our bathroom, leaving the door open. I washed my hands and dried them on one of the towels provided. My reflection in the mirror was stern, almost fed up. I had pictured this night for months, even before I had asked her to marry me, but it never played out like this. We would have been all over each other by now, but that wasn't how it was going to be, not tonight.

My head dropped, and I closed my eyes, almost anticipating the cries, sobs from our room as she began to break down. I took a deep breath and straightened up. How was I going to cope on my wedding night holding my new wife while she mourned the loss of her best friend? Her lover if that's what he was? I turned to walk back out.

"Hey, you." Grace stood blocking my way.

I leaned back against the sink unit. "Hey, you."

“I didn’t want any more to drink because I think I’ve had enough already, and I want to remember what our first time together was like.” She managed to force a half-smile from her mouth. Her hand reached up towards my chest as she walked closer.

I watched her, and she looked beautiful. I put my hands on her waist and looked into her eyes. I had never noticed before how dark the outer rim of her iris was but only on the one side. “Do you still want this? We could wait until.”

“Shh!” she put her index finger to my mouth then let it fall away to be replaced by her lips. They had gently, touched mine but I moved forward, pressing harder.

My mouth opened further, my tongue gently exploring her mouth before I brought it back. I was taking my time now, no one was going to disturb us, and I felt relaxed.

Everything forgotten, I had married Grace, and she was the one who had initiated this.

My hands moved over her body, I kissed her gently at first, but I had waited a long time for this moment. My shirt and tie were discarded as she unbuckled my belt. I needed to slow things down. I wanted to be the one taking control. I held her against the wall and kissed down the side of her neck, moving back just enough that I could see her face. I wanted to remember every part of tonight, especially how she looked. I pressed back into her mouth, my tongue once again meeting hers. I wanted her, but I needed to make sure she wanted me just as much.

I let go of her and stood back.

She smiled. Not her put on smile, but her breath-taking, infectious smile. The one I had longed to see. “Will we go through to our room?” She asked.

I didn’t need to think about my answer now. Grace wanted me. I walked her backwards out of the bathroom as we continued to kiss. The light from the bathroom lit up the bedroom just enough that we could still see what we were doing. I moved behind her, kissing the back of her neck from her hairline down to her shoulders. I was like a child at Christmas unwrapping my new toy. The floral smell of her perfume only adding to the desire I felt for her right now.

There were a couple of hooks to start with and a small zip that I hadn’t noticed. I pulled it down slowly, exposing the bra fastening first, but I let the zip continue its journey over her soft, delicate skin until it reached the bottom. I let my fingers trace the route the zip had just made, my mouth next to witness for itself what my fingers had already experienced.

I stood in front of her. She was still smiling, and I wrapped my arms around her and pulled the sides of her dress down, watching her strapless bra come into view, slipping it down further over her stomach, then to the matching pair of lace pants and suspenders which held up her stockings.

She put a hand on my shoulder to steady herself as she stepped out of the dress. I put it over onto a chair for her. She crossed her arms in front of her, trying to hide herself until I was back with her.

"The boots really set off the whole look." I laughed, looking at how crazy she looked.

She laughed with me. "They came with the underwear," she joked.

I kissed her, my hands wanting to feel every part of her. "Sit on the bed." I knelt down in front of her. I pulled at her cowboy boots, removing them one at a time. My hands moved over her legs, pulling them apart so I could get closer to her, kissing her.

Her hands were in my hair. She helped me remove my trousers before we moved further onto the bed. I laid on top of her, our legs intertwined as we kissed and touched each other.

There were things I wanted to do to her that I couldn't before because I knew if I went there, I wouldn't be able to stop, but nothing was holding me back now. She was my wife, and we had waited a long time for us to be together like this.

I ran my tongue along the inside of her thigh before I tasted her, moving against her. Her breathing was hard, and her back was arching at the thrill of what I was doing to her. "I want you," I said, kissing her stomach.

"Wait." She pushed me on to my back and knelt beside me, leaning forward kissing me, then her mouth moved away from mine, kissing the side of my cheek, my throat, my neck, down my chest, stomach as if she had taken a large knife and decided to cut me in two. She was slow and methodical. Every kiss meant to build the anticipation I felt, her tongue always there first before her lips surrounded the kiss effortlessly.

My fingers ran through her hair, she looked along my body, searching for my eyes. "I love you."

"I love you. I'm sorry about everything today. Forgive me?" She pleaded.

I placed my hand at the side of her face. "There isn't anything I need to forgive you for; you've made me an incredibly lucky man today, certainly not something you need to apologise for." I kissed her.

She moved back down my body, wanting to please me with her mouth, her tongue finding every hidden delight.

"Come here." She did what I asked, and I moved on top of her body, finding my way inside her for the first time. I could feel the tiny goosebumps appear over her skin. I kissed her as I moved inside her, pulling her closer; our union together would never be broken. I would never let anything come between us ever again.

"I love you, Grace."

She cuddled into my chest, our breathing regulating before we could speak. I wrapped my arms around her, holding her. "Can I ask you something?"

"Of course." She ran her fingers along my arm.

"Do you think we could try for a baby?"

"I think it's a bit late asking, but yes, I would like to do that with you." She smiled. I pulled her back into my chest. I couldn't have been happier.

I lay facing her. She was so beautiful, and she was mine. I couldn't stop touching her, letting my fingers run up and down her arm, playing with her hair. I couldn't get enough of her.

"I have a question for *you*." Her eyes dropped.

"Sounds serious." I kissed her.

"Why didn't you turn round?" She looked up at me.

I pulled back and looked at her quizzically. "Turn round when?" I had no idea what she was talking about.

"When I came into the church, and when I was walking down the aisle, you didn't turn round. Was there something wrong?" I could hear the emotion from earlier rise again in her throat.

"Oh, Grace. I'm so sorry." I opened my eyes, lent up on my side, and kissed her. "I was so nervous I didn't want to turn round in case I completely lost it."

"So, you weren't angry with me?" she held my hand at her face.

I had felt so let down in the morning. My focus was entirely on that kiss and my anger at Gabriel, but as soon as I took my place at the front of the church, all I could think about was Grace. I *was* nervous when I heard the music play and the sound of everyone turning in their seats; it was all I could do to stop myself from passing out.

I sat up, pulling her up to face me. "I could never be angry with you. You have made me so happy today. I love you," I kissed her before pulling her close. I wanted to hold her like this for the rest of our lives.

Her arms draped over my shoulders, her lips kissing me gently. "I love you too."

She had fallen asleep, but I had wanted to stay awake. I wanted to watch her. I pulled the cover slowly away from her hands and down her body, resting it at her hips. She moved on to her back, her hand went up to her face but rested on her pillow, next to her, I sat myself up on my elbow, my other hand gently touching her stomach where I hoped our child would be starting its creation inside her.

Her hand found the back of my head. "Hey, you. What you up to?" she asked groggily. "Go back to sleep." I didn't want her to know how important this was to me.

She placed a hand on top of mine. "I hope so too," she said as sleep stole her back and away from me. I cuddled her into my body, holding her close.

Chapter Forty-Eight
Gabriel

I sat in the back of the taxi as it drove away from the wedding and away from Grace.

What had just happened? Why had things ended as bad as they had? Why did I agree to leave and not stay until I had the chance to talk to her, to explain, why I had to leave? She was never going to forgive me for this. I had never seen her look like that. And what was that handshake? Did she hate me that much, after everything we had been through, or did she hate me because of everything we had been through?

The taxi stopped, and I looked over at her house, remembering the first time we had met. From then on, we had become friends, more than friends. The first time I held her in my arms and the first time I had kissed her, the first time I had slept with her. All the firsts, good thoughts, but there were bad memories too. Amelia and Oliver, demon entities who had tried to kidnap Grace and take her away from me forever. Then today. Watching her marry Daniel and wishing it was me, then the look on her face as I left.

I couldn't turn around as I walked away from her. I wouldn't have been able to make it out the door if I had seen her face start to lose its composure. I knew it would have been wrong, and Daniel would probably have hit me, which he would have had every right to do, but I would have walked over to Grace, wrapped my arms around her waist, pulling her next to me, a hand escaping to hold her face and I would have kissed her. Not some quick, fleeting kiss but a passionate kiss that had enough force behind it that she would have been under no illusion of what was happening.

When I had finished, I would pull back, take her hand, and walk her out the door, out of her wedding, and away from Daniel. There would have been shouts and protests, but she would have walked away from Daniel and towards me.

Wouldn't she? It was a question that would be left unanswered because I did none of that. I walked away, broke her heart, and left her with Daniel.

I walked towards my house, taking one final look at the street before walking inside and closing the door behind me. Michael was already waiting in the lounge.

"Hi. I take it you know what happened?" I slumped onto the couch opposite.

"That's why I'm here."

"I thought as much. So, am I in trouble then?"

"You're not in trouble, Gabriel. It was never going to be an easy mission. We needed you to come."

"What about last night?"

"We didn't anticipate how much you loved her. We didn't think you would go through with it."

"It could have changed everything?" I let my head fall back against the couch.

"It could have, but we were able to pull it back. The mission was a success, Gabriel. Grace and Daniel are going to be great together." Michael smiled his approval.

"What about the demons?"

"They're gone. Once you come home, there will be no reason for them to hang around here." He paused, realising what I was asking. "She's safe; nothing bad is going to happen to her."

I nodded my head, glad to hear that everything was going to work out for Grace. She deserved to be happy, and even if it wasn't with me, I couldn't want anything more for her. "I'm glad."

"Are you ready to go home?" Michael stood up and extended his hand for me to take.

Was I? Was I ready? I knew I needed to leave, but what if, just maybe, I had left something here I would need to come back for? I smiled wondering if my last night with Grace was going to produce the one dream I had always longed for. I replayed over our last night together, hoping our child would be starting its creation inside her. It was a thought. I smiled and shook my head. I stood up. For now my time on earth was at an end.

"I'm ready."

The End